ONE SMALL SQUEAL

ONE SMALL SQUEAL

THE PIG AND I MYSTERIES

DONNARAE MENARD

To Farm Girls Everywhere

Chapter One

"You're probably all smug today, aren't you? You don't have to go out in the rain to go to work. Or wear pinching shoes, or deal with that Neanderthal that can't figure out how to mow all of the lawn, not just the middle." She paused, looking around the room, then out the window at the yard. "You know I love you, but this is all getting to be a bit much. Working, dealing with the house stuff. Maybe we should move into a condo. After all, we're not getting any younger."

She walked across the kitchen to pour the last of the coffee into a go-mug. "Yes, I shut the coffee maker off. Listen, the dog is fed. I made sure the back gate is closed. It's supposed to stop raining in the next hour, and even though it's not legally summer yet, it's going to get muggy. The air will come on at ten. I've made plans for this weekend, so rest up."

With one last look around to make sure she had everything, she left the bright chrome and gunship-steel kitchen and walked through the mudroom, go-cup and briefcase in hand. The last thing she did before she picked up her umbrella and walked out the door was to pat the closed lid of the fifteen-point-five-square-foot chest-style freezer.

"I'll see you tonight. Bye, love."

The appliance, slightly dented and always locked, hummed along until her vehicle was out of the drive. Then it stopped. Dead.

Chapter Two

It was a surprise to all the residents when a billboard sign appeared smack-dab in the middle of the roadside border. The rather garish sign depicted a toothy woman and a man with a cocker spaniel smile. The pair framed the offer of prime real estate lots in the soon-to-be-available Bright Water Circle development.

"The plan is for thirteen houses," I said to my daughter Melanie.

"I saw the sign." Melanie carefully balanced a tall ceramic coffee cup and a plate of toast. Then she expertly maneuvered around her pug, Lilo, and my corgi. "It's a workday, guys. I have to get signed in. Let's move it along."

I snapped my fingers, but Royally wasn't about to take his eyes off Melanie. Both dogs continued their urgent skipping dance all the way down the hall, toenails clicking and clacking like an old-fashioned train, then came to a dead stop as their breakfast courier stepped over the dog gate and escaped.

Melanie had moved home to our tiny farm after the unexpected passing of her father. She had taken up residence in the two rooms on the western side of the house. What had at one time been the dining room and parlor were now her bedroom and office, with a pocket door that connected the two.

Without so much as a sighing whine, both pooches bolted back toward the long kitchen. There was every chance I would have a bite left for them to share.

On the outside of the heavy screen door, Buttercup issued a soft *ooh-hoo*. Via the handicap ramp, the four-hundred-fifty-pound porcine was in a position to see me share the scraps with the dogs.

"No bread for you, porker. Carrot sticks only," I said, as I opened the door and let the pig into the house.

The thick wooden farmhouse door had always kept Buttercup out, but she had learned early on how to work the lightweight screen door. A few weeks earlier, she had been inside when some deer new to the neighborhood had taste-tested her evening grain. Without further ado, Buttercup had burst through the door, literally ripping it off the hinges, and launched herself off the fence-free deck. She hadn't broken any bones but suffered a limping injury for several days. Changes had to be made.

Melanie contacted a contractor friend, and I went to the bank. The deck was enclosed with a fence of closely placed pickets, with a human-only gate to the steps. A pig-friendly ramp, complete with a gate at the low end, had also been installed, as well as a screen door with a heartier framework and metal mesh that covered the bottom half. Buttercup had mastered the ramp, but the new door fit snugly enough that she couldn't get the rooter at the tip of her oval snout disc underneath to pull it open.

The humans knew it was just a matter of time, but the dog gates in the house kept Buttercup out of Melanie's quarters and the living room. Maybe they hoped the new metal door would be a deterrent.

"Here you go." I offered two carrot sticks, one at a time.

The pig's tail whipped back and forth in glee as she accepted the treats. She kept her head high so her buddy Royally couldn't snatch one away.

The dog, the pig, and I exited the kitchen door. There were other animals that needed to be fed. Lilo, Melanie's pug, and the four resident house cats watched as we left. But as the felines searched out the sunniest window, Lilo sat outside the gate. Eventually, her faint whimpering call led Melanie to open the gate and let her into the office.

Chapter Three

"There's a notice in the *Valley Daily* touting a grand opening showing at Bright Water Circle today." Melanie turned her laptop so I could see the ad. "What exactly does that mean?"

"I'd say it's an open house like any other," I replied. I'd finished working in the yard and gone back inside to make lunch. "Though what they'll have to show besides wild shrubs, I'm not sure."

"Hmm." Melanie closed the laptop lid and reached for her green goddess salad dressing. "A couple of days ago, I went out to meet Missy and Heather for brunch. There were guys out there. Surveyors, I think."

I nodded and went back to the job that entailed trying to convince Mavis that her meds were actually a yummy snack. An hour later, after I finally accomplished administering the appropriate medication into the cat, blessedly receiving only mild wounds, I went outside again. My intention was to weed the flower beds at the end of the driveway. It was a rare phenomenon to arrive there without either a dog or pig escort.

I stood at the end of the drive and gazed across the ancient orchard, feeling the sun warm on my back and the gentle breeze that encouraged play instead of work. Instead of a casual stroll across the road to find a stump I could rest on among the wild hay and rye, I wandered down the road toward town.

Calwin Mountain Road was a dead end, culminating in the turnaround at the edge of the National Forest. Currently, only three houses stood along the mile-long stretch, so there was never much traffic. I passed the house where young Shane Davis had lived with his elderly parents until Buttercup unearthed the remains of a man Shane had believed was a rival for Melanie's affections. After the medical examiner's apprentice had been arrested, his parents left the valley. There were new people living there now. Thus far, I hadn't struck up a neighborly friendship with them.

At one time, long ago, the riverbank ran high and wide here. There had been a house with a barn that tilted into a washout. Both were old and ramshackle. When a heavy winter storm blew down the barn, both buildings were razed. The property had gone back to a more natural state, with the exception of the trash, which escaped the business dumpsters and made its way across the road. There were always bits caught in the tall grasses and sumac that had grown in.

The ladies from the Preservation and Historical Society showed up twice a year to clean the area up. This allowed for a clear view of the Moat Range on the far side of the river. The Moats ran the entire length of the valley on the west bank. The view was breathtaking. The selectmen had approved the cost of half a dozen granite and wood benches. It was a prime spot for a casual picnic or late-evening canoodle.

Prepared to turn at that point and return to the wild collection of weeds, I paused. I had expected to find a single vehicle parked in the overgrown lot, but there were tent awnings set up. At least three, two white and one royal blue. Over the tops of at least a half dozen cars, I saw the dark red of Stan the Hot Dog Man's food truck. A refurbished UPS special. I could barely hear his Dixieland jazz music.

My feet walked on. Before I knew it, I stood inside the first of the tents. Easels held an overlarge view of the site plan, house choices, and lists of available local amenities. The next tent had two folding tables. Christine Gillespie, my bank representative of choice from the local bank, was hard at work as she attended to a young couple endeavoring to fill out an application while also being attentive to a squirming three-year-old. As I walked through, Christine waved. With a quick wave back, I moved on. Christine's frustration at trying to speak over the toddler's cries was plainly evident, and I wanted none of that.

Under the last awning, in the royal blue tent, a tall, slender woman passed out brochures and invited newcomers to walk around the site.

"The lots are already surveyed out and marked with corner ribbons," the woman told them. "Each is numbered, and you can come back here to see the specs and prices of those you are interested in." She handed a young couple bottles of water and waved them out into the sunshine.

She turned to where I was standing. "Hello! I'm Racheal Gerrish. Welcome."

Behind her, set on another easel, was a circular picture of a younger, smiling couple. The marquee ribbon identified them as Racheal and Richard Gerrish of Gerrish Real Estate.

Before Racheal could launch into her sales pitch, I held up my hand.

"I'm not really here to buy," I said with a smile. "I'm Doris Flynn. I live at the end of the road. I'm just curious, I guess. So, I walked up for a look."

"Well, Doris." Racheal smiled warmly. "I'm glad you did. You should definitely check everything out. Walk around, have a hot dog. They're free. If you have any questions, come on back." After she handed me a bottle of water, the Realtor turned to another pair of new arrivals.

I ordered a *Hurry Up Heartburn* complete with chili, onions, and spicy mustard from Stan, and did just what Mrs. Gerrish had suggested. Except I didn't look at the lots so much as I did at the other people. These could be new neighbors. How were they going to feel about Buttercup and keeping our neighborhood peaceful? At the end of the circuit, I paused for a moment to take a good look at Racheal. She looked a lot older than in the poster picture. Maybe she was just tired or had gone sour on selling real estate. The hard lines and thin smile didn't shout welcome.

Suddenly, a round, wet slab of baloney smacked the side of my knee. I knew that slimy bit of pig anatomy and didn't react, but on the other side of the tent, Racheal almost jumped out of her skin.

"I tried to stop her, Mom." Melanie strained to hold the big Hampshire pig back. "I really did, but she knew you'd walked down here. It was all I could do to get her harness on her before she took off."

Racheal rushed forward and seemed to move in reverse at the same time. Her face was pale under the makeup that had been applied by an expert's hand.

"What is *that*?" There was an edge of hysteria in her voice.

The nearest couple turned to stare. Still seated at her table, Christine smirked.

"It's okay." I took the harness lead from Melanie. "She's friendly."

Right then, Buttercup became aware of the Stan-mobile. The hot dog man was known for passing out Porker Specials to kids at town events. The specials were half a hot dog roll slathered with ketchup, relish, and mustard. Buttercup didn't like onions, and she wasn't allowed meat. At events Buttercup attended, kids would stand in line to feed her the free half a roll Stan passed out.

Stan was one of Buttercup's favorite people. He loved her as well. The Porker Specials were great for his bottom line. While people waited for a free half roll to feed to the pig, they'd buy their own hot dogs, chips, and whoopee pies.

Scree, scree. The pig called to Stan to let him know she was there.

"Nope. Home. Go home," I said, pointing up the road.

Standing between her and the hot dogs, I used my knees to push her away. To get her to turn, I had to point Buttercup right at Racheal. From the way the Realtor reacted, you'd think I'd pointed a loaded semi-automatic at her.

The woman let out a shrill little screech. The hair stood up on Buttercup's back, and she took off like a shot. Believe me, I got in all my running exercise with this pig on a leash, and also when she wasn't on a leash. Fortunately, she was only good for short bursts.

Chapter Four

Melanie strolled into the yard a while later with a suspicious mustard stain on her blouse.

"I don't think Buttercup made a good impression," my daughter said, as she nodded toward the sunbathing pig.

"Well, duh. Why didn't you just give her a cookie and lock her in the pen?"

I was a little hot under the collar and pulling weeds out so fast, I'm sure a few pansies were sacrificed.

"I wanted to see what was going on down at the open house, too. And it's not safe for a young lady like myself to wander around out here in the wilds, or near the paved roads." Melanie intoned a deep southern drawl, complete with downcast eyes and that smart-alecky cherub-bow smile she uses to get Noah to jump through hoops.

I could have thumped her.

Melanie went off with Lilo and Royally yipping happily at her heels. The two dogs made enough noise that Buttercup roused and trotted off to see what all the excitement was. Like maybe a snack. I might have heard the screen door close, but don't quote me on that because I was pretty deep into bad thoughts and the consideration of what might happen to our quiet little road when thirteen houses went in.

As a matter of fact, it wasn't until the Beamer stopped six feet from where I knelt that I realized it had traveled up the road. Startled at the proximity of the front bumper to my forehead, I sat back on my haunches. Racheal Gerrish had a white-knuckle grip on the steering wheel. Her eyes darted from place to place around the yard.

"Is it safe to get out?" she asked through the half-open passenger window.

I levered myself up from the ground. "As a matter of fact, it is."

She exited the car with the same care as Rambo when he stalked through the forests of Guatemala, looking for Godzilla.

"I don't mean to barge in, Mrs. Flynn. Doris. But I wanted to chat with you for a few minutes. I had hoped to do so earlier, but you had to…leave."

I tried not to grin. My recall wouldn't tell me how long Gerrish's Real Estate had been in the valley, but I just knew this woman considered the suburbs to be out in the sticks. "I was just ready to go in for a cold drink. Would you care to join me? Or maybe coffee?" I pulled off my work gloves and stuffed them into my back pocket. Leaving them on the ground was the same as giving Buttercup permission to rip and shred.

As Racheal stepped out from behind the car I was struck by what a tiny waist she had. Her dress was of a shiny fabric you don't see today, and of a style popular in the 1950s. Deep round neck, longish full collar, tight bodice, and a full skirt that ended an inch beneath the knee. I knew there was crinoline under there. And though she should have been wearing inch-and-a-half pumps, she had selected patent leather ballet shoes dyed to match her outfit. A wise choice of footwear, as she had stood in the sand and dirt all day instead of on a carpeted floor. I was awestruck at how elegant she looked.

Through the living room window behind me, I heard Melanie ask, "You want to go outdoors, big girl?"

Still enthralled with the shimmer of the lake blue fabric and pale pink-and-lavender hyacinth floral pattern, I hesitated just long enough for Racheal to get around the front of the car—and for Buttercup to race down the ramp.

The pig snorted a greeting, the woman screamed, and the big skirt went up on the hood of the car.

Yup, I was right about the crinoline.

"For the love of Pete," I said.

Buttercup came right over to where I waited, but her shiny black currant eyes were on all those yards and yards of fabric, just waiting to be ripped asunder. There was a reason the clothesline had been moved into the fenced-in garden plot. And it wasn't to keep the woodchucks away.

Racheal began to make noises that sounded like a possible lawsuit. Melanie charged around the corner. Now there were barking dogs in the melee. After dumping a fistful of miniature chocolate chip cookies in my hand, my daughter scooped up Lilo, quieting at least the pug down.

"Hold on, Racheal. Wait just a second." I waved my hand in front of Buttercup. She caught the scent of the cookies and turned her attention away from the hysteria on the BMW. "C'mon, Buttercup. Come with me. That's a good girl."

As the pig and I moved across the yard toward the barn, I stage-whispered to Melanie, "Get her off the car, into the house. Don't let her leave."

I tossed the leftover chips of cookies into Buttercup's big outside pen, scattering them around. She followed immediately, as this type of snack hide-and-go-seek was her favorite game. Then I hurried back to the house.

Irritated whines came from Melanie's bedroom, and the door to the cattery was closed. The previously well-appointed, elegant Realtor was seated at the table, a tall glass of iced tea clutched in her hand. She looked quite frazzled. While I apologized profusely, I got a cool washcloth from the bathroom and handed it to our guest.

"I'm sorry," she said. "It's just that animal is so big." She dabbed at her face and neck, leaving the cloth pressed against the pulsing vein on her neck for a few moments.

Melanie inched away. I let her go.

"Don't apologize," I said. "I should have realized as soon as she heard you speak; she'd want to come outside and check out what was going on."

Racheal stopped patting the washcloth against her long, swan neck. She seemed to grow taller, thinner. Or at least her neck did. Her perfectly modulated voice had acquired a squeak.

"Go outside? From the house? You let the pig in the *house*?"

I could tell from the way her eyes darted around on the floor that her feet were already on the move up to the rungs of the chair. This was the type of situation where I'd learned to speak softly, offer encouragement, the same way I do when the humane society drops off a new dog. I held my place, careful not to make any fast moves.

"Let me explain. Buttercup isn't a farm animal. She was raised to be a pet. The people who had her before me thought she was a pot-bellied pig. But she's not. Here she is treated like one of the dogs. She gets to come into the kitchen. She has her own kennel space outside. She has house manners. But just like the pug and the corgi, she gets excited. And she is big." I waited until Racheal looked less like Alice did after gazing into the elongating mirror, then added, "If she makes you nervous, she can stay out in her kennel. Really, it's okay because once she gets done with her snack, she'll have a nap."

"Like a cat?" Racheal whispered.

"Exactly, except without the elaborate bath. I don't have her pool set up today."

"Ah-huh." Racheal's eyelids dropped to half-mast. She obviously thought it was a joke about the pool.

I put a plate of full-sized oatmeal cookies on the table, sure that she would be insulted to be offered the same ones Buttercup loved. "So, you wanted to chat?"

Racheal gave a little shake and transformed back to realtor mode.

"Yes. I would have come up sooner, but my husband was at a closing. Sometimes they take a long while. This one had a hang-up on the final inspection." Before I could respond, she went on, "But in regard to this development, often while we go through the permit process with the town, I hear from abutting neighbors. This time, there was nothing. In the interest of being good neighbors, I thought I'd reach out to the people here on Calwin Mountain Road and see if any of you had questions."

She smiled at me across the aged pedestal kitchen table. I could see the offered olive branch, but to be honest, I didn't think it extended to any type of friendship. Our acceptance would make it easier for her to find new owners for the intended lots. If she had come right out and said her ride up the road was to discern if we were pig farming up here, I would have been more ready to believe her. Now it was my turn to sit back and cool my jets.

"Well, currently there are only three houses on the road. The one directly across from where you want to put in houses, the next one up the street, has new owners. I don't know them. The last house beyond that is where we live. And beyond is all state land. In the National Forest, there's a small place to park and trails."

Knowing the old duffer who owned the orchard across the road from us on the river side, and the meadows that separated the development from the ancient apple trees, had at one time talked about selling, I avoided mentioning that undeveloped land.

"We've been here for a lot of years," I went on. "This place has been in my late husband's family for generations. We don't farm, but I am permitted to kennel four difficult dogs while they're screened for placement. Also, eleven cats, plus my own. I guess you could consider this a not-for-profit business." I figured all of that information was sufficiently convoluted to stop her questions.

"What is a difficult dog? One that's bitten someone?"

"Possibly, but they're not difficult for me. These are specific breeds: pitbulls, German shepherds, Dobermans, rottweilers, breeds like that."

"Oh, my!" The stretched-neck thing had started again.

"Don't be alarmed. We don't get dogs unless there is a solid chance they can go back out to new homes. The cats never go outside because of the natural predators. Bears, coyotes, foxes. As a matter of fact, currently, I only have one difficult dog in residence. But I have a full house of cats, and they're all senior citizens."

"You must be pro-no-kill, then?" Racheal looked around again. This time, probably for fuzzballs as opposed to pig poop.

"Exactly." I nodded to the interior screen door. "The cattery is a separate room. Mostly, they nap, but each has time out among the people daily. A few are emotional support animals and spend the day loafing at GreenBriar Nursing Home."

"Well, that's totally unexpected. But wouldn't you be more comfortable in a facility out of town?"

"This *is* out of town," I said dryly. "National forest on two sides, floodplain and river on one. The nearest neighbor is half a mile away. And as far as being comfortable, this is my home. I don't charge a fee for the animals' care.

People donate food and care sometimes, which is great. But the long and short of it is that this is what we do. And we don't plan to move."

My friendly tone had started to evaporate when I caught on to Racheal's hint that my operation might not work well with hers.

Before another flag could hit the ground, the screen door opened, and the tall, impressive Sheriff Everett Neddel entered.

"I picked up a blueberry pie at the bakery for supper," he said. When he caught sight of Racheal, he swept off his hat. "Ma'am?"

The Realtor got caught up in Neddel's black Irish looks and swallowed hard. She also quickly concluded that he and I might be friendly. I didn't even have a chance for introductions before she was up and out.

* * *

"I give up," the sheriff said, planting a light kiss on the top of my head. "What just happened?"

Everett Neddel and I were still pretty new to each other and semi-romantic. I still called him by his last name, for crying out loud. The sheriff was also a fairly recent—as of about a year ago—addition to the valley and still had to learn who was who.

"That was Racheal Gerrish of Gerrish Real Estate. They're the agency that wants to sell the lots up the street. I walked up there today to check it out, and Buttercup followed me."

"Oh." Neddel had also suffered a little shock at my choice of house pets.

"Don't get nervous. She was on a leash. Melanie brought her down."

Neddel made a little phfft noise. He didn't believe either of us had control over our porcine friend.

The clatter of dog nails rushed down the hall.

"I heard that," Melanie said. "I'm on my way to pick up Imogene and Rufus. They've probably had all the senior-citizen love they can stand for one day. How about if you order up from the Rib House, Mom, and I'll swing in on the way back? Slaw and Red Bliss Potato Salad. No fries."

"That does sound good." Neddel's big blues got even rounder. "And garlic

13

bread, the cheesy kind."

I kept a credit card right by the phone for just this type of emergency.

Chapter Five

A couple of days later, I walked Buttercup up and down the road. Both of us needed a little exercise, and because I had a new dog, I couldn't take her with me while the hound and I got used to each other. Duke was some kind of Red Ridge cross. He had come to me from Berlin with an older female named Delish. As long as she was here, he was not easy to manage. But she was a brute that needed to go somewhere with a human physically stronger than I was, so Duke stayed. Immediately, his Big Boss attitude slipped, and he became easier to handle. I'm not sure why. Maybe she egged him on or called him a sissy in dog language. Newly neutered, but still with attitude. He had the exceptionally long snout of a Red Ridge, but some kind of musty blue color that might come from a Plott hound. I know he was originally from the South, so anything was possible.

Fortunately, he was barely a year old and really wanted to please. I'd left him out on the steel cable overhead run to work off some energy. He had a new high-impact chew toy to toss around, so I knew he'd be good for a while. I didn't trust him around the cats or even Royally and Lilo yet, but I had hopes.

Back before my husband Ian's sudden passing, he had gotten me a dogcart—or a goat cart, whichever you prefer—and fitted it out for Buttercup. Back then, she'd been a lot smaller, and for every parade we'd make her an outfit and decorate the cart. She actually got really excited when I took it down from where it hung inside the barn. The vet and I decided she was at maximum weight for me to handle and for her own health. Now we did laps up and down the road to keep her there. With her harness on and the cart behind her loaded with concrete blocks, she was slower and easier to keep on the straight and narrow.

I noticed as we passed the Davis house that their name had been painted off the mailbox. No new name was added. I went up as far as where the tents had been set up for three days.

They were all gone now. The grass was trampled flat; the hot dog mobile pulled out. Somebody had done a good job of picking up all the trash left behind.

"I'd say Racheal hired a cleanup crew so that when the lookie-loos come to scope out the offering, they'd see everything clean and fresh," I said to Buttercup.

As I came back by the Davis house, I heard a screen door slam. A towheaded boy of around four whipped down the driveway toward us. The door banged again, and a woman came after him.

"Andy!" she called. "Andrew, stop right there."

The child reacted immediately. In this day of passive parenting, I was surprised. I reined in Buttercup.

"Hello," I said to the boy. My eyes flickered toward the sandy blonde woman, whose hands rested on his shoulders. "I'm Doris Flynn. I live up the road. This is Buttercup."

As this was our second lap, my big girl was content to stand in place, though she stretched her snout out to see who was there.

"I'm Eve Saucier. This is my son, Andrew."

"Hello, Andrew."

"Did you see my daddy?" Andrew asked excitedly. "He was on TV!"

I could see Eve pale.

"No, darling. That was just somebody who looked like Daddy."

The little boy turned around, looking up at his mom. From the set of his shoulders, it was obvious Eve was in for an argument. I elected to move along.

"Maybe I'll see you another time," I said, and nudged Buttercup with my knee. "Home. Go home, Buttercup."

It had gotten warm while I was out in the middle of the dirt road.

Thankfully, my porcine buddy was glad to head back to the shady and damp mud pit in her pen. Hot afternoons spent in the wallow were usually followed by a chilly hosing down. Fortunately, the pig seemed to enjoy both.

As we moved on, I took one last look at the woman and boy. Behind them, I spotted a terrier of the Jack Russell sort in the window of the house, obviously up on a piece of furniture. Andrew may have ignored Buttercup, which I thought was odd, but the dog was interested.

Instead of taking Duke, my boarding dog, out for a leash lesson on the road, or even in the old orchard across the way, I decided to go up the ridge behind the house.

"Okay, Duke." It was an effort to keep my own nerves at bay. "Let's talk about how we will not rush wild animals. Particularly bears and porcupines. And maybe if you come across a body today, we'll just ignore it. Okay?"

This was the same ridge where Buttercup had found human remains months earlier. I hadn't come up here since then, but now it was time to move past all that evil. Duke wore both a harness and a restraint lead in the event he got rambunctious. He was pretty excited and wiggled from nose to tail. I kept a firm grip to keep him in line and myself on task.

"What a good boy you are."

I coaxed him along with both my words and a few well-timed snacks. Even though I kept him close, I let him sniff and mark as we went. We came back down from the ridge after half an hour, both panting. I put him in the pen with the small blue kiddie pool and left the hose on so it would fill up while I went looking for a cool drink.

Melanie and her friend Missy Shaw sat in a shady corner of the deck, a pitcher of lemonade at hand. I could hear Buttercup complain because she didn't have access to the pool.

"That's pretty funny," Missy called out to me. "There's a chicken race behind you."

"It's all about food," I said with a laugh. "They had to be kept in the coop while Duke was on the run this morning. I don't know how well he accepts them."

"Pig–1, Dog–0? Or is it dog–1, chickens–0?"

"Pretty basically, either." I dropped into a chair. "How come you're out here in the middle of the afternoon?"

The young woman in her ferny-green top and khaki shorts looked back down the road and frowned. "I had to do a home visit for a new child who is due to come into the preschool program. He's never been in any type of daycare or preschool, so he'll enter at the kindergarten level. We want to make sure he's ready, you know? At the same social level as the other kids."

"A new kid who lives out here?" Melanie asked.

"Andrew," I said.

"Do you know him?" Missy turned to me.

"Actually, I just met him today. We didn't have much of a conversation. I thought he'd be all excited to see Buttercup, but he was too busy telling me about his dad."

"And therein lies the problem."

"How so?" Melanie asked.

Missy twitched in her seat uncomfortably. "I just spent an hour with Andrew and his mom for a home visit. All he talked about was his daddy being on TV. He was obsessed, yet his mother led me to believe his father isn't in the picture now. Hasn't been in a while, and they only recently moved here."

"Like never, or newly not there?" I asked.

"Don't know. She wouldn't expand on it." Missy put her empty glass on the table. "But they're from the other side of the state. I can't see how his father would be on television unless he's a politician or criminal."

Melanie and Missy, who had gone to school together, walked off. One on her way back to work, and the other to shut off the hose while Duke frolicked in the pool. My own thoughts drifted to supper ideas and the possibility of a short nap. Eve and Andrew Saucier were far from my thoughts.

Chapter Six

Well, the gate at the bottom of the ramp was a good idea," Neddel said, as he expertly flipped hamburgers and grilled chicken off the gas grill on the deck. Below, Buttercup paced between the bottom of the steps and the ramp gate. "I thought you said you never feed her meat."

"I don't. But she is an omnivore. And she knows there's food up here. If you don't think she can't smell Italian dressing, ask Melanie about the big tossed salad fiasco." I held open the door so that Neddel and his platter could enter. "Too many mosquitoes out there tonight for my liking."

"Once again, consider spraying," my erstwhile beau said.

"No chemicals, thank you. We want to put up a Martin birdhouse," I said.

"Aren't those a little big to hang in a tree?" Neddel tries to act like he's a country mouse, but he's more a city rat.

"They go on a tall pole out in the open," I said. "What are you doing on Sunday?"

Melanie's Cheshire cat smile gave away my intentions.

"Nope," Neddel said. "Busy. Sorry."

"Coward," said Melanie.

"Get Noah to help," Neddel said while he mayonaise'd up a hamburger roll.

* * *

Later, Neddel and I walked around the yard in an ineffectual attempt to work off the burgers. While I tucked Buttercup and the hens in for the night, Neddel wandered over to Duke's inside run.

Each of the four chain-link fence enclosures had an outside run and an inside pen. There was a levered door so I could shut them in or out as I needed. Duke had free range back and forth. He was from the city, so being able to go outside day or night helped him get used to country life. His barking sometimes woke me, but only because I listened for him in case he panicked. My neighbors were too far away to be bothered.

Buttercup, on the other hand, was shut inside at night. She had proven that if she was in the outside pen and an intruder—squirrel, raccoon, or bear—trespassed, she would do her darndest to get out of the enclosure and run them off. When she was safely tucked inside, she wasn't bothered by the need to oust nighttime visitors.

Exiting Buttercup's bedroom, I watched Neddel outside Duke's pen. The dog's tail wagged slowly. I knew he watched every move Neddel made, heard each whispered word, and waited.

"Sit," Neddel said, giving the hand sign.

Duke sat.

Neddel squatted down to be level with the dog.

Duke stood up.

Neddel stood up.

"Sit."

Down squatted Neddel.

Down went Duke's butt.

Up came Neddel.

Up came Duke's butt.

This time, Neddel didn't speak. He gave the hand sign.

Duke sat, but barely. He wasn't sure. In his mind, it was probably getting confusing. As soon as Neddel made a move to squat, Duke was up again. Neddel never said a word. He took a step back away from Duke. A big step. Duke whined. He wanted Neddel to come closer. Neddel signaled. Duke failed to react. Neddel took another step back. The lightbulb went off in Duke's head, and his butt slammed to the floor.

"Good dog," Neddel said as he took a small step forward.

Next, Neddel signed for Duke to lie down, and the dog reacted immediately. Neddel took a step forward, and Duke held. Neddel took the second step and waited. Only Duke's tail moved as it slowly swept the floor behind him.

Neddel squatted, but never reached toward the dog. Then he started talking, man-to-man.

"You did a good job, Duke. But you need to remember what you learned. If you want to be part of the team, you have to be one of the players, not a bigshot."

I went back to the house. I wasn't sure why, but Neddel was giving Duke a lesson. I let him have at it. Half an hour later, Neddel came in, said goodnight, and drove away. He seemed pretty pleased but was distracted. I wanted to ask what was going on between those ears, but I held back.

"Did the two big guys have a moment?" Melanie asked from behind my elbow.

"I think so." I couldn't help but smile.

"Isn't that cute?" Melanie went away laughing to herself.

Way back when Duke and Delish, the big female dog, had arrived, Neddel had been wary of Delish. Even though Duke took all his cues from the older pit-bull-boxer mix, the sheriff had said the young male had potential.

It seems that now Neddel was seeing something in Duke that I wasn't.

Chapter Seven

Since Ian's death, I had isolated myself at the farm. Oh, I still went out, but not to attend social or town events. For a long time, we thought Melanie had Lyme's disease. When she was diagnosed with multiple sclerosis, it was a shocker. Then the MS bloomed twice, and hard right after the death of her father. Because of that, she'd moved back from the city and worked from a home office.

My daughter had become a homebody. Noah had been her on-again, off-again boyfriend. But that changed. They had gone to school together. He had known her when she was gregarious and well aware of her likes and dislikes. She was vocal about her sudden fear of being someplace and falling or having an episode. Noah rose to the challenge and unearthed new adventures she would enjoy. He also took the time to light a fire beneath the butts of her old schooltime chums, letting them know she was home and ready to be part of the community. A few, like Missy, were married and had children, but they had often been in our home as kids. They knew us, and they returned. They welcomed her back. She joined them for many excursions, but always took her trusty collapsible cane. If something didn't come out well, like the cove beer party where she got roofied, no second chance was taken.

Melanie had also accepted the chore of shopping, which I detested. The farm and I had settled into a routine where I was comfortable after Ian's death. It changed again when Melanie returned. Then a new twist was added when Sheriff Everett Neddel came to town. A hot commodity for many local women, single and not, but I wasn't on the lookout for romance.

I probably never would have availed myself of his attention if it hadn't been for Buttercup. She was the one who found the body on the ridge above the town. And somehow, she was the one who had stayed, if not in the center of the entire investigation, at least on the inner rim. Now, Neddel and I moved cautiously ahead in our relationship. Melanie warned me that it was I who stood on the brake.

"Some warmer body is going to come out the winner here," she had prophesied when I continued to send him home at night.

"I can't help it," I'd said. "I just can't see the world beyond the farm."

"You need a job," she'd declared.

Then she got Noah to agree with her. They both went to work on me, starting by circling ads in the help wanted section of the daily. Or they'd left sticky notes on the fridge and sent texts and cellphone shots of every HELP WANTED sign they saw. When I still hadn't moved fast enough, Melanie had enlisted Neddel's help.

All this explained why, on a bright, sunny day when the lawns were still moist from the previous night's rain and every shade of green imaginable glistened in a merry way, I stood in the kitchen in a pair of pressed cotton trousers, a comfortable, short-sleeved blouse, and shoes made for walking.

"You look great, Mom! You're going to knock them dead," Melanie enthused. She was pleased as punch that she had gotten what she wanted: I had found gainful employment at the Agency on the Aging.

"For crying out loud, Melanie." I feigned shock. "The basis of this job is to make sure they aren't dead!"

Melanie giggled and handed me a brown paper bag. It contained a sandwich, an orange, and a power bar.

When I was ready to get into my car, I saw Duke watching from the outside section of his pen. Ears at attention, a questioning look on his face. He wanted to go. Buttercup and Royally, my Pembroke Welsh Corgi, snuffled around the edge of the woods line, oblivious of the fact I was about to leave them to Melanie's care.

It was like the first day of school, but I was the one getting on the bus. Or into the Jeep, as it were.

My new part-time job was as a field agent for the Agency on Aging County Office. South of the village, about seven miles from the farm, it was located in a three-story building that had at one time housed a wood processing and furniture mill. It had closed forty years prior because the acreage that surrounded the plant had been classified as a hazmat zone. Then, to the surprise of the town's residents, the property had been bought up by some goody-two-shoes entrepreneur half the continent away. Soon it was sterilized, revamped, and opened as leased office space.

I had to admit it was a beautiful area that overlooked the winding Saco River, the White Mountain Valley, and the Moat Mountain range to the west. Nonetheless, this was ten acres I would never have considered stepping foot onto.

"Let's just hope they actually got this place clean and I don't glow by the end of the day," I muttered as I got out of the Jeep.

My directions had been to go directly to the third floor, where I would be buzzed in and show identification. There was an elevator the size of my shower. I took the stairs. The young woman at the desk, Heidi, told me I would meet with Tom from personnel, and then she had been instructed to take me directly to Mrs. Henderson's office. The lowering of Heidi's voice and a side glance at the mention of Mrs. Henderson raised the hair on my arms.

Tom, on the other hand, was pretty jovial. We filled out forms and chatted about the weather. He gave me a tour, which included the employee entrance, a much newer and larger elevator, a cafeteria with one candy bar machine, the restrooms, and finally the locker room. Then we zoomed back up to the third floor, where we hustled down an inner corridor. He knocked twice on an unnumbered door, swept it open, and said my name. Then he disappeared. Poof. Like magic.

"I had expected you before this," the woman behind the desk said as she rose.

There was a wide window behind her, and the woman kept getting taller until she covered it. My brain screamed that I was in the presence of Supay, the Inca God of Death. Mrs. Henderson had to be six feet tall. She was built like a refrigerator with a head, and had heavy, pendulous breasts, but no butt. Her voice was deep and unfriendly. It was barely ten o'clock in the morning, and she already had a five o'clock shadow on her wide chin and along the upper hairline of her jowls.

The woman was terrifying.

She looked me over, taking in my slacks and blouse. Comparing my outfit, I was sure, to her two-piece suit with its straight skirt, single strand of pearls that were almost choker tight, and one-inch pumps.

I was her new, specifically-middle-age requested employee, and she found me lacking.

"Mrs. Flynn," she began.

"Doris, please." I smiled.

"Mrs. Flynn," she reiterated.

I groaned inwardly. *This was so going to hurt.*

"I'm sure you're aware that your time here is meant to cover the maternity leave of one of our more *mature* employees."

Mrs. Henderson gave a sniff that let me know exactly how she felt about a woman who, at thirty-plus years of age, had decided to have a child.

I nodded.

She pointed to a chair, and I sat, but not as gracefully or silently as she did. For the next thirty minutes, she explained that I would do home visits to verify that some of the frailer members of our community still breathed. Also, I would check that there had been no changes in their circumstances that would make them ineligible for the agency's services.

"You have been assigned office space on this floor, near the elevators. Ms. Lemper will take you there shortly. You will arrive no sooner than ten minutes before your shift, collect the day's visit log and the necessary files, make your calls, and return here. Under no circumstances are you to take files home with you."

"Yes, ma'am," I said.

"You will use your own vehicle. Every Friday, you will be required to return Form 1164 to accounting. If you are going to be later than four o'clock, you may submit electronically. I am sure Mr. Reynolds has explained everything else to you?"

"Yes, ma'am," I repeated.

Even as I agreed, she pushed one of the buttons on the keyboard located on the side extension of her desk. Within five seconds, I swear, there was a knock, and Heidi stepped into the room. It must have been an illusion of the light, but it seemed her thin, youthful body trembled.

"Mrs. Henderson?"

Nope. The high pitch of Heidi's voice indicated she knew she was in the presence of the dragon, and death was imminent. The trembling had been real.

My assigned office space was a cubicle in a general-use office. My retired military issue desk was against the wall, away from the windows, but so close to the elevator that the rattling would interrupt any telephone conversations.

Heidi's job description included time allotted to instruct me on how to access the computer file that I would use to find my list of contacts.

"You download the list, gather the files, and make physical contact," Heidi explained.

"So, I won't know until that morning which client I see? How do I schedule visits?" I asked.

"The idea is to just show up. These people are supposed to be homebound."

"And if they aren't home?"

Heidi shrugged. "Two attempts. Negative results mean a loss of services. You will have six to ten contacts to make daily." She looked back down the corridor, then stooped to pick up a scrap of paper. "Doris, I can call you Doris, right? You need to be clocked out by five-thirty. You only get today to find your way around, so I suggest you make the most of it. I have to go back to my desk, but I can help you from my computer. Just buzz me."

By noontime, I was pretty much on top of what small amount I needed to know within the building. According to the download, I would be assigned six contacts to make that day. Each one came with a list of specific items that I needed to witness proof of.

I told Heidi that I was on my way out.

"All you need to do is meet, greet, collect info, and beat feet to your next client. Oh, and you need to be back and off the clock by five-thirty," she said.

I drove toward VFW Street, chuckling. The young woman's warning had sounded just like the fairy godmother's for Cinderella.

My first stop was easy. Arnie was an old man, crippled by both rheumatoid and osteoarthritis.

"The door is open," he called out.

He was in a recliner near the window. The table beside him held a radio, a book, a couple of bottles of water, a bag of snacks, and a remote. The television played a twenty-year-old sitcom.

This was one of six apartments in the building. When I'd come through the front door, I could smell the reek of urine and worse. In this apartment, I knew where the stink came from.

"I'm Doris from the Agency on Aging," I said. "Do you always leave your door open? Is it safe?"

His smile immediately disappeared.

"I'm sorry," he whispered, and I believed him. "I didn't mean to fall down and make a mess on the floor. I really didn't."

I took a quick look at his file. The report stated that on multiple occasions, he had created a mess that required a special homemaker visit to clean up.

"I don't understand," I said.

I didn't, really. The report sounded like I was walking into a cesspool with a deranged, senile old man. But when I looked around, I saw a shabby, cluttered apartment that was basically neat, except for the area around his recliner. The kitchen table was clean. There was some evidence of crumbs and spills on the counter and breakfast dishes in the sink.

Arnie explained that he had limited mobility. His hands and feet were crippled. Homemaking came in for one hour every two weeks. He did the best he could.

I asked if I could look around.

He said yes, and I went into the bathroom and the bedroom. It was obvious he didn't sleep in the bed. The bathroom needed to be bombed out and replaced.

Back in the living room, I asked Arnie the questions on my list, which to me made no sense. Had he had breakfast? Did he sleep through the night? Could he get to the bathroom on time? Then I asked him who usually came in and helped him.

I had a problem leaving and only succeeded when he dozed off. I had been at the first house for an hour. Far longer than I would be able to if I needed to make six visits in a day, which included travel and paperwork. All in eight hours.

As it was, I made two more visits. One was a half-hour drive on mostly dirt roads. Another elderly person, alone all day, and wanting to chat. My last visit was closer to town. By the time I got there, the neighbor had returned with the husband and a to-go supper. They weren't interested in my hanging around.

At five o'clock, I sat at my desk, feverishly trying to type my notes. Two other people who sat nearby did the same thing. There wasn't any hi, how are you, welcome chatter, just get done and get out. At five twenty-nine, we all rushed for the time clock. I was relieved to drive away. But when I considered the day and the closing up, I wasn't sure if I felt like some monster with no heart, or a jilted lover left at the altar. Sad, inadequate, mortified, all that, and angry as well. No wonder I'd been hired with my skimpy skills; no one in their right mind would want this job.

* * *

"I need a shower," I said as I walked past Melanie and Noah. The two of them smiled as I passed them.

Supper was on the table, but I couldn't stop. I knew they wanted to hear about my day. None of my three visits had been good. At least I didn't think so. What had I accomplished?

"You look pretty exhausted," Melanie said when I came downstairs. "How did your first day go?"

"It was terrible."

My eyes filled up. I had signed a non-disclosure clause, which prevented me from speaking to anyone about my clients. Melanie had a similar contract with her company, but she was stronger than I was. Before I could stop myself, I spilled my guts.

Noah got up and let Buttercup inside. She'd been making noises of rejection since I'd gotten home. The pig walked over, laid her disc on my knee, and asked me what was wrong in low, chortling coos.

"As a special gift," Noah said cheerfully, though his eyes belied that sentiment, "I'll do the dishes."

"Okay," I sniveled.

I took the bowl of leftover salad and a big dog biscuit and headed towards the barn. Melanie walked with me as far as the chicken coop. She would shut in the biddies and go back to help Noah. Buttercup woofed along, telling me about her day. She knew the salad was for her and forgave me everything. Especially because I had already poured Italian dressing on it. Once it was dumped in the trough in her bedroom pen, I turned my attention to Duke.

Melanie could let the hens, house dogs, and cats, and even Buttercup out and interact with them in the yard or in the house. But the humane society dogs were different. She was not to let them free or to enter their enclosure. I didn't feel that would be safe and strictly forbade it. Instead, just as I did, she would sit in a lawn chair outside their pen, talk to them, maybe work where they could see and hear her. It was good that they had even this little bit of interaction with another human besides myself. I had no idea how even Duke might react. My daughter's handicap made her vulnerable.

I snapped a harness, collar, and short lead on him, and we walked around the yard. He needed to burn off energy, and I needed to release my angst. We walked fast until I was huffing, and he wasn't pulling on the lead. Buttercup made the first circle and then sat down and waited for us to finish.

This was not the job I'd thought I signed up for. My first visit, Arnie, had been the absolute worst, but the other two weren't much better. Opal was an old woman living with her daughter, who worked outside the house. The daughter had two teenagers who weren't concerned about their grandmother. They lived in the middle of nowhere. If an emergency call went out for them, it would take twenty or twenty-five minutes for help to arrive. At the last house, Mrs. Bell had been home, but Mr. Bell had been taken by a neighbor to a doctor's appointment. I'd asked about the unregistered car in the driveway. Mrs. Bell said she didn't drive, and her husband wasn't physically able to.

"I thought there was more assistance, home visits, something more than this out there. I never realized people are so isolated," I told Duke. "This was my first day, and I already don't want to go back."

"So…are you?" a deep, slightly gravelly voice behind my shoulder asked.

"Yip!" I yelped and jumped to the side.

Duke reacted immediately as well. Though his tail went between his back legs, he gave a growl that sounded vicious. In the fading light, I could see his lips roll back far enough to expose the glisten of pointed teeth and a ridge of red gum.

"Easy, Duke," I said. "Easy. It's okay."

I put my hand down, but didn't quite touch him. Then I stood still. He knew me well enough to consider me a shield. The top of his head slid into my palm. I moved in slow, even steps back toward his home pen. Neddel, who had immediately realized his mistake, held back. Once Duke was in the pen that he considered his safe place with its familiar flannel bed and big dog biscuit, Neddel entered the barn.

Duke stopped chewing, watching him with wary eyes. I was seated in a lawn chair that faced Duke, twenty-four inches from the chain-link. It was important that if he'd had a bad episode, that I didn't desert him. He needed to know that I'd be there. The second chair was a foot further away. Neddel slid into it. He remembered what I'd told him way back when Duke and Delish had arrived and kept his hands relaxed on the armrests where Duke could see them.

I had removed the doghouse in the home kennel when Duke first arrived. He didn't need to hide anymore. But right now, he was backed as far into the corner as he could get. He had his treat. There were no loud noises. Normally, the radio played constant rock and roll. With Duke still settling in, quiet jazz at low volume filled the barn. No possible weapons that could hurt him were in sight. No brooms, shovels, sticks of any kind. He waited.

"I thought he and I had come to an understanding," Neddel said quietly.

"You might have. I don't know why he reacted that way. But I have to tell you, it takes more than a single good time to make a marriage work."

When I started speaking, Duke looked at me, a question in his eyes.

"Yes, you're a good boy. It's okay. No one is going to hurt you."

Duke moved his golden eyes to Neddel, who took the hint.

"Good dog, Duke. So, Doris, how was your day?" He asked in a quiet voice.

"I think we should talk about something less stressful right now," I answered.

"Okay. How's the rent situation at the Martin house?"

I laughed. Setting up the Martin house with Noah and Melanie had proven to be quite an experience. It would have made a funny video. We'd dug an enormous hole, set the base in the ground, and filled it with concrete. The pole was positioned in the base, and we strung lead lines to hold it just right while the cement hardened. Lastly, exhausted by our efforts and with a continual fight to keep the dogs and pig from excavating, we covered the whole base setup with soil. A finished project, and we were proud of it. However, we had yet to see a single martin.

I said, "It's been less than a week. But some very pretty and tiny songbirds seem to have moved in."

"Really? Was that expected?"

"Not at all."

I switched the radio to the sixties station. We sat quietly, listening and humming a few bars here and there. Eventually, Neddel's fingers reached out to entwine with mine. Duke relaxed. When Neddel spoke to him, the dog moved to a place close by. I left the two of them so they could have another guy talk.

Chapter Eight

My week rambled past. I learned more about the agency, met more elderly residents, and considered several times that I should retire. On Saturday, I might have taken a couple of naps.

Sunday was clear and sunny. Even though July 4th was officially tomorrow, the parade and fireworks were to be held today. The powers-that-be voted in the change, as there was a good chance more people would be able to enjoy the festivities that way. Most of our tourist trade would have to be at work early on Tuesday morning, and therefore fly away home by 9:00 Monday evening.

A small carnival was set up in Schouler Park with rides and games. For the past couple of years, I'd sat out the three parades in town. This year I promised Melanie I'd attend. And if I was going, so was Buttercup.

She knew something was up and had her high game on. Both she and Royally had been bathed the day before. She'd gotten a good rubdown, been treated to body lotion, and had her whiskers trimmed. Royally had been trimmed and brushed to excess. He was so fluffy it was hard to tell where the actual dog was in all the fur.

The enclosed horse trailer I'd borrowed to transport Buttercup was in the yard, attached to the jeep, and filled with straw. She just knew she was going for a ride, maybe because I hadn't let her into her outside pen. Or possibly because I'd loaded up her harness and red, white, and blue superhero costume. Royally was already in the truck, whining to go.

I lifted Buttercup's cart down from the rack. She was doing the math. It all added up: she would get to go this time, and it was sure to be fun.

"Do you want me to drop the load gate on the trailer?" Noah asked after he helped me load the cart on the roof rack.

"No. I need her to use her potty first. Go inside. I'll call you when we're ready."

Buttercup ballet-stepped after me out of the barn. Duke was pressed against the wire but ran outside for a better look. The pig went right to the trailer, but I'd walked over toward the bramble area she used for a bathroom. I snapped my fingers and pointed, a signal for her to go into the brambles. She snorted and looked back at the trailer. I didn't make eye contact. Duke woofed. When I turned toward him, she decided it was better to get done and get out of the yard before I decided he could come as well.

* * *

"You're sure you don't want me to wait?" Noah asked as we drove to the staging area for the parade.

"No, take the truck and trailer back to the house. We're supposed to end up on that side of town, so we'll walk home from there."

I pulled into the Our Lady of the Mountains Catholic Church parking lot to a spot where I would have room to drop the load-gate.

"You guys have a good time. Buttercup and I will be looking for a nap by the time we get done," I said, and sent Noah on his way.

Missy found me as I hooked Buttercup into the traces. Her four-year-old Sammie would ride in the cart and toss candy. She'd walk along beside him, as I needed to stay beside Buttercup.

"Okay, Sammie," I said, once he was seated with a bucket of candy between his knees. "Royally doesn't get any, got that? And don't throw the candy at Buttercup, or she'll stop."

"Okay." Sammie nodded so hard I thought he'd topple over.

"Between his short legs and fat belly, Royally isn't going to last long walking. He wants to start on the ground. When he lags behind a little, pick him up and sit him on the seat with Sammy." I told Missy.

"Will that make the cart too heavy for Buttercup?" she asked.

"No, she's used to loads of up to two hundred pounds of cement in there. I bet the cart, Royally, and Sammie won't equal one-twenty-five."

After we were assigned our spot, we got in line. Soon the parade music started.

Buttercup was a pro. This was the one type of event where she waited for a command. She knew what she was supposed to do. Her tail thrashed back and forth. The oval at the tip of her snout was raised and quivering.

"Hep," I said, and she stepped out.

We took a left onto Main Street and walked past the John Fuller Elementary School. That was the first place Buttercup wanted to turn off. She knew the kids. Then she wanted to stop down near Schouler Park. The Stan-mobile was parked near the carnie rides.

"No," I said, "keep on."

I walked with my knees right beside her big, triangular black ears. She bumped me once, then again with another good one to let me know she wasn't happy. We might have had an issue right there, but a couple of people who recognized her started to yell her name.

Let's face it: in the literal sense, Buttercup's a ham. In a couple more steps, I realized that Melanie stood among her friends as they coaxed Buttercup forward. To help me out, my daughter yelled, "Cookie!" Buttercup recognized Melanie's voice. The big ham-ster knew the cookie was for her.

I could see the lumber building at Hancock's Supply. That was the parade's end. We were almost there when a ruckus happened on Buttercup's off side. On the front edge of the spectators, a woman in a blue sequined tuxedo tried to corral a Jack Russell that had taken a dislike to some guy in the crowd.

The dog darted in and out, on the attack. People yelled and tried to get away. I actually considered leaving Buttercup in the parade to see if I could help. Then I realized the dog already wore a muzzle. His nutty owner had brought a dog with an attitude to the biggest public gathering in the village.

I knew Dolores, one of Neddel's deputies, was somewhere behind me riding her Morgan-Palomino cross. When she rode up toward the Jack Russell, the dog spooked and ran into the street. And he ran right into

Buttercup's side. Like, bang! Splat!

The pig didn't like that. She jerked and tried to turn. The cart hampered her, but Royally, who was still afoot, decided that he should maybe help her out. His way is to try to herd her where he wants to go. Missy grabbed Sammy and got out of the fray.

Now the cart was on one wheel. I fought to keep it from turning over as I wrestled with Buttercup at the same time. To be honest, Royally was pretty much making his own decisions for a few seconds there.

The woman was in my face, screeching at me. She scooped up the Jack Russell and darted backwards half a dozen steps.

That's when I realized it was Racheal Gerrish.

I was sweating all over. I knew my blood pressure was on the rise, and I couldn't help myself.

"Be quiet," I ordered using my big dog tone.

She blinked, but her mouth didn't shut.

"You're riling up the animals, alarming the spectators, and scaring the children. You want to see that in the paper alongside your business logo?"

That did it. Her jaw snapped up, but her eyes were still giving off sparks. Buttercup gave a yank, and I turned back to what she was doing.

The entire episode lasted only a few minutes. Dolores and her horse were between me and Racheal. I did all I could as the parade moved on. I grabbed Royally and plopped him down in the cart, where he continued to sound off. Then I strong-armed and kneed Buttercup so she faced the right way and pulled a peanut butter snack bar out of my pocket. Instant attention-getter. We were back in formation, maybe a tad behind where we should have been, but headed toward Hancock's.

Some clown on the sideline yelled out, "Geehaw, get along, little piggy!"

I laughed and waved and mentally blew him off.

We made it into the Hancock Lumber parking lot, and I wrangled the pig and cart off to the side.

In the back of the cart, I carried my duty bag. It was like an emergency medical kit, containing anything I might need for an animal while I was out. There was also a gallon of water. Using the collapsible bowl and gallon jug,

I gave both dog and pig a drink and a chance for a little rest while I chatted with some of the other parade participants. I thought a little positive PR might be a good idea right then. Nobody said a word about the incident with Racheal or about Buttercup leaving the line, so I assumed it was no big deal.

Twenty minutes later, it was time for the almost two-mile walk back to Calwin Mountain Road, then from there to the farm. Noah had taken the truck and trailer home. I could have called, but the traffic was barely moving, and there wasn't really room to park and load. It had started to get warm, so we weren't in any real hurry. There were always people who came for the parade and then went home to their family barbecues. Later, the whole kit and kaboodle would return at dusk for the fireworks, so there was a fair amount of exiting traffic.

I got across Route 16 with no issues. People drove by and blew their horns or yelled out hi to the pig. All the usual fanfare. There weren't a lot of people on the sidewalk, so I steered us there because it would be safer.

Up ahead, I could see two people walking. A woman and a child.

The small child was tired. They slowed down. At one point, he stopped, but she tugged on his hand and he kept moving. I was almost ready to detour into the street to pass them when I realized it was Eve and Andrew. The new family from next door. They still had almost a mile to walk. It didn't look like the little boy would be able to go much further.

"Hi, Eve," I called out.

She turned. Andy flopped down on the ground.

"Well, you're pretty ambitious, to walk all the way into North Conway for the parade," I said. I tried to remember if I'd seen a car in their driveway. There was a garage, so maybe?

As if in answer to my thoughts, the little boy whined, "The car won't go."

"Ah," I said. By now, I had reached them on the sidewalk. "I'm going to pull over right here so Buttercup can rest in the shade for a bit. How about if you join us, and when Buttercup is ready to go, you can ride in the cart? Buttercup and I walk right past your house on the way home."

I specifically spoke to the child, a move I hated from others when Melanie was young. He immediately brightened up and jumped to his feet. In the shade of the cherry tree in front of the Christmas Loft, I poured water into two paper cups from the duty bag. From a package of peanut butter crackers, I gave one to Eve, a second to Royally, and split the last four between Buttercup and Andy. While he sat in the cart seat with his snack and Royally made sad puppy eyes at him, I slathered a little sunscreen on Buttercup.

"Why are you greasing the pig?" Eve asked.

I laughed aloud. I heard a lot of comments with regard to Buttercup, but that was a first. While I explained about the pig's tender skin and sunburn, I packed up the cart. With the lead in my hand, I took my position at her right ear.

"Home, Buttercup," I commanded. "Go home."

She could sit but not lie down when she was in the traces, so she heaved her ample butt up. Though her hooves clicked and clacked like high heels, we continued on our way.

Andy didn't talk about his father today. He was too busy telling Royally that he had a dog, Prince, who couldn't go with them to the parade. I listened with a half-ear, because somewhere in that walk, Eve started to talk. Letting her ramble led to some interesting information.

I'd been right when I'd told Noah the critters and I would be tired out by the time we got home. He and Melanie beat us there. She had the lawn sprinkler already on, snacks, and cold drinks ready. Buttercup was all about a treat and a nap under the sprinkler, whereas Royally took his to a hole he'd dug under the picnic table. My treat was iced tea, along with the fried dough Melanie had brought home. I took them to a shady corner of the deck where the gate kept my four-legged buddies at bay.

"Huh," Noah said. "I thought they'd be all over you for that fried dough. I even suggested to Melanie that she get two."

"Did she?"

"Nope."

"Good thing, because then I'd have to eat them both. Bad for the critters' hearts." I peeked over the rail and saw just the butt end of Buttercup headed into her home pen. "They're both down for a nap. If you shut the water off, the chickens will canvass the area for fresh bugs. Worms, ticks, whatever they can find."

Noah's nose sort of scrunched up. Not for the first time, I told myself that farming wasn't in his blood. Melanie brought out plates of cold salad and sliced chicken. I told them how I had come across Eve and Andy.

"You might want to mention to Missy for her preschool paperwork that I don't think they have a lot of money. Andy's father was supposed to join them here, but they haven't heard a word from him in a while. She's waitressing down at Bea's in the mornings and hopes to find some kids to babysit after school come September. They came up from Nashua."

"You got all that info in half a mile?" Melanie asked.

"Closer to a whole mile, actually." I pushed my empty plate away. "I think she's lonely. Probably didn't realize all she spouted off."

"Has she reported the father missing?" Noah asked.

I think Noah is a Sheriff Neddel wannabe.

"They aren't married. I don't know how that works. There also seems to be some kind of undercurrent, like he might have been recently divorced. Andy is four years old. If this is his biological father, there could be a can of worms I don't want any part of."

Melanie nodded. "True that."

Right about then, I dozed off and woke just in time for animal feeding. With the parade, carnie, and fireworks, I knew Neddel was going to be busy with work and such, so I allowed myself a nice long shower. I turned the barn radio up a little and went to bed about the time the first rocket went off.

Chapter Nine

It came as an early lesson on my new job that my half-hour lunch couldn't be spent snoozing under an apple tree somewhere. Otherwise, I wouldn't make my entire contact list. Also, Mrs. Henderson's rule about not arriving earlier than ten minutes before a shift was bogus as well. There were two other full-time outreach people who did what I did, five days a week. One worked specifically with vets and medicals at extreme risk. The other, a woman named Maryann, was doing the same work I was.

By the time I pulled into the lot every day, they were already out on the road. Maryann told me I could sign in and out anywhere if I used my iPad. In all the years she'd been there, no one had ever checked to see if her physical files were back in place at the end of the day.

"Are you serious?" I asked.

"Yep. Mrs. H. only takes half an hour for lunch. She's out of here by four-thirty, regardless."

Maryann was my age and a wealth of information. She filled a cardboard box with more files than she'd get to in one day. When she caught me looking, she told me she had a regular schedule.

"I thought we were doing the same job," I said. "The way I understand it, there is no regular schedule."

"Well, yes, and no. Basically, it's the same people every thirty or sixty days. That's the part that makes it regular. So, unless there's a special needs call or something, I know where I'll be for the next couple of days. My range is south and west, mostly." She kind of bit her lip. "Also, talk to Heidi. The computer gives you cases at random. Here. There. Miles away. Heidi can tighten things up so your calls are closer to each other on any given day. Less running. Unless you're into a larger Form-1164 gas return and a chance of never catching up."

I was only going to be working three days a week. Therefore, taking files home might not be a good idea. But less distance between calls would be a relief.

"Sure, I can take care of that," Heidi said when I asked. "Are you applying for the vacant full-time caseworker position? I could help you with the paperwork." She looked hopeful.

My brain screamed, *absolutely not!* But aloud, I explained my animal responsibilities. Already, I felt I'd been shirking lately in that area.

The week after the Fourth, I got Arnie's file again. He had taken another header. The Visiting Nurse had stopped in and made sure he was alright. Even though it would have been easiest to do him first, I shuffled the file to the end of the stack, that way I would have more time to visit with him. Melanie met me outside of his apartment with an overfilled plate of leftovers and my house cleaning bucket.

"Are you sure you want to do this, Mom? You aren't supposed to be cleaning and doing laundry, are you?" she asked.

"Just this once. He doesn't want to go into a nursing home. I don't think he really has to. I just need to figure out what he realistically needs."

While I did his home visit, and he stuffed his face, I cleaned—well, tried to clean—his bathroom. I'm not sure how come I hadn't vomited by the time I was through forty-five minutes later. Whoever had cleaned up had missed a lot of blood. I knew he'd cut his head, but holy cow! I'd rather clean up monkey poop smeared on the walls than blood dried on the baseboards.

"How come you don't get more home care assistance than an hour every two weeks?" I asked Arnie as I stripped off my rubber gloves. I had my butt parked on top of a newspaper on the sofa, and a bottle of water from my bag in hand.

"The woman who used to come here? Lori?" Arnie looked for a place to put the empty Tupperware down. I slid it into my bag. "She told me if I was too needy, I'd get shipped off to a home." He spoke in a high whisper and had a scared look in his eyes.

I wasn't sure what to say. Was he needy? I looked around. I didn't consider this the best place for him, but he'd been here a while and was happy. How much could I ask him without getting him all riled up?

"You know, Arnie. I'm new at this job. I don't want to jump to any conclusions, but you're new to me, so I don't understand all the facets of your life. But if you keep falling down, if you can't keep up your place, it's going to be out of both your and my hands."

"I don't want to be locked away like some old piece of luggage. Used and forgotten," he said.

"I don't want you to be either. But changes are going to have to be made."

Arnie shook his head and looked away.

"I've got friends who come in and visit. I can sit here in this window and watch the neighborhood. There are kids, families."

He sounded despondent. I walked over to see what he could see. It wasn't all that much. Did he really have friends? He and I were going to have to have a sit down and dragged out, I knew it.

I need to decide exactly what I'm going to ask and who I can contact; I thought.

"See that little blue split? New people. They've got a terrier. I thought it was a couple, but it seems to be just the woman."

"Are you just trying to divert my attention?" I asked. "I'll let it ride for right now, but there will be conversation. And stop spying on your neighbors. The last thing you need is a neighborhood woman to report a peeping tom."

I turned away to pack up my stuff. "Arnie, I think I'll check around about the housekeeping thing, okay?" At his worried look, I added, "Take it easy. I won't mention any names. I'm new, so the other people in the office share info all the time."

He smiled and nodded. Then he waved goodbye and turned back to the window.

The next day, I was scheduled to be off, but I already had a plan that included sneaking into the office for a little tete-a-tete with Heidi.

Before I pulled out of Arnie's parking lot, I checked to see if Melanie needed me to pick up anything on the way home. I saw a message from

Nedell. He wanted me to stop at the sheriff's office.

"I'm kind of stinky and sweaty," I warned as I came through the door.

"Yeah, I heard how you'd gone all bleeding heart," he said.

At my raised eyebrow, he explained that he'd forgotten I would be at work and called the house. Melanie had reported what she considered to be my questionable actions. Needless to say, I wasn't impressed even though I knew she meant well. There have been many times I've gotten caught up in other people's drama. Invariably, I end up suffering as well.

"If your plan is to dump on me, how about I go home and have a shower? And maybe supper? That way, I'll be strong enough to fight back," I groused.

"Nah," he said with a smile. "It's not my business. Melanie just wants to make sure this isn't some old con taking advantage. But that's not why I called you." He clicked away on his computer and then switched on the small TV on the shelf behind him. "I had you stop in because I found this short feed from the parade on Deputy Dolores's body."

The segment lasted a couple of minutes, and then only because the deputy had continued to deal with Racheal Gerrish after the parade had moved on. A point I hadn't been aware of because I'd had my hands full with Buttercup and Royally.

I watched as Dolores dismounted and faced the enraged Realtor. Racheal had her Jack Russell in her arms. I could see why he wore a muzzle. He growled, snarled, and tried to lunge. His body posture was combative and rigid. I don't know if he was still angry about the pig, didn't like the horse, or whatever the issue had been before Buttercup and I had come upon them, but he looked like he was about to stroke out.

"Well, he definitely needs anger management," I remarked.

Nedell turned up the volume. Racheal was on a full-volume rave about Buttercup! The woman screamed in Dolores's face that if her dog needed to be muzzled, something should be done about the pig.

"It's a dangerous animal," Racheal declared. "Not only did it come at me while I was speaking with a potential client at the parade, but it charged me out of nowhere and attacked me at a sales function that I had set up a few weeks ago."

I think my jaw might have fallen.

"Seriously?" I asked. "Buttercup was on the lead. Stan was there. She wanted a Porker Special."

"Was this the day Ms. Gerrish was at your house when I arrived?"

"Yes, but Nedell, that's not what happened," I sputtered.

He held up his hand for silence. Full cop mode. He had paused the recording, so I didn't know what happened after that ridiculous accusation.

"Before you go off half-cocked," he said, "I want you to know Dolores brought this to my attention because she thinks Racheal is a powder keg. I have to agree, she has a lot of the signs of being volatile. I've invited Racheal to come in. I think it will be better if she's here in person to view the tape. Then I can see what she has to say. If she continues in that vein, I'll tell her she needs to fill out a police report."

My temperature rose. "She'd better rescind that threat," I said. "Make sure you tell her statements like that could get her in court for defamation of character."

I immediately felt bad. Nedell was only trying to help me, and I was coming unglued all over his office. Even though I knew I should apologize, I couldn't squeeze out the words. Instead, I sat there like a petulant third-grader.

Nedell pursed his lips. "I'll call her now. I'll get back to you later."

In the car, I called Melanie to say I was on the way home.

"Sit down at your fancy computer and find out everything you can about Racheal Gerrish," I said.

"From your tone, this doesn't sound good," my daughter said. "But I'm on it."

Chapter Ten

Melanie was ready for me by the time I pulled into the drive. Unfortunately, there was a whole host of animals that still weren't used to my being gone all day on a regular basis. I tried to slip away to change out of my good clothes in my bedroom, but on the first floor, a chorus of barks, mews, and a couple of woofing grunts called me back to where I'd be in reach. The easiest choice was to have a seat in the kitchen while all manner of critters milled around on the floor. I could dispense snacks and pats, get sat on, get slurped on, and be welcomed back into the fold.

I tried to explain to Melanie about Nedell's tape, but there was a lot of interference. Buttercup finally settled in one place when I slid the long-handled back scratcher down her spine. The dogs lay on my feet. One cat draped across my lap, while a second had wound itself like a fur stole on my shoulders. The third took a spot on the table, directly in front of me. Once she had pushed my coffee cup away, she refused to give up her spot.

I repeatedly told them that I needed only a few minutes. No one listened.

"They don't like your new schedule," Melanie said.

"You poor little babies, starving, unloved." I cooed as I got up and started to lay out bowls and grub.

As soon as I turned my attention to all the furbies, I had to raise my voice to be heard over the hubbub.

"It doesn't make any sense to me why this Gerrish woman is wound so tight as far as Buttercup and I are concerned. We're nobodies," I said.

Deserted by all the four-legged critters—including her own Lilo—for the food lady, Melanie opened her laptop again.

"Okay, here's the basic information," she said. "Racheal and Richard Gerrish worked in a successful partnership in the Nashua area for fifteen years. A while ago, they separated their part of the business from the Lang Agency. I don't think it was really friendly, because there isn't any of that oh-I-miss-them-so-much crap on social media. More like, the Gerrishes were here today and invisible tomorrow."

"Okay."

The tray of cat dishes and I disappeared into the cattery. I barely got the door shut in time to keep the dogs and pig out.

Melanie kept talking, upping the volume, until I was back.

"The Gerrishes, as a couple, relocated here to the valley. They opened their own agency. I read on Racheal's feed that they were ready to give up condo living and buy a house. She talks like this is the wonderland they've always been looking for. Now they want to, you know, be part of a community, and not just in a business sense. On the other hand, she also did this continued two-bit reach out, which invited her previous clients, or those she hadn't been finished with, to sign up so she could continue to be their *Ace in the Hole.*"

"Ah-huh."

Two small dogs done. Bowls for Buttercup and Duke in hand, I stepped outside, where I had put the boarding dog out on the steel run for some exercise. I left his food and water where he could reach them.

"Isn't this fun? It's like a picnic," I cooed as he buried his face in the bowl.

Buttercup was already in the home pen. Regardless of where I walked with her bowl, she knew where her trough was. Too tired for much else, I filled her trough, gave her water, and scattered a couple of fistfuls of unsalted peanuts around in the straw. That would keep her busy until she was ready for a nap.

Duke was done and ready for his Milk Bone and bed.

"Thank God," I whispered.

Inside, Melanie busily mixed tuna salad. "Is soup and a sandwich, okay?"

While she worked, she finished her tale of the Gerrishes' business move.

"I don't know how much they got for their condo, but I have to tell you the photographs were fab-u-lous." Melanie stirred soup, cut sandwiches, and used her foot to push the house dogs out of the way. "I'm kind of surprised they didn't buy a house on Pear Mountain or Glen Ridge."

I was too tired for corgi or pug antics. I lifted both dogs over the baby gate in the hall entrance and out of the kitchen while I listened to everything Melanie had uncovered.

"Yes. Instead, they purchased a split off of Stark Road in Conway. A fixer-upper, Richard called it. However, company-wise, they moved into that house-turned-office on Route 16, where O'Brien Realty used to be. They actually bought out the business when the old man retired."

"So, even though there wasn't anything said about Lang buying them out of that agency, they still had enough bucks to purchase a house and buy out a solid business?"

"Right." Melanie sat down and switched screens. "But this is where I started to really wonder. The few media posts Richard put out were about what he had done to fix up the house. The picture shows a modular. Looks like it's in a mobile home park. He had a list of things it needed. Where he bought what, blah, blah, blah. That was months ago, more than six. Which made it sound like they were really buying into being local."

Melanie paused barely long enough to not choke on a sip of iced tea.

"Everything Racheal has put out since they got here and took over Mountain Realty—now The Gerrish Agency—is business-oriented. But it's like she doesn't realize she could get some mileage out of what Richard is doing at their own home. For her, it's all about what's new and happening in the valley. Where she's dipped her toes. Stuff like that.

"Then, if you read down the comments, there are a couple of posts where people, some of them past clients, ask Richard questions. All were answered by Racheal, who was very lighthearted about the fact that he is very busy because he has to travel back and forth to Nashua as he ties up the loose strings of their business there, which supposedly they're all done with."

"Ah-huh," I said again. "What are the chances he and a female realtor in Nashua hooked up, got caught, and he and Racheal had to leave?"

"Nope. I never found anything about friends. There's some chatty stuff about clients, business associates, a lot about the Langs. But if they're the other couple involved, you should know they are Mr. and Mr. Lang. Gay couple. Plus, there is absolutely nothing on their website about him, like Richard dropped in, helped us out, we had drinks, nada. They, like the Gerrrishes, are very prolific on social media." Melanie sat back, with the last bite of her sandwich in hand. "I totally believe that if he went back there, they would have said something about it because prior to that, they were such great buds."

"Are you thinking, Mr. and Ms. Gerrish have called their wedded bliss off?" I asked.

With the dishes in the sink, I removed the baby gate. Hysterical floor-surfing dogs frantically checked for errant crumbs.

"I am for a fact," Melanie said. "Now that I've given you all this Gerrish family information ad nauseam, let's talk about why Ms. Gerrish might not be so happy with you."

I couldn't help but roll my eyes. Melanie is a ferret for facts. I couldn't stand all this, but I would need to be fortified. In self-defense, I pulled the tab on a can of A&W Root Beer.

* * *

"I bet I'm on the top of Racheal Gerrish's do-not-invite list because of Buttercup's visit to the new housing site." I didn't realize until just then how tired I was. Dropping my butt into a seat alone was work.

"Yeah, I don't think that helped," Melanie said.

Deftly keying, she brought up the town's webpage and skipped down to where it offered taped town meetings.

"Okay, look at the planning board meetings from over a year ago." She pointed with a pink and white French manicured nail. "There's a woman who looks surprisingly like you seated in the front row every time that the posted agenda mentions the development of the Calwin Mountain Road/Saco River project."

I groaned. When the owners had announced the property would be for sale, I'd started my campaign. Basically, the area was designated a floodplain. But we all knew that big bucks could grease palms. There were greedy people everywhere. The only way to keep some shyster from buying and building was to be present and remind the board about the zoning. There had been a lot of hoopla, and the project had been on the agenda of the twice-monthly meeting for a while. Then the project seemed to have been abandoned. I no longer needed to attend every zoning board meeting. Obviously, a mistake.

"What you mean is that Jared Cross is no longer interested in the sale of the entire property to a single buyer who will develop the land. He's hired The Gerrish Agency to sell individual lots. Then the new owners can do what they want."

Melanie nodded.

"That's impossible." The flat of my hand came down hard on the table. "It takes a lot of work to put together a development. Then there are all those permits."

"Here's the thing," Melanie pointed out. "If you read the paperwork you brought home from your day in the meadow, you'd see that Ms. Gerrish is perfectly clear that this is a *proposed* development. She offered a substantial discount to people who get in now."

"Oh. Yeah. She gets interested parties, goes back to Zoning, they feel there's a need, and voila, suddenly it's legal to build there." I should have gone for coffee after all. And maybe a couple of heavily frosted cupcakes. "I don't like her."

"I'd say, Mom, she doesn't like you either."

Melanie left a board meeting video up on the screen. I watched it play out and noticed a few people nodding their approval whenever Racheal Gerrish got up and spoke. It was one of the few meetings I was absent from.

"It's a cinch that Mr. Cross warned her about you. She probably watched these same tapes. I mean, know your opponent, right?"

I nodded.

"She wants to sell expensive house lots on the river. You live next door with a large, free-range pig. What are the chances she'd find you undesirable?"

After Melanie had gone off to TV movie land with the dogs and cats, I released a new set of cattery residents to wander the house through the night. Then I went up to my bedroom to watch more of the tapes. Eventually, I realized that Racheal had occupied a seat in the back of the room during a lot of meetings. I started to backtrack. Months before the Gerrishes had moved here, Racheal was there. A literal pain in the rear. Often, a thin, fair-haired man was beside her. I caught moments when they whispered together. When the agenda item that pertained to Calwin Mountain Road had been cleared, the couple left.

"It seems," I said to Royally and Poppy, who had taken spots which held my ankles down under the covers, "Racheal Gerrish knew who I was long before I was aware she existed."

There was a small expulsion of noxious stink. Royally's indication that, whatever the problem was, it wasn't important.

I pushed him away. Perhaps just this one time, I should consider the offensive.

Chapter Eleven

My day off proved to be pretty hectic. Even working three days a week, I found I had to speed the rest of my time up considerably. My time with Nedell fell into that category, and I felt bad about it.

"It's not like I'm complaining," he said. "But does your visit to my office today mean I haven't been out to the farm often enough? Or maybe too often?"

I stood across the desk from where he sat. He looked impressive in his uniform, all starched and pressed. He'd had a recent haircut, shaved clean, and smelled so good. I tried not to smile. But I felt a slight rise of pride that he would come down my road to court me. I took a deep sniff.

"What is that spice, masculine scent wafting my way?" I murmured.

There was a little blush on his cheeks. Was it because of what I'd said or due to the officer who manned the desk and who tittered because I had walked straight past him with a breezy good morning? I'd come to the sheriff's department to make this meeting more professional, then totally ignored all protocol. My ears burned. I was sure the flush was migrating down to my cheeks.

"This is a professional call," I said, a lame attempt to get my feet back under me. "Even though Racheal told you it was a misunderstanding, Melanie pointed out that, in the event Ms. Gerrish files a formal complaint, we should also provide our statements."

"You told Melanie about the tape?" Nedell sat back.

His eyelids slid lower. A pen held at chest height rotated in his hands.

Hmm. He shot me a look that suggested an error on my part.

I fished for excuses. "I was angry. You didn't tell me it was a secret. She's basically my office manager."

"Office manager?"

"She keeps track of my schedule."

"Right." He put down the pen. "I did speak with Ms. Gerrish. She told me that both episodes were blown out of proportion due to her stress and offered an apology."

"What stress?" I asked.

"It seems her husband is away a lot because he works at the other branch of their company." Nedell smiled. "She didn't file a report."

"But you documented it, correct?" I asked. *What other branch? Melanie said they severed ties with the Mr. & Mr.*

"That's the way my job works," Nedell said. "There's always a paper trail."

"Perfect. Like I said, here is a statement, written individually by both myself and Melanie in regards to the day Racheal met Buttercup. There is also a sheet on the foofah at the parade."

I knew Dolores had written a statement, because she'd told Melanie so when they ran into each other in the produce aisle at Hannaford's. She'd also apologized if she hadn't been attentive enough to what my needs were at the time.

"That darn little dog! He about drove Mayfaire nuts," Dolores had complained. "He's a big horse, but normally so easy to handle. I was ready to arrest the mutt."

"What are you up to tonight?" Neddel called me back to the moment.

A little smile curled the edge of his mouth. He leaned across the table, catching the tips of my fingers. I tugged, but he pulled himself closer until he was lying on the desk. His lips pressed against mine. I finally pushed him away, sure that besides being breathless, I was blushing as well.

"Zoning board." With a wave, I was gone. There was no way I'd miss another meeting.

It was barely nine a.m. From the sheriff's office, I drove over to my new workplace on my non-workday.

Once in the lot, it was all me trying to be Sam Spade and find a place to park away from the cameras. Then, a stealthy advance to the stairs instead of the elevator. That way, I could scope out the lobby before I ventured in.

No Mrs. Henderson in sight, but Heidi was busy at her desk. She had one stack of papers and another of 8 x 11 envelopes in front of her. The phone rang, and she keyed up the headset. Even as she answered questions, her fingers were still busily stuffing and sealing.

"Hi, Doris," she called out when I slithered into the room.

"Sh," I whispered, as I made the down-low sign. "I need some information."

"You're safe. Mrs. H. is out of town at a departmental meeting. What's the skivvy?"

I explained about Arnie and my concerns.

"That's a bummer. There are options. It's too bad that lazy Lori couldn't get off her duff to help him out. It was her responsibility to make sure the client gets what they need."

"Why wouldn't she?" I asked.

"For one, any extra offer would mean paperwork for her. For another, in not signing up clients, she saved the agency money, sort of. There are a lot of older employees who still believe that not using the resources makes them look better."

The phone rang. While she spoke, I noticed the next envelope was addressed to Calwin Mountain Road. To Eve, no less.

"I'll email you some information to read," Heidi said. "Do you know how to access it from off-site? There's a lot. You might not have time to read it all here. There's also contact information there for the different aspects of assistance available."

She looked sorrowfully at the implication that I might have to do research on my own time.

"It's not a problem for me to work a little at home." I smiled. "Hey, is this envelope for Eve? I go right past her house on my way home. How about I drop it off, save the agency a little postage?"

"That would be awesome," Heidi said. "She's applied for assistance downstairs." This was my first indication Heidi had anything to do with the other agencies in the building. "We need this back in ten days, or she'll miss the window for this quarter."

"Glad to help. Thanks for the information."

I skipped out of there, right up until I was in the parking lot. Who knew when the Henderson Harpie would return? I could still get caught. By the time I made it to the first stoplight, I had a heavier coat of sweat than the weather called for.

Chapter Twelve

When I pulled into Eve's yard, I noticed SAUCIER had been printed on the mailbox in black magic marker. There was a tiny pile of sand beside the garage, and Andy zoomed a plastic Batmobile around in the dust. Prince appeared from nowhere, gave a couple of hard barks, then belied that sentiment by extreme tail-wagging.

"Hi Andy. This must be Prince."

The kitchen door was open, and Eve stepped out. "Good morning, Mrs. Flynn."

"Oh, my goodness, Eve! Doris, please."

Without waiting for an invitation, I mounted the steps and held out the envelope.

"I work part-time with the Agency for the Aged in conjunction with DCYS." If I talked fast enough, she might not realize the two departments were separate entities, and I couldn't be affiliated with both. "It's time-sensitive. I thought if I brought it out instead of mailing it, we might be able to get it back before the quarter closed." I smiled and shrugged. "Your decision, of course."

She glanced past me. Andy was busy. Vroom, vroom. Batman roared through the dirt.

"That would be awfully nice," she said. "I have tea."

"That would be awesome."

* * *

The paperwork was straightforward. Invasive but clear. In my guise as a representative for the state, Eve was eager to provide information and answer questions she normally wouldn't share with others, if I would guide her through the forms. Was it wrong to misrepresent myself? Yeah, maybe.

We'd been at it for a while, two cups of tea anyway, when Andy came in for a snack. Eve went to get the copy of her previous year's tax filing. While we waited, Andy and I talked about the parade, and I petted Prince. The daily newspaper was on the table. Eve must have been reading it when I arrived.

"Who's a good boy?" I cooed to Prince.

"That's my daddy," Andy whispered. "I'm not supposed to tell anybody. It's a secret. If Santa Claus finds out I told anyone, he won't come."

I almost snapped my neck as I sat up. Andy stood solemnly beside the table. His small hand splayed out on the newspaper. Beneath his grubby little fingers was the ad for The Gerrish Agency, complete with a picture of Racheal and Richard. He sat at a desk. She stood behind him. They both smiled invitingly to all the real-estate-hungry suckers out there.

As Andy stared at the picture, I took a very good look at him. His brown eyes were moist. He'd lost his smile. But now I could see he was the spitting image of Richard.

I heard the thunk of Eve's heavy sandals as she approached. Gently, I pulled the paper free and flipped it over.

"Here's another cookie for you, and one for Prince," I whispered. "Why don't you take him outside so he doesn't get crumbs on the floor?"

I watched him go down the step and hoped he'd forget about the picture when Eve sat down.

"I hope this is the last thing we need," she said.

I hoped so too. My brain was reeling. I'd come here mostly trying to help, but a little curious, okay, nosy. What I ended up with was a bomb blast.

Chapter Thirteen

"You did what?" Melanie demanded, with a look of sheer horror on her face. "Mom. That's beyond invasion of privacy. That's… that's…I don't know what."

"I know," I said. Now that I was safe in my own kitchen, I had to admit that I felt some guilt. "It's not about Eve. It's, I guess, Andy. He's like a waif. Even when he's happy, he's sad. Missy said he's had very little interaction with other children. Even when his mother has to work, a sixty-year-old grandma comes in and watches him. They don't have a car that runs. What'll happen when winter sets in, and she can't walk to work and the store?"

I may be soft-hearted, but Melanie is beyond me. Her bottom lip trembled. Little red dots appeared on her cheeks, just below her eyes. A sure sign she'd start to cry soon. I reached out and touched her arm.

"If we can figure out how to help her and Andy, even a little, they might be okay."

Melanie sniffed. "All right." She got a notepad and pen from the counter. "What should we do?"

"First, you need to realize she's waiting for a man who likely won't come back." I had my own copy of the newspaper. "At one time, she was the receptionist at the Lang Real Estate office in Nashua. She and Richard had an affair. She continued to work even after Andy was born. Richard remained part of their lives, but on the sly. Somewhere along the way, Mr. Lang jokingly remarked to Richard how he and Andy had the same coloring and round head."

My tongue ran over my wet lips.

"Racheal must have had her suspicions. She brought the hammer down on Richard, because Eve told me he suddenly wasn't with her anymore. Then Racheal threatened to fire her."

"Oh, my God," Melanie whispered.

"Only intervention by the Mr. & Mr. owners stopped that. Eve worked for them. There was a big row. Eve said it was more than she could handle, so she quit. But the whole situation created instability in the workplace. Richard—or Dick, as Eve calls him—moved them up here. He owns the house. I gather Racheal doesn't know. He and Racheal had secretly planned to separate from the Lang Agency. If they could on their own find a listing that would lead to a big launch, you know, so their fledgling new office would get some recognition."

I chewed the inside of my cheek. Had my memory of Eve's words been right?

"The meadow," Melanie said.

"Exactly," I said.

"What went wrong?" Melanie asked.

"I don't know. Neither does Eve. She hasn't heard from him in months. They had a code, and she sent email messages, but the last time it was Racheal who answered. Eve doesn't dare do it again. That's also when he stopped depositing money in Eve's account for her and Andy to live on. She doesn't know why Dick went back to Nashua. She said the entire setup got flipped over backwards. Dick and Racheal were supposed to open a branch here, but Racheal would stay in Nashua. He'd come here. His plan was, once they were in separate locations, to file for divorce. Then he and Eve would be a family."

Melanie shook her head, still doodling on the pad. It was part of her thought process. I went outside and put the lead and harness on Duke. We both needed a walk.

Instead of our usual hike up the road, we took the ridge path that wound up and above Eve's house. I think we were barely out of the yard when Buttercup realized we were gone. Snuffling wasn't all that big snout of hers was for. She tracked us down in minutes. Maybe she could join the K9 corps.

Without a lead, she was free to roam while Duke and I stayed together.

Every time I went out with an animal, I wore a black pouch on my belt that held very small snacks. It never took long for an animal to recognize it, even the poultry did. My plan was to make this hike a workout with Duke, but unfortunately, every time I gave him a command, Buttercup circled back to be part of the snack pack. And she hadn't come alone. Blanche and a few of the other biddies had trailed after her. The upside was the realization that Duke wasn't interested in the chickens.

We got to a place where I could sit on a stump while Buttercup, the biddies, and the dog could root around, with Duke still on the lead. Periodically, I would call him back, then tell him to sit. When he responded in a positive manner, he got a snack, as did Buttercup. If nothing else, the dog got a lesson about how to share.

Through the branches below, I could see Eve's backyard. Andy was back playing in the dirt. Eventually, his mother came out and scooped him up. He squealed with glee as she spun him around. Duke came to attention. Even Buttercup lifted her ears. She gave a little snort that said, *what just happened?* I knew we needed to head home before the pig went down into the yard to check.

I clucked to her, but she was still facing in the direction where she had heard Andy, while Duke, on the lead, was pulling back towards the farm. I couldn't get back on the other side of her, so I went for the second-best thing. I resorted to singing a ditty.

"Oh, I wish I had a peanut butter cracker!

That is what I'd really like right now.

And if I had a peanut butter cracker,

I'd share it with my favorite little sow!"

Immediately, Buttercup's interest in the unknown squealer vanished. She took the lead and led us all home.

* * *

When Noah showed up for supper, I asked, "Are you scheduled to work tomorrow?"

"Nope."

Noah worked at the bank. Every fourth week he got Wednesdays off, but he has to work on Saturdays.

"Good." I smiled at him in a way that made him gulp nervously. "I've got a project for you."

* * *

My first chores the next morning were to clean out Buttercup's pen and Duke's kennel. Then I fed more weed from my fenced-in garden spot to the biddies. I was deep in thought about the meeting the night before. I'd driven over to the town office, only to find out that the development at the end of Calwin Mountain Road wasn't on the agenda. I needed to think about which member of the committee I could squeeze for information.

Melanie and Noah were out on recon. Gerrish Realty was holding an open house in the prestigious Pear Mountain neighborhood. I wanted to know what their modus operandi was. He did that; she did this; did they work together to reel in the awestruck sucker fish? Neddel showed up before their return. I rushed out of the barn when I heard the car with the expectation of a Melanie report. I might have been a little short with Neddel. As soon as I realized what I'd done, I felt terrible. He was so kind, and I really did like him. As compensation, I offered food. Just like Buttercup, he followed me into the kitchen.

"I figured you'd have some catching up around the homestead to do today," he said. "Thought I'd help out a little, maybe take Duke for a walk up into the national forest."

I looked up the road. Because there were so many trails above the farm, I didn't usually go there.

"It'll be someplace unfamiliar to him," Nedell said, then with a sly wink added, "It's a cop interrogation trick. You know, take him out of his comfort zone and watch his reaction."

"Sounds good," I said. "He'd love that. Thanks."

We hooked the snack bag onto my boyfriend's belt, with only a minor amount of canoodling. I warned him three times not to let the dog loose. Then I took the pig into the house so they could get away without her.

Buttercup was good inside until I pulled the vacuum out of the closet. She put her snout against the bottom of the screen door and let herself outside. Cats disappeared into the cattery, and I was left alone to hunt down dust bunnies. On my hands and knees, I sweated up a storm, cussing at wads of dog hair that lurked far under the sofa. I wasn't aware of the kids' return until Melanie touched my shoulder.

I screamed, "FOR THE LOVE OF UNCLE MIKE!" before I launched myself over the vac on a direct collision course with the bookcase.

Both Melanie and Noah fell backwards. Noah scrambled back as far as the kitchen. Royally and Lilo, shut in Melanie's room, started to bark loudly. That, of course, raised the *skree, skree, skree* from out in the dooryard.

"Ouch!" I cringed and struggled to my knees, rubbing my hip where I'd made solid contact with the maple bookcase.

"For crying out loud, Mom. You almost scared me to death."

Noah was more considerate. He rushed back into the room to help me up and inquired if I was all right.

It wasn't hard to tell that the gate at the bottom of the ramp hadn't been closed, because a large, maybe four-hundred-fifty-pound object was head-butting the kitchen door. It's a good thing I had a solid oak one installed. Once the vac was off and the pig was in, we were all in the kitchen, beverages in hand, getting down to the dirt.

"Listen, Neddel is out on a nature walk with Duke." I looked nervously over my shoulder. "He could be back anytime, and you know how he is."

Noah cocked an eyebrow.

What I'd said sounded like it didn't bode well for my personal relationship with the sheriff, yet he continually showed me that he could be proven to be the right guy. A different type of knight on a white charger. The perfect Mr. Right-Hand-of-the-Law. Neddel, like Ian, my dead husband and Melanie's father, shared the same attribute: always warning me about myself. My daughter totally understood the need to proceed with caution. How long would Neddel tolerate my use of the Eleventh Commandment? Do now, apologize later.

Melanie leaned across the wooden expanse. "There were a lot of people at the open house, so it wasn't like Gerrish could radar in on us. At least, I don't think she did. She was the only representative from the realty office there, so she was pretty busy."

"You should have seen it, Mrs. F. It's a beautiful house," Noah sounded all moony.

Melanie nodded. "Richard wasn't there, but Racheal's pretty smart. The place was well-lit, impeccably cleaned. There were fresh flowers, a coffee station with small pastries. The whole enchilada."

"Hardwood floors. Two and a half baths, one en suite. Oh, and a water closet off the rec room in the basement." Noah sounded like a brochure.

"I thought the event would be kind of chintzy, you know, here's the brochure, look around, with only her there. But get this. Christine Gillette from TD Bank was set up in the TV room. She had finance applications, propaganda. Mom, she's another smarty. She knows all the answers, and she can multitask." Melanie was obviously awed. "There had to be nine couples milling around or filling out forms."

"I don't know who did the landscaping, but every outside angle was perfect for the house and the view." Noah had a rapt look on his face that started to worry me.

"Wait, a second." I held up my hand. "Noah. You know this was a fact-finding mission, right? That you weren't there to actually buy a house?"

The light came on in Melanie's head. She looked at her beau with terror in her eyes. He'd been sitting up straight since he sat down, but sagged at my words.

"I know," he said. "I don't think I've ever been in a mansion before. It was…I mean, I got kind of overwhelmed."

"It's not a mansion, honey," Melanie said. "Just a big house for rich people."

"Not us." He sounded sad.

"No, not us." She rubbed his arm a little and offered him a cookie.

While he nibbled, she told me she'd asked specifically for Mr. Gerrish.

"She blew me off the first two times, but the next time I spoke up, she looked at me funny. Then I remembered she'd seen me before. So, I waved to an imaginary person and tried to move away, but she cut me off."

I'd been casting worried glances toward Noah, but now my concern was fully for any danger Melanie might have put herself in.

"I whispered that I was asking because Noah's father was going to be involved in our purchase wherever we go, and he has some serious hangups." My daughter had a self-satisfied grin on her face. "Don't worry. When I signed in, I used Aunt Dorothy's name and address."

"Well, the Gerrish Agency contacting Dorothy won't be a problem." I sighed. "She's been dead for three years."

"I'm so sorry for your loss," Noah said.

"It's okay, thanks, Noah. She was my aunt, more than ninety years old, and lived in Wisconsin somewhere. We hadn't seen her in twenty years," I explained.

He looked questioningly at Melanie.

She shrugged. "My address book is in my purse. We always sent her Christmas cards."

"Did Racheal tell you anything about Richard at all?"

"Nope. Well, the same thing she's been saying right along. He's working at their other office in Nashua."

"But there's nothing online about them having a second office?" I asked.

"Mom, I've scoured the web. I can't find hide nor hair of Richard Gerrish anywhere."

Melanie broke her last carrot stick into small pieces to feed them to Buttercup. The pig had been poking her for several minutes.

"He's got to be somewhere. How about you get me the telephone number for Mr. & Mr. Lang?"

I just knew Neddel would come back while I was on the phone. But I couldn't force myself to wait. When the receptionist answered, I asked for Richard Gerrish.

"I'm sorry," she said. "Mr. Gerrish is no longer with this agency. Would you care to speak to one of our other Realtors?"

Laughing self-consciously, I explained this was a personal matter. "Can I leave a message for him?"

I wanted the woman to verify if he still worked there or not; instead, she countered with a question.

"Can I put you on hold for a moment?"

And click, she was gone before I had a chance to answer. It didn't take long for a man to come on the line. Out in the driveway, I heard a vehicle pull in. Melanie went out to stall Neddel.

"This is Mr. Long," the man said. "I'm sorry. Who is this?"

"My name is Doris Flynn…"

Noah made frantic slicing movements across his throat. I waved him off.

"I work with a local nonprofit. Mr. Gerrish has always been a supporter. I was reaching out because we hadn't heard from him in a while." I repeated the apologetic laugh. "In this business, we need to be careful we don't ruffle any feathers. I wanted to make sure no one here offended Mr. Gerrish."

"I'm sure you didn't." The man was quite smarmy. "Richard and his wife actually moved out of the area."

I could hear Melanie talking on the deck.

"Thank you for your time," I said smoothly. I hung up the receiver with two seconds to spare.

Noah collapsed in his seat.

"What's up?" Neddel asked when he came in.

"We're just taking a break." I stood, dusting off my hands. "I've got work to do in the cattery, and then I have lawns to mow."

"What's wrong with Noah?" Neddel whispered.

We watched the younger man race out to where Melanie could protect him. As the official family shopper, her afternoon was designated. She'd be gone for a couple of hours, and Noah seemed eager to go with her.

Neddel and I went out to the barn, where he watched me coax my vintage mower to fire up. When it was chugging in a manner that didn't sound like it was going to stall, Neddel climbed aboard. My old ride-on Cub Cadet mower isn't fast, but it gets the job done, so replacing it isn't warranted. Neddel thinks it's hilarious that the biddies follow him, running in their side-to-side way and scooping up displaced bugs. To add to his amusement, last spring a friend moved out of state and gifted us with two Peking ducks. All in all, there's some serious waddling. Even I stopped working for a bit to watch the show.

Finished and sweaty, we headed across the street and through the orchard to the riverbank. Royally and Lilo were afraid of the moving water. They paced the shore, whining out a warning as Neddel, Buttercup, and I waded in the shallows.

"Come on, guys. Come in," Neddel coaxed.

"It's not going to happen," I said. "Lilo's always been afraid. Royally got swept away a few years ago. I really thought for a few seconds we were going to lose him, but he got caught on a snag. Now he won't even go in the lake."

We stayed in the shallows, sunning on the bank and watching Buttercup. She was, I think, chasing minnows.

"Neddel, if somebody wanted to disappear, totally disappear, what would it take?"

"I guess it depends on how deep this person wanted to go."

At my confused look—I'd never considered there were depths to disappearing—he explained.

"People disappear for a lot of reasons. They're usually running from the law. Or due to financial or family issues. If they figure all they have to do is leave town and no one will follow them, then they don't try so hard to cover their trail. If the mafia or Feds are after them, they do a lot more."

"Like?"

He shrugged. "Buy a new identity. You know, with a social security number and fake credentials."

I leaned back on the wide, smooth river rock, considering what he had just said. Nedell had started picking out stones and skipping them across the surface of the river. Each time a skip made a little splash, Buttercup snapped to attention. She didn't seem to make the connection between his arm swinging and the darting stones. Though they were oblivious of each other, I watched them both. In a move that would have made a breaching whale envious, the pig launched through the ripples after a particularly loud skip.

"Crap!" Neddel yelped.

He lunged into the river, and I barely caught the tail of his t-shirt to drag him back.

"What are you doing?" I asked.

"She's going to drown." He was still pulling away.

"The water is only eighteen inches deep," I pointed out. "When she realizes you aren't throwing fish, she'll be back."

Neddel's brow furrowed into concerned wrinkles.

"Oh, that's so sweet," I cooed. "You're worried." Then, because I didn't know when to shut up, I added, "If she'd been in distress, would you have given her artificial respiration? Pinching her nose together might be a challenge, but pressing your lips to hers would be easy."

What a look he gave me! Without a word, he climbed the bank. He stood there for a moment, back to me. I was all set to apologize when he twisted back around. There was a shine in his eyes. Shaking his head, he laughed loud enough so we all stared at him.

"Yeah," he said. "I can see that in the paper when the EMTs show up. *SHERIFF KISSING PIG.*"

Without thinking, I threw my arms around him. He hugged me back, then kissed me breathless. Letting go, he called the dogs, who were thrilled to be leaving, but Buttercup and I lagged behind. She's slow sometimes, and I was bemused; I could barely breathe. I guess I shouldn't have been surprised when, in the driveway, Neddel suddenly remembered something he had to do and left.

"You let him go? Mom. You should have thrown him down on the riverbank and had your way with him," Melanie told me later, after I'd related the conversation.

Stamping my feet, cussing under my breath, and basically throwing a Terrible-Two Temper Tantrum had no effect on the lecture my daughter was giving me. It was, however, another log on the jam, keeping Noah, who seemed to be suddenly worried I was going senile, away from me. At this rate, we were never going to bond. If he became my son-in-law, they wouldn't be coming to my house with the kiddies for the holidays.

I finally decided I'd take Duke out for some training. I wouldn't get anything else done this afternoon, anyway. I left Royally in the house and scattered peanuts across the back lawn to keep Buttercup busy. Then, Duke and I drove off in a cloud of dust. I slowed down as I went by Eve's house, noting that the ten-year-old Elantra was still parked in the drive. Like the rear end of my jeep, Eve's vehicle was coated bumper to bumper in dust. There were no signs of movement.

There was a nice dog walking trail in Whitaker Woods, so we went there. I kept Duke on a short lead, and things went well. On the few times we encountered others, I pulled off to the side and held his collar.

"Dog in training," I warned.

The other dog walkers kept their precious ones to the far side of the trail. There might have been a little growling and a few whines, but there was no lunging. From Duke, anyway. A good sign. When I was sufficiently worn down, we got back in the car and drove past Neddel's apartment building. His POV wasn't there. Next stop, the sheriff's office. Duke and I walked right in the front door.

"Hi, Doris," Deputy Delores said. "He's in his office. I don't know what his issue is, but he's got his grumpy on."

"Bummer for you," I said sympathetically.

"Yeah, I'd give anything for a football game on his TV today." She laughed and turned to a radio call coming through dispatch.

I gave a quick knock and cracked the door. "Do I need a white flag?"

Melanie would have been proud of me. If I'd dare tell her what I was doing.

"Neddel, I need to ask you honestly about what happened this afternoon," I said. "When you kissed me, I thought you kind of, you know, liked me. Then you took off like a scalded cat. To be frank, I don't know what happened. Did I do something insensitive?"

"No, it's nothing you did, Doris. I like you as well. I'm just not sure if either of us is ready for any type of relationship."

He looked away, lips pursed. When he turned back, he just looked sad.

"I should have asked, not assumed."

"You did nothing wrong." I felt my cheeks pink as I continued. "To be honest, I enjoyed it."

As soon as I uttered the words, I wanted to leave. I can only take so much romantic tension at a time, and I was at the finish line. Before I could go on, I'd need a little break. While I was talking, Duke had gone around the desk. His head was on Neddel's knees as the sheriff fondled his ears. It wasn't hard to see they had something growing between them.

"Listen, Neddel. I have a couple of errands to run. You don't want me leaving the dogs in the car, and I don't quite dare take Duke in public places. Would you be willing to watch Duke for a bit? I can come back later, or you can drop him off."

"If you won't be gone long," Neddel said.

He was smiling at Duke like they were best buds. On my way out, I waved to Dolores and drove over to Taco Bell, where I bought a couple of mega meals.

When I knocked on Arnie's door, there was no answer. I immediately thought the worst. When I gently twisted the knob, the latch released, but my throat caught. I eased across the room, greasy bag and king-size root beer held out in front of me like a shield.

The old man was lying cock-eyed in the recliner, mouth open, his cup of coffee spilt on the floor. I stopped breathing.

Then, like the phoenix of legend, that old buzzard jerked upward, let out a hacking cough that should have woken the neighbors, and gently drifted off again.

"You absolute jerk," I cussed under my breath, but right then I decided it was time for a real doctor's visit, not just VNA, but somebody who was going to order a chest X-ray, check out his collection of meds, and help me decide what he needed.

I left after cleaning up the coffee. One meal went in the fridge; the other went on the table beside him, along with the soft drink. I probably should have left a note. Instead, I'd give him a call a little later, so he'd know who'd been inside. While I was at it, I'd ask who his primary physician was. If he gave me flak, I'd tell him I thought he'd kicked off and was ready to dial the funeral home when he woke up.

I wasn't quite ready to go home, so I followed my thoughts and ended up on Woodland Grove Road, cruising slowly past where Racheal Gerrish lived. A wheelbarrow and gardening tools had been left on the side of the driveway near a patch of red cedar mulch and a fledgling red maple. Through the open garage door, I could see the rear ends of two vehicles.

"Huh, must be Mr. Gerrish is home," I said to myself. "I wonder where the missus is?"

Then I considered what they could be doing if he'd been staying in Nashua for a while. My ears and cheeks heated up. I was turning into my great-aunt Audrey, a dirty-minded peeping Tom. I drove home.

Neddel had beaten me there. Duke was in the outside part of his chain-link enclosure. Busy with a big beef knuckle, he didn't bother to look up. Royally yapped from the deck. If he hadn't gotten a bone to chew on, he was probably giving Neddel grief. Buttercup was the only one who stirred when I pulled in. It could have been because she was so happy to see me. More likely, it was because the supper hour was nigh.

"There's my good girl," I enthused.

Her tail wagged. She gave a happy woof and leaned heavily against my leg to move me toward the ramp. As soon as I lifted the latch, she had the gate wide open and was on her way up, leaving me in the dust.

"Cooking in here," Neddel called through the screen door. "Pig stays out."

Buttercup didn't like that. Melanie stepped outside with a wedge of watermelon in hand.

"Get it, Buttercup," she said, tossing the melon over the railing.

Buttercup thundered down the ramp. It was hers. She was having it. And if Royally didn't move his shimmy-shimmy butt, she was going to run him over.

"You didn't give Royally a bone?" I asked the three people working around the table.

"I'm saving it for when we sit down for supper," Melanie said. "We're all set here. You get to feed the cats and the stock."

So, what's new? I wondered.

Chapter Fourteen

On Monday morning, when I arrived at work, there was a message on my computer from Heidi. *See me.* After I'd called Arnie, I'd left a message on Heidi's line stating my concerns. It was a roll of the dice whether she had an answer for me, or if one of my coworkers had complained I was a bleeding heart. Either way, I was headed there anyway to deliver Eve's paperwork.

I had already gathered that Monday mornings were always hectic. But it seemed to me, as I squeezed out the employee access door and was confronted by a large crowd where multiple people spoke at once, that this was a particularly difficult one. However, once I burst through the maze of tightly compacted, overly stressed bodies, I realized the issue was that everyone was packed in the same quarter of floor space. I immediately moved to a position behind the empty desk adjacent to Heidi's and approached from the rear.

Across the room, two starched and pressed state troopers, complete with wide-brim hats and holstered service revolvers, stood in front of the window. I didn't know if they were really good actors or just well-versed in ignoring the nervous masses. One held a file that they both seemed intent on.

"Heidi?" I whispered out of the side of my mouth.

Her desk phone rang. Holding one finger up to me, she lifted the handset. "Yes, Mrs. Henderson?"

She spoke not a word, but after replacing the receiver, did something I'd yet to witness. She got up and left her desk to march over to the troopers.

"Gentlemen? Mrs. Henderson will see you now," she said in a low voice.

As soon as Heidi closed the boss's office door behind the two lean, arresting machines, the crowd migrated toward the rows of seats.

I handed over Eve's paperwork while inclining my head toward the hollow wood door.

"Later," Heidi hissed. Then, in a more normal tone, she added, "Regarding Arnie Shaw? When you submitted your report, which I have to tell you was much more extensive than I normally see…"

The information had been a lot to read and decipher. I wasn't sure whether I should preen or cringe.

"…I emailed it downstairs to the EIT. Emergency Investigation Team. They're going to want to talk to you. Either here, or via telephone." Heidi looked up at me inquisitively.

I hadn't known this would be the outcome and needed a few minutes and more information to make a decision. I bit my lower lip. The elevator door swooshed open. More general need applicants.

"I'll meet them here," I half-whispered.

"Good choice. I'll schedule." Heidi looked past me, a smile on her lips, dread in her eyes. "Good morning, Mrs. Pike. What brings you here today?"

I left the way I'd come in without making eye contact with anyone else sitting there. Downstairs, Maryann was shouldering her bag, ready to hit the streets.

"Did you hear that Mrs. Henderson's husband is missing?" she asked.

Well, that explained the visitors.

During the time I was visiting clients—and according to my estimation, asking the wrong pre-programmed questions—I got a text from Heidi. She had forwarded the forms the investigator wanted completed before the end of the day. My meeting was scheduled for Tuesday at two.

I needed to forfeit my last client visit to be back at my desk, or those forms weren't going to get done. I sent Heidi a text asking her to reschedule.

In the office parking lot, I cruised slowly, looking for any vehicle that was New Hampshire green and bronze, or a trooper who might be undercover.

Nothing. I think I was actually disappointed.

If I thought Eve's paperwork was invasive, I was struck shell-shocked dumb by what I was asked in the paperwork from the investigation team for Arnie. I wanted to help him, but this needed to be done by someone who had seen him more often than I had. It was appalling how many times I keyed in the word "unknown."

On the drive home, I flicked on my directional signal just before VFW Street, but decided at the last second it wouldn't be a good idea. That was when my cellphone chirped the dedicated Melanie ring. I pulled over.

"Are you on the way, Mom?" Melanie asked. "Cliff from the Humane Society is looking for you. He said you were supposed to call last week."

"I just passed there. I'll go back."

It took so long to get turned around that I almost missed Cliff, who was leaving for the day.

The guy kind of reminded me of a young Arnold Schwarzenegger. I think it was the teeth. We spent half an hour talking about a program he was putting in place with the local summer camps. They'd be busing kids in from a few of the local summer camps. He and his people would teach domestic animal husbandry.

"Kids get handed puppies, kittens. They don't know the basics of taking care of these animal babies. Worse than that, sometimes parents opt for adult animals, which will be easier. They have no idea what habits their selection already has and will be brought as luggage." He leaned against the hot metal of his truck without flinching. "The idea was broached by the local scoutmaster, who's looking for a place for scouts to earn badges. You said you wanted to help out. Are you still available?"

We had talked about this a long time before. To be honest, I'd completely forgotten.

"I had to go back to work," I said. "I can give you Wednesday and Friday."

Cliff pulled a notebook out of his truck. "Let's see what I've got. Okay. Wednesday, two to four. Friday, nine to eleven. We've got limited space in the building, so we'll be outside."

"That explains the big wedding tent over in the dog walk area." I nodded in the direction of the large, pristine, white canvas-and-nylon structure.

His eyes followed mine. Neither one of us knew what to expect when the buses pulled in, and were probably both contemplating what would happen in that covered but grassy area. This was a pilot project. I think we were both nervous about it.

"See you Wednesday," he said, jumping into the truck.

"Wait!" I said as the truck pulled away. "*This* Wednesday? Day after tomorrow?"

* * *

I traveled home in shock. My quiet life was flushing down the drain. I'd had a pleasant schedule before I took this job. Time to read the paper. Weed the garden. Converse with chickens. And dogs. And pigs.

I pulled in to find Buttercup and Royally waiting. No Duke barking. Before I could walk over to his enclosure, Melanie stepped out onto the deck.

"Neddel showed up twenty minutes ago. He took Duke up the mountain for a workout," she said.

I must have looked surprised, because she was quick to ask if that was all right.

"Yes, I guess," I sputtered. "He never said he'd come over."

Even though I'd been kind of pushing Duke in Neddel's direction, and allowing them bonding time, this was the first time he'd taken the initiative for them to have a boys' afternoon.

Royally jumped up, getting his dirty pawprints on my trousers. I squatted to give him a rub. He had to share my attention with the cattery cats, house cats, Buttercup, Duke, and now, even Neddel. It was hard for him, and I knew it. Now that I was on her level, Buttercup could get her muzzle in my face.

"Phew, bad breath," I said, trying to push her away.

She immediately expelled a loud, lingering fart with a tremendously bad odor. Even Royally darted away from her.

"Yeah, about that." Melanie was still on the deck. "I don't think that mashed turnip you put in her breakfast was a good idea."

Leaving the pig outside, we went in for a quiet iced tea. Buttercup could get onto the front porch because the lawn sloped across the front of the house. On the high end, the ground was level with the old decking. The tall, old-fashioned windows had a sash eighteen inches up. I sat in the armchair with the window open, and the pig rustled around on the porch, accepting bites of carrot as I doled them out. Telling Melanie about my busy day helped me shake off the lingering tension from work. I wasn't the type who waited. If something needed to be done, I wanted to be on it. Now.

"Can you believe she's a Mrs.?" I asked Melanie, referring to Mrs. Henderson. "She's got great-aunt spinster written all over her. I'd like to see the guy who took her on."

My daughter looked thoughtful. "I've seen her around, but never with a man. Maybe she's a widow."

"Nope. Maryann, who works with me, said Mr. Henderson works right here in town."

I couldn't remember ever having seen Mrs. Henderson anywhere. But then, if she wasn't directly in my sphere, I might not have noticed. A voice called from outside.

"Hello, the house! We're here, and we brought art!" a voice called from the driveway.

The dogs started barking. When I got to the kitchen door, I saw Melanie's friend, Missy, wrestling with the gate latch to come up on the deck. Buttercup had her pinned there, and the two-year-old in her arms wasn't sure how she felt about the pig. Sammy was working on climbing over the barrier. With one hand, he waved a piece of yellow construction paper over his head.

"I brought this for your fridginator," he called.

"Refrigerator," his mother and I both corrected at the same time.

Everyone came into the house. Buttercup found a place to nap on the deck, and Sammy explained my new piece of art.

"It's thank you for the pig ride," he said. "Mama said I had fun."

Missy rolled her eyes.

"What's this big moon taking up half the picture?" I asked.

"Pig butt," he said proudly.

"Ah-huh. Well, the black crayon was the right color for Buttercup's butt."

I produced a roll of tape, and we selected a spot on the front of my fridge. Then, while he and his sister played with the cats, the grown-ups gossiped.

"Missy, do you only work with the children through the school?" I asked.

"Yes, and the county outreach project. I have an office in the same building you do, but down a floor."

I didn't realize I was staring as I tried to phrase my questions about Eve in my head until Missy snapped her fingers in my face.

"Mrs. Flynn, what are you thinking about that's going to cause me to lose my job?"

"How can you say that, Missy?" I asked.

Missy was Melanie's childhood friend. We were comfortable speaking with each other; therefore, I wasn't worried she'd take offense.

"Experience," Melanie said.

Missy accepted my invitation to supper. I sighed with pleasure to have Missy sitting at our table again. While Melanie and Lilo played with the tykes, Missy and I rustled up some grub.

"It seems like all I do now that I'm working again is prepare food in one way or another," I said to Missy. "People, then animals, then people again. It just goes on and on."

"Noah and I made burgers the other day." Neddel stood in the doorway.

"Don't let the pig in," Missy said. "She's having some kind of toxic gas attack."

"Perfect." Neddel pulled the door tight behind himself.

I have to admit, he might get on my nerves, but there are just times he's spot on as far as helping out, even when it includes Buttercup. Though he wasn't a fan of dispensing meals in the cattery, he had the outdoor feeding pattern down pat. He stepped outside, holding the bowls high and schussing my porcine friend along. I watched them go with a little jealousy. She wasn't carrying on like he was the enemy, and she was setting up boundaries. She often does that with new people. Yet, she was trotting. Tail high in the air. Both signs she was happy.

Am I being replaced? I wondered. *Is this what happens when you go back to work and your family has to depend on someone else?* I looked over at Melanie, biting my lip.

"When you were little, Melanie, and I went to work, did that make you love me less?" I asked.

"What? Are you kidding? Heck no. I knew you'd come back. After the first couple of days, I was so excited to be playing with the other kids. I bet I didn't even know you were gone." She went back to tickling Sammy, who was breathless with laughter.

"I know what you mean, Mrs. Flynn." Missy cut into my thoughts. "I feel the same way. At noontime, I call the daycare, hoping one of the kids is close enough for me to say hello. Dave doesn't get it." Her eyes were so sad. "He thinks I'm overreacting. But I'm not." She turned to me. "Am I?"

I shook my head. "One day, Melanie will understand. For me, I always remember. When I see people like Eve who are so insecure with everything, I worry the stress will crush them."

Missy gave me a little hip bump. "Is she your next crusade?" She tried to laugh, but there was a little hitch in it.

We might have dissolved into sobbing dishrags, but Nedell was back, and supper was hitting the table. As we ate, Neddel talked about his trip up on the mountain with Duke. He pointed out the dog's strong points and some others that needed work. I think he was right on the edge of telling me that he wanted to take Duke for his own, which would have been awesome, when the cellphone attached to his belt chirped.

His eyes took on a distant, unseeing glaze as he listened. I knew it was a mechanical message going out to all the law enforcement in the area. Sometimes, it was nothing. This time, even as he continued to listen, he was rising from his seat. One hand patted his back pocket to verify his car keys were there. Halfway to the door, he finally lowered the phone.

"Sorry, I have to go. A body was found on the back side of Mount Chocorua." Neddel's face was grim. The details must have been particularly nasty. "The medical examiner, your friend, Dr. Lombard, is on her way."

"Who's dead?" I asked.

"Don't know."

"No ID?"

"No." Each word took him closer to the door.

"Young or old?"

Chapter Fifteen

Melanie and Missy were cleaning up, doing their girlfriend chatty thing. I could have stayed, but I felt it was important for Melanie to strengthen the bonds between herself and her childhood buddies. For a few moments, I stood and watched. I missed that, having close friends of my own. Back in the day, I'd had plenty. Then Ian had become enough to fill my time. And Melanie. I'd given up working. Somehow, everything else had faded. Sure, I had lots of casual friends, but no one I could dial up and spill my guts to. I was glad Melanie had Missy. I couldn't help smiling, even though on the inside it felt a little sad.

Duke had gotten plenty of exercise with Neddel, so I put Buttercup's harness and lead on her. Unfortunately, she'd already had supper and wanted to laze about. It was like trying to get a teenager to clean their room.

I got the pig as far as the lawn, where she sat down. Plop! No lifting that butt until she wanted to. I snapped off the lead, but left the harness in place. Then, swinging the strap, I strolled down the driveway and headed up the road toward town.

I got as far as the lilac bushes. At that point, I was out of her sight. She wasn't having that. No one else was outside, and I was gone. Worse than that, I was singing the piggie snack song.

"Oh, I wish I had a little piggy cookie.
That is what I'd truly like with meeeee.
'Cause if I had a little piggy cookie,
Buttercup would be right by my knee!"
The thundering of hooves on hard-packed dirt was a signal I was about to

get bulldozed. I swung around, ready for the worst. Buttercup set the brakes three yards away, coming to a full stop with her quivering disc against my right front pocket. Only a thin layer of denim separated her from the peanut butter cracker, which I dutifully handed out. I should have bought stock in Keebler. Snapping on her lead again, I continued down the road.

We drew abreast of Evie's house. There was a new car in the yard, a small SUV with all the hallmarks of a grandma-mobile. A frond of plastic flowers attached to the on-roof horizontal antenna. I could see a very large stuffed teddy bear in the rear-facing car seat. The in-state plate read NANA 1.

I slowed down, allowing Buttercup to graze on the side of the road. In the house, Prince sounded off. When the pig indicated the area was picked over, I might have accidentally dropped a few peanuts among the bracken. Eventually, the barking alerted someone that we were outside, and Andy popped up in the front window. The little boy's face broke out in a wide grin. That forced me to smile back until he disappeared and I realized he was headed my way. Sure enough, the screen door at the kitchen entrance slammed shut, and he raced up the drive.

This time, the woman who called him back was not his mother.

"Stop right there, young man!" The order, which came from an elderly voice box, was hard and sharp. And it got immediate results.

The woman followed Andy to where he stood, poised for a second flight. She appeared to be in her mid-sixties, dressed in jeans and a short-sleeved plaid shirt that looked like faded L.L. Bean.

"You do not ever, and I mean *ever*, run out of the house like that! Do you understand?"

I knew she was right, but I felt bad. If I hadn't smiled and waved, he would have stayed, standing on the sofa and looking out the window. I raised my hand.

"Hello. I'm sorry. It was our fault," I said.

Buttercup had raised her head. She didn't advance, but she was looking. By now, the woman had Andy by the hand. He was tugging on her as he pointed toward us.

"See the pig? She pulls a wagon, and I got a ride! She's my friend," he chirped.

And I was obviously chopped liver. But his declaration had the woman taking a squinted eye look at us. Then she took a single step forward.

"I know you. You're the woman with the cats."

I didn't respond. Yeah, I had cats. But I was sure this lady had never been inside my house.

"It's me! Angie!" She released Andy, who took the initiative and moved toward us again.

I still had no idea who she was.

"Slowly, Andy. Don't rush her," I said, stepping closer to Buttercup's head. "Say hello, call her by name, and use a smiling voice."

"'Kay," he said.

Squatting, he whispered a greeting to Buttercup.

It was funny, really, because standing up, he was barely taller than the pig. Angie approached us, also smiling, though nervously. When she was close enough, she touched the top of Andy's head with her fingertips. That small amount of contact kept him where he was. I wondered what it took to have that much control over someone, and felt an icy breeze on the back of my neck and knees.

"It's nice to see you," I said, hoping to crack the tension. "Are you watching the neighborhood small boy today?"

It seemed to work.

"Would you care to come up?" Angie asked.

It was obvious she thought I'd identified her, but I still wasn't sure. I looked up the drive, knowing there were no outside seats. Only the small pile of dirt. I hesitated.

"How about," I countered, "we go over into the meadow? There's a nice place to relax in the shade, and Buttercup can see how many grasshoppers she can catch."

"I can catch grasshoppers!" Andy enthused.

"I don't want to take him near the river." Angie sounded nervous again.

"We won't go there. But right under that first couple of apple trees is an old wooden bench. We can sit there," I said.

"This is nice," Angie said when she was seated. Andy was engaged in watching Buttercup root. "I wonder who put this here?"

"Actually, my husband did, right after we got married. I come here often to keep his memory strong."

I didn't tell her that attached to the seat behind my back was a tiny brass plaque that read: IAN & DORIS, K.I.S.S.I.N.G.

Angie told me she remembered Ian. Now, I was even more confused because she was so familiar. I just couldn't put my finger on exactly who from where. Her question opened the conversation for her to start talking about her own dead husband, which led to the state of her current affairs, and the need to earn a little cash money. And therefore, her coming to watch Andy five days a week. That also let me know Angie wasn't family to Eve, but hired help.

"Mind, Eve works breakfast and lunch at the Blueberry Muffin, so she's usually done by two. That gives me the rest of the day. Today she's working through supper. Somebody called in sick. She'll be wiped out by the time she gets home." Angie had busy fingers: brushing, patting, folding a blade of grass. "Poor tyke. Doesn't have anybody here. His mama's gotta work, and she's not strong. Then there's his father. Phfft. Some men just aren't made to be daddies."

I nodded while she ran on at the mouth. She was good at sharing information she probably should have kept to herself, but not careful about what she said in front of the boy. Fortunately, Andy was so engrossed in trying to find a grasshopper, he wasn't listening. I didn't have the heart to tell him they wouldn't be big enough for him to find until August. When I realized Angie had finally gone silent, I spoke up.

"I know what you mean about the money. I'm still in my own house, but you know. Taxes, maintenance, heating oil? I just went to work for the Agency for the Aged."

That got an immediate response.

"Oh. You work with Edith Henderson, that poor woman." Angie shook her head, all sad and despairing.

Chuckling, I said, "I don't know what you mean. She seems pretty together to me."

"You didn't hear? About her husband?"

"I don't know anything about her husband," I said, feigning surprise, hoping Angie would share more gossip. "I don't know much about her at all."

Buttercup stretched out in the sun. Andy pouted, disappointment on his face.

"She needs a little rest, sweetheart," I said. "Come around on this side of her. You can sit with your back against hers. She won't even know you're there."

Andy smiled again, shoulders up around his ears like it was a secret. He tiptoed around the pig and settled into the grass, playing with a Matchbox car he took from his pocket.

"Well, you know," Angie said when I turned back to her. "He took off. Just gone. Left the business. Told nobody. I gather he didn't even bother to take his things."

"How could that be?" I was actually a little shocked. "This is a small town. Well, except for the tourists. That's the kind of talk that runs like wildfire."

Then I thought about Eve's Dick. He was gone as well. Maybe it was a male menopause thing.

Angie nodded. "It's not like they live in town, being as they're down on the Kancamagus Highway," she said.

She knew the dirt, and I was about to get a shovelful.

"Edith Henderson inherited that defunct chalet motel a mile or so down there. Even before her father passed, it was nothing more than a run-down collection of boards and shingles. She lived alone in the main building for years before she took up with that man. He wasn't from here. Then suddenly one day, poof, she's sporting a ring and a foreign husband who doesn't even talk English."

I still couldn't picture this guy.

"Are you sure?" I asked.

"Oh, yes. She set him up in the old salt barn, repairing cars."

I knew that building. The town had built a new sand shed behind the police and court building on the East Conway Road. The tiny, dark brown structure near the warden's station on the Kancamagus Highway that the town had used for a hundred years was almost invisible among the forest trees. The building and lot had gone on the block and been sold.

"Foreign cars, right? Mazdas, Volvos, vehicles like that?"

"Exactly. Myself? I always buy American." Angie sniffed.

I bit my lip. Her SUV was a Hyundai. Looking down, I saw that Andy, leaning back against the warm pig, was sound asleep.

"I didn't realize that the mechanic's name was Henderson," I said.

"I don't think it was. That's probably the English version of whatever communist name he came with." Angie hissed, disgusted at what she knew.

Right then, I should have stopped her. The more she said, the louder her backwoods attitude got. It was like holding a conversation with my grandfather. He'd been from the Midwest, and he had the most biased attitude I'd ever encountered in my entire existence. If you spent two hours with the man, you knew why my father didn't go back to his hometown after his military hitch was over.

"Edith met him at one of those Bible-thumping tent church meetings. Some snake-oil-selling, smooth-talking preacher latched on to her, got her to take on a green card husband. Yup. That's exactly what happened. Now their four years are over. He's a card-carrying American citizen, and he's done with her."

Angie shook her head. I didn't know what to say.

"She's my friend, and I love her dearly," Angie said. "But the woman is a fool. Spent all her hard-earned money on that sneak-thief, and now he's gone in the night."

Buttercup roused. Angie suddenly realized where we were, and maybe what she'd said, because she jumped up.

"My goodness! Eve will be home anytime. Best I get her boy over there."

I didn't want her to wake him up, so I said, "I'll carry him. He's sleeping. So lovely."

"Oh, I can get him. He doesn't weigh anything." Angie squatted down and scooped him into her arms.

They were gone without a by-your-leave. Buttercup rubbed against my leg. She was ready to go home as well.

On the way, I told the pig, "Angie said Edith Henderson was her friend, but from the way she talked about her, I'm kind of glad Angie and I are only casual acquaintances."

Buttercup gave a snort that ended in a little toot. I leapt out of range. Those little bursts were deadly.

I got all the critters buttoned up and ready for bed. Noah and Melanie were scarfing up popcorn, deep into the Bruce Willis movie marathon. After I packed my lunch for work the next day, and laid out my outfit—the one with no dog footprints up to the knees—I sat in bed, cybersearching.

I didn't bother with Richard Gerrish, but I looked for Eve Saucier. Nothing. Racheal Gerrish went on for pages, so I clicked past to Edith Henderson. I thought it an odd coincidence that both women had a husband/boyfriend who had casually walked away. Once again, I came to a dead stop.

"Crap," I said to Royally, who was trying to sleep. "I should have asked Angie what Mrs. Henderson's maiden name was."

I cleared the search bar and typed in "Angie." I got shut down. Again.

I had never figured out how she knew me, though toward the end of our conversation, she had seemed slightly familiar. I didn't know her last name, or where she might have worked before babysitting Andy. If I could figure that out, maybe I'd realize who she was.

"Well," I said, powering down the computer and sliding it to the floor. "I'd make a lousy private eye."

Chapter Sixteen

The next morning, I walked into the cubicle area for the field contact agents, which is what we got to call ourselves in the Agency, to find Hector lying across his desk, whining.

"Why?" he said. "Why? I don't want to."

Hector was kind of a Sasquatch. All anyone ever sees of him is his backside leaving. Maryann said he's really good at his job. Heidi told me he was a fast worker. I'd been doing this job for a couple of weeks and didn't know how you could be both fast and good.

"What's going on?" I asked.

Maryann was both talking on her phone and keying into her iPad.

"New director," she mumbled. "Short-timer, but doing a meet and greet."

"Why?" Hector's voice was muffled because his lips were pressed against the desktop blotter calendar.

"Good morning." A new voice spoke from the employee entrance.

Hector came off his desk like his moist lips had touched an open light socket.

"These are our field agents," Heidi said calmly. "Hector, Maryann, and Doris. People, this is William Bennett. Mr. Bennett is going to be the acting director for the agency while Mrs. Henderson is on administrative leave."

Before anyone could ask a question— I knew I wanted to—Heidi and Mr. Bennett were gone.

"Well, that's that! I'm outta here."

Hector and his flapping briefcase exited the building at amazing speed. Maryann was only slightly slower. Which, of course, left me.

I didn't feel like I had to race the others to the parking lot. I only had two contacts that morning, due to my interview in the afternoon.

Then I looked at the addresses, and I wasn't happy. One was in Chatham, twenty miles on bad roads. The other was on the far side of Albany, almost in Chocorua. Also in the exact opposite direction.

"Who plans this stuff?" I groused.

Mrs. Henderson had been very clear that these were supposed to be surprise visits. I closed my mind to that dictum and dialed the phone. The grandson who answered explained the client in Chocorua was at Memorial Hospital.

"Phfft, glad I called," I told myself, loading my attaché with both files

I was glad to learn the client was there for scheduled surgery, and not because she'd fallen, poisoned herself, or been mauled by a bear. I enjoyed a mediocre cup of hospital coffee while we had a pleasant chat, and I filled out the required paperwork. This was a good interview, it seemed that after her surgery and recovery period, this woman would be more stable on her feet.

In Albany, I met Mrs. Hurst. She was so pleased to have company stop in, she'd made us cinnamon toast. She was eighty-eight and actually pretty spry.

"I don't cook much, dear," she said, laying the plates on the table. "My granddaughter doesn't want me to use the stove while she's at work."

She had a thermos of coffee to hold her through the day. I had a tea bag in my purse and quickly found a small pot to heat water in. It worked out wonderfully.

"I'm very happy here in my home, and I enjoy my alone time." She patted the cat, who strolled around on the table, checking out the crumbs. "I watch my shows. Take a nap. Meals on Wheels brings me lunch. Then the school bus comes. My great-granddaughters make us a snack. They aren't alone, and neither am I. My family takes very good care of me."

I had to agree with her. The house was clean, warm, and inviting. She had a lovely bedroom on the first floor and was able to show me exactly how to work the remote. It's a cognitive test. She had me wave to the camera in the living room that kept track of her. To be honest, as I drove away, I wondered how come she was on my list.

"I'll have to ask Heidi," I mused.

I was at the traffic light on NH Route 16, where the Kancamagus Highway meets it, when I realized I was in the wrong lane to make a left-hand turn. But that didn't stop me. Probably a good thing there was a lull in traffic because I shot across four lanes.

I drove all the way to where the tumbling-down Chalet Motel melted away into the red pines. The entire center structure, plus the guest room wings, sat in an overgrown parking lot lower than the road. A fairly new sedan had been pulled up close to the front door, and a new pickup truck was parked off to the side.

I didn't see a single person or critter, and I cruised by the place four times. At the corner of the main building, where it fell back several feet to the front of the motel room's wing, was a big doghouse. I only got a quick look, but I could tell it was shabby and had been there for years. Weeds grew around it, too, so no pup made his home there.

I followed the Kanc almost to the turnoff for the forest warden offices. There was a mom-and-pop gas station, the kind that sells cigarettes, beer, and sometimes has a hotdog grilling machine, across the road from the defunct salt shed.

"I bet the hot dog business dried up when the town plow guys got new digs," I said aloud.

The lights were on in the gas station, and a couple of pickup trucks were parked in the lot. I could see the back of a woman's head right below the scratch ticket dispenser. And yellow crime scene tape across the walk-in door on the side of the salt shed.

Without turning on my directional signal, I pulled into the lot and whipped around to the back of the building. For five or six minutes, I sat in the Jeep Liberty, barely breathing, cellphone in hand. I waited to see if some busybody from across the street would mount up to see who was hiding out back. I had my alibi all laid out in my head. I was on company time, and I needed a break. This seemed like a good place to park, maybe check my texts, and defrag as I really had no other reason to be here other than I was incredibly nosy.

Nobody showed up.

I got out of my vehicle and moved up close to the building. In one small section, there were three windows. Every one of them was thick with grime. I rubbed my fingers on the glass, but the crud was on the inside.

"So, this probably was the office," I said to myself.

There was only one thing to do. Bold as brass, I walked around the corner and up to the side door crisscrossed with police tape. I tried the doorknob, knowing it would be locked, and it was. But the door was loose.

There was maybe an eighth of an inch of wiggle room. I put my shoulder to the nasty, grease-soaked wood and shoved hard, still twisting the knob. When the door creaked open, I took one more quick, and guilty, look around and ducked under the tape. I was inside.

It didn't seem prudent to wait and find out if I'd been seen. This would surely be my only chance. I started darting around, trying to look at everything.

It seemed *Mr.* Henderson was exactly what Angie had said. The guy who worked here fixed cars. There were three of them inside, two parked bumper to bumper on the far wall. All three of the vehicles were in some stage of disassembly. Everywhere I looked, I found discarded tools. There was an oil stink that was gag-me-thick. Surprisingly, no girlie posters hung on the walls.

The office door was open. Inside, I found a desk as filthy as the floor out front and an old chair. Nothing else. No file cabinet, hot plate, or computer. There was evidence that somebody other than me had been rifling around because the desk drawers were all pulled out and left hanging. One had been upended on top of the desk with its contents strewn on the wooden top and floor.

It wasn't hard to pick out the spot where, at one time, a file cabinet might have stood. It was the only place on the floor that wasn't the same color as the aged, paneled walls.

I had been looking for a picture, the kind guys have taken where they're leaning against a fender, arms and legs crossed, wearing a huge grin, and a bicep-exposing t-shirt. With nothing in hand for my efforts, I returned to the front, walking out of the office and around the nearest car on its far side. There I found a big, red Snap-On two-tier tool chest. My dad used to keep all kinds of receipts and Field & Stream articles in his tool chest. Maybe I'd have better luck there.

This old, chinked-filled wooden building was really close to the road, so dust was an issue. It was no surprise that every tool, even those inside the drawers of the tool chest, was covered with a heavy layer of coarse grit. While I was opening drawers looking for papers or receipts, I heard the heavy slam of a vehicle door. Inching over to the roll-up door, I peeked out the corner of the window. I…could…almost…see…

My cellphone went off with a shrill ring that echoed through the salt shed. Throwing myself backwards brought me into contact with a precariously stacked pile of wrenches. There was no catching them. They tumbled downward, ringing as they hit each other, clanging against the side of the five-foot-tall metal toolbox, and finally crashing into a new heap on the floor. I scrambled towards the door.

I was almost outside when the cellphone rang again. I pressed answer to snuff out the attention-calling ring.

"Yes? Hello? Hello?" My voice was as high as the call tone had been.

"Doris?" Neddel said. "Are you alright?"

I was gasping and unsure if I was scared or just startled. After swallowing hard, I said, "Yes, I'm fine."

"Where are you? You sound funny."

Rushing to get back to my car, I drew a deep breath before answering. This didn't seem like the best time to stop and explain to the cop in my life what I was up to.

"My brain was deep in mental math." I tried to chuckle. "You know, figure out the best route for a client. The phone startled me, that's all. What's up?"

"You said you might be getting done early today. Could you stop and pick up Duke? I've been called down to Tamworth, and I can't take him with me."

"Sure. Leave him in the office if you have to leave before I get there." *Maybe Duke won't destroy the place.* "How did you get him with you?"

"I thought I'd give him a try, you know, in case." Neddel didn't say anything else, but I knew he meant in case he decided to keep him when the dog was ready for adoption. "I'll see you in a while."

I was only five minutes from the agency office. It took me longer to make myself presentable in the ladies' room than it took to drive there. For a job that didn't have any wasted minutes, I was really blowing the hours today. While I fluffed and buffed, I considered what a waste visiting the salt shed had been, and only then wondered how long the interview was going to take. I hoped not long, if Neddel was waiting with Duke for me to get there. I called his office, but the phone went directly to the message board.

"I'll get there as quick as I can," I said. "But I'm not quite done for the day yet."

It was twelve-fifteen when I walked up to Heidi's desk. I had over an hour to use up. A woman I didn't know was seated there. She glanced at my badge.

"If you're looking for Heidi, she's down in the cafeteria. It's her lunchtime. She'll be back at twelve-thirty."

I gave her a silent wave and made a U-turn. Tom, whom I'd met on day one as my tour guide, had breezed me in and out of the cafeteria on said tour. Even though I'd never returned, I knew where it was.

"Hi Heidi," I said as I walked up. "I didn't think you ever left your desk."

She blushed slightly. "Well, to be honest, normally I don't. Or when Mrs. Henderson would go to lunch, I'd sit in her office. But with Mr. Bennett, the new guy here, I thought it smart to let him know up front this is my time. You know, so he wouldn't take advantage."

"Yeah, I get it," I said. Mrs. Henderson must have done exactly that. It was too good of an opening for me to pass up. "I'm surprised Mrs. Henderson would take a lunch." I chortled. "I take her to be the type who is willing to work a twelve-hour day for ten hours of pay."

Heidi smiled back. "When I first came here nine years ago, that was the way it was. Back then, she was Ms. Greene. She always went out at lunchtime. She has a dog. Or at least she used to. I think she went home to let it out. Then she stopped. I figured the dog had died. She didn't leave, arrived early, stayed late. I mean, it was brutal. When she got married, she got liberated. From the job, I mean. She started to take a half hour. Twelve to twelve-thirty. I think she was having lunch with her new hubby."

I pressed my lips together. I wanted to know about the guy, but I didn't want to admit that I knew he was gone.

"He must have worked close by," I said, eyeballing the pay-as-you-snack box.

Heidi shrugged. "I guess."

"Have they been married long? I mean, were they still honeymooning?" I did the Groucho Marx eyebrow wiggle and wondered if I was pushing this act too far.

"Oh, my God! Don't go there!" Heidi was really blushing now. She picked up her things to get back to work. "It's been like, five years. She's very quiet about her life."

For the next while, I reviewed the cases of the clients I had thus far met. Some had been on the list for a while; others were new. Spending time doing an in-depth read about who the clients were, what they needed, and what had been offered so far took up more time than I'd have to dedicate on a normal day.

I did find Mrs. Hurst's file. Six months before, she had lived with her daughter, who suffered from a mental illness and only worked part-time. Mrs. Hurst's care had been spotty, and a place was being sought for her when her granddaughter stepped forward. For one year, we would monitor Mrs. Hurst on a monthly basis. After that, revamp her visits.

I really hoped Mrs. Hurst's current situation continued to work out for her.

The alarm on my cellphone rang. Time for my interview with the investigation team on Arnie's file. I gathered my notes and went down one floor to the conference room. To my surprise, Mr. Bennett was there. I expected a question-and-answer forum, but the woman who headed up the meeting wanted me to relate a narrative of findings. I hadn't prepared for this and wanted them to see the situation the way that I did, but not to believe I had taken more than a professional interest. This was not my strong suit.

"In your words, Doris," she said. "Tell us about your visit with Mr. Shaw."

I tried to keep on task and to the facts. I passed out my personal notes, as well as copies I had just run off that had been left by the previous outreach agent.

"He's in good spirits and well able to understand, just physically challenged by the damage to his hands and feet from the arthritis. I don't believe that he needs to be in a nursing home, but I do think he would benefit from senior housing where there are other people his age. Or if he stays where he is, having housekeeping, a little physical therapy, and maybe VNA to help him understand about taking his meds and keeping himself physically, ah, clean, would improve his quality of life."

"Why do you think his case was so badly misconstrued?" Mr. Bennett asked.

Okay, so this guy was my new boss. When he spoke, I realized he was the reason I felt so nervous. I hesitated for a moment and reflected on what I really wanted to say.

"Like many older people raised in a different generation, he carries a belief that if he can't take care of himself, he will be a burden to society," I said. Sounded good so far. "He told me he's afraid that being found needy would mean he'd have to go into a nursing home situation, and he's terrified of the idea."

Okay, that was pretty close to the actual conversation.

There were a few more questions, mostly about if he drove, had friends where he lived, and appeared to understand everything I said to him. Then I was dismissed. It felt like I had been there more than an hour, but actually it was thirty-five minutes. I zapped a cup of water for tea while I considered how different this job was from my expectations. From my desk, I shot Heidi a message that I'd had a pooch client emergency at home and was leaving for the day. I didn't wait for an answer.

At the sheriff's office, Duke was lying under Dolores's feet at the reception desk.

"He's such a good boy," she cooed, and passed him a peppermint candy.

Chapter Seventeen

Duke was on the overhead run, playing with Buttercup. The pig wanted to know how come the dog had gone for a ride, and she hadn't, when Neddel pulled in. Dressed in old jean shorts and knee-high barn boots, I was mucking out.

"Oh, you have all the fun," he said.

I paused for a welcomed break. Neddel was carrying a tin of kitchen sink cookies and offered me one.

"I didn't realize when I went back to work how many chores would be waiting when I got home at the end of every day. It's a good thing I didn't take a full-time job."

Buttercup had come running when Neddel pulled in. They were on the outside of the pen while I was on the inside. I realized my boyfriend was kind of dancing around.

"What's going on?" I asked, peeking over the fence.

People walked through all kinds of stuff on a daily basis. Buttercup was always interested in the smells coming from the bottoms of people's shoes. Normally, she just snuffled around, but today, her disc was running up and down Neddel's pants leg. She was even ignoring the cookie tin.

"What's with her?" he asked.

There was agitation in his voice. I didn't want him to not like her.

"No. Buttercup. Back," I ordered.

She didn't listen.

"Did you have pizza for lunch?" I asked. "There's some smell in your jeans that she wants to know about. What kind of laundry detergent do you use?"

"I had a turkey grinder for lunch, and I didn't wipe my hands on my pants." He moved aside again. "No. Buttercup. No."

It was as if she couldn't hear him. The snuffling continued. He climbed up to sit on the fence out of her reach. She's taller than he thought. Neddel had just settled on the planking when she reached up with her snout and goosed him. He came down on my side of the fence.

"Whoops," I said.

He looked ugly.

My eyes went from him to her and back. With Neddel out of range, Buttercup moved away. Her tail was thrashing from side to side, which meant she wasn't happy. Then I realized that, as a single man, Neddel lived more frugally than a guy who had somebody taking care of the home stuff for him.

"Are those the same jeans you wore yesterday?" I asked.

"Yes," he said, sounding a trifle miffed.

"And you left here and went to a body dump, right? Maybe got out of the car? Walked up to the scene? Stayed longer than three minutes?"

"Oh," he said, turning to look at Buttercup, who shooed chickens away from where she wanted to lie down. "Yeah. All that. By the way, your friend Doctor Lombard says hello."

"Tell me about what you found," I said.

While I mucked and shoveled out, Neddel got a wheelbarrow of fresh sawdust from the enclosed holding trailer and shoveled in.

"A couple of young guys were out on four-wheelers, horsing around. They came across a discarded freezer out at the edge of one of the forest service roads and were using it as a jump. From what I could see, it had been offloaded at the top of a small rise. Sometime during the flooding last spring, the sandbank washed away, and the freezer tumbled over when the four-wheeler launched. The lock is damaged, but it looked like it was set at one time. I'm willing to bet it gave way when the freezer rolled over."

He took the tools over to the outside spigot to rinse them off.

"When the freezer rolled maybe a second time, the shifting weight inside flipped the lid," he said, finishing his tale.

"Let me guess. Cold storage for unwanted human pieces." *Disgusting.* My nose wrinkled.

"Just one piece. At least, I think so. It was hard to tell because it was pretty mushy," he said.

"Gross." I rinsed my barn boots and kicked them off so they'd dry on the deck.

"Why don't we sit out here in the sun for a few minutes?" I asked. "I could use the vitamin D boost."

Neddel was sprawled out in the Adirondack chair, eating another cookie, when I came back outside with two tall glasses of raspberry lemonade. Once I was comfy, with the sun warming my face and knees, I started with my twenty questions.

"These are pretty good cookies," I said. "Where did you get them?"

"A woman left them at the office," Neddel said. "Dolores told me to take them because she didn't need the calories." He chuckled.

I turned the tin over. There was a note taped to the bottom.

Enjoy the snack, Sheriff. Homemade especially for you. Patty Monson.

I almost choked. Patty Monson! Divorced for the third time, always on the hunt for a new man. And obviously on the move again. The bite of cookie in my mouth turned to sawdust. When Neddel turned away, I tossed the rest of the sweet over the deck railing.

Neddel offered the tin, but I shook my head. Instead, I changed gears.

"How big was this freezer?" I asked.

"What? Oh. I thought we were done with that." Neddel might have started dozing off. "We didn't finish up there until about three this morning. Let's see. Not big, but a chest-type freezer, maybe fourteen or fifteen cubic feet, just big enough for an adult male to fit in. White. Fairly good condition, but old enough so it was a little rusty on the bottom. The motor cage showed signs of leakage."

"You said the body was a, what? Dinosaur?"

"Phfft. You aren't real good at interrogation, are you?" he asked. "Adult male."

"Old? Young?"

"Let's see if I can head you off on this one. Save some time, maybe get us to where we're eating supper earlier because I'm about worn out," Neddel said. "Doctor Lombard, your friend, will probably be calling you as soon as the facts are verified."

"Why would she call me?" I asked.

"She specifically asked me where you were, and what time I thought you'd be arriving at the drop site."

"Really?"

His words had perked me up. This could be my in!

"Yes, Doris. She did. I told her you hadn't been issued an invitation, and I'd shut off my cellphone so you couldn't track me."

I felt myself blush full-blown scarlet. Before Neddel could comment on that, I told him to get back to the description of the remains.

"As I said, according to Doctor Lombard, adult male, Caucasian. I'd say from the way he was packed in, average height." Neddel swirled his lemonade. "No way to discern weight because the body was, like I said, mush. There was some darkish brown hair. Eye color was indiscernible from where I was."

"What was he wearing? A suit?" I asked.

"Naked."

"Tattoos? Scars? Birthmarks? Teeth? Anything?" I ran out of ideas.

"Doris. Mush. End of statement." Neddel handed me his empty glass. "What's for supper tonight? I left some steak tips when I came by this morning to pick up Duke."

"Let me go look."

I probably should have been chagrined at what he'd just told me, but I was mostly annoyed. There were at least a couple of local guys who had shown up missing. Neddel's body in the freezer could be one of them.

The bag of marinating tips was in the refrigerator, along with a good-sized green salad. Courtesy of Melanie, who thought I ate lettuce only if cold meat, cheese, and two slices of bread were involved.

Neddel was giving me facts, but didn't seem inclined to want to connect the dots to either of the men I knew were missing. While the grill heated up, I skewered beef, onions, peppers, and chunks of tomato, and discreetly sent a text message to Dr. Rose Ann Lombard.

Neddel is holding out on me. Waiting for details. Possibly missing local.

My cellphone dinged.

Missing like dead? Or missing, like ran away? Neddel said he had a runner.

Phfft. That was a disappointing turn of events. Frustrated with the cryptic texting, I didn't bother to answer. The bigger issue was that when I went back outside, I thought Neddel was sleeping standing up. One quick topple and he could have been grilled. I had to smile. He looked kind of cute, all defenseless and droopy.

* * *

I put a plate down in front of Neddel. Fat and juicy steak tips, roasted to pink in the middle, served on a bed of fluffy, garlic mashed potatoes. On the side was a crispy green salad with Russian dressing, the kind Buttercup and Royally could lap up all day long, and that makes me want to upchuck. Crusty rolls, choice of beverage, and me. What more could any red-blooded male want? I thought I'd try for a little more intel. Ian had been easy. He talked in his sleep. I didn't know about Neddel. Every time I thought about seeing him sleeping, I got all embarrassed.

"How come the state police came down to speak to Mrs. Henderson about her missing husband and not you?" I asked.

Neddel had his first bite almost into his mouth. He paused, shook his head, and proceeded to continue moving his fork upward. I waited, not touching mine. Second bite. Sitting across the table, Melanie sat there, moaning about how delicious everything was. She wasn't even eating any meat, just carrying on. I still waited.

"Okay, Doris. I give up."

Neddel continued to slice his beef, but he was making eye contact.

"And you were doing so well at ignoring her," Melanie said.

"Quiet, you," he said. "I did speak with Edith Henderson. A couple of times, actually."

He took a bite. I laid my fork on the table.

"I took the initial call. If you wait, you can read about it in the paper tomorrow or the day after," he suggested.

"Or you can just tell me," I said.

"Oh, look at the time," Melanie exclaimed. "I'm missing the national news."

She and her plate disappeared down the hall. The tapping of Lilo's feet could be heard as the small dog put in a frantic effort to stay with her master, as well as in spill range if the plate should overturn. I knew Royally was considering it, but he stayed with his chin and drool, right on the edge of my knee.

Neddel watched Melanie go with envy.

"A while ago," he began.

"How long?" I interrupted.

"Months. Late last summer. Edith Henderson's husband disappeared. She called to report it, and I was the first contact."

"You waited months to get back to her about Mr. Henderson?" I was aghast.

"No." He looked at me with the same disgust he did when Buttercup did piggy things. "I went right over to speak with her and fill out the incident report."

"Sorry," I said. Then I filled my mouth with salad so I wouldn't interrupt again.

"She said that, even back then, he'd been gone for a while. She had waited to file a missing person report because she thought he would come back in a short time. According to her, he said a few times that it wasn't unusual for men in his country to go off for some downtime and be gone for weeks."

"I thought that was only in Australia," I said. "They call it a walkabout or some such. It can last for years."

Neddel shrugged. He was finishing up his shish kabob. I pushed the serving plate toward him. To my surprise, he ignored it.

"Mrs. Henderson isn't worried so much that he isn't going to come home as she is concerned that something bad might happen to him while he's gone. That's why the staties got involved."

"Because his wife is worried that he's going to get into trouble?" I asked. "If that was the way spouse disappearances worked, you'd be handling those types of calls twenty-four seven."

"Extenuating factors." Neddel sat back in his seat. "Ivan is from a communist country. He looks like a foreigner, and as soon as he opens his mouth, you know he is one."

"She told you that?" I asked.

"No, I've had other interactions with Mr. Henderson in the past. He had a file from before I arrived here."

Now I was pushing away from the table. "How? I mean, why? I never heard of this guy before all this. I read the paper. If he had some, oh, I don't know, clashes with the law, it would have been on the police blotter."

"Maybe," Neddel said slowly.

"Or?" I asked, going all squinty-eyed.

"It might have been withheld from the paper if someone had a good reason for it not to be seen. Or if a member of the family held enough power to ask for it to be withheld, and be given that courtesy."

His brows were drawn together. I was sure he hoped his cellphone would go off, and he'd be able to run away.

"Are you going to explain that last bit, or am I going to get a crowbar and pry it out of you?" I asked.

Neddel raised his head, and there was a look in his eyes that I thought might be anger at my intruding on his work. Instead, he leaned back and laughed. Loud.

"I heard a while back that you had a tendency to be tenacious," he said.

Now I was the one fumbling.

"Who?" I demanded. "Who said that?"

"Oh, someone around," Neddel said with a shrug.

He'd stopped me cold with that remark, and while I was still listing possible guilty parties in my head, he started speaking again.

"A while ago, some Ukrainian students worked in the area. Overall, they did well. However, a small fraction of locals pushed their anti-communist viewpoints to the forefront. Going so far as to run ads asking people to avoid businesses that employed these people. These youths were brought here because they were needed in *our* workforce. It never really amounted to too much, but after one season, none of those students returned. Others came, stayed one season, and then they were gone. It came up at a selectmen's meeting because fifteen miles away, across the border in Maine, the same men and women return from Mexico, El Salvador, and the Mediterranean, year after year. Those people don't need to be retrained, and they know their way around the area. Why is it foreign workers will return to Maine but not here?"

"Because South American countries aren't connected to communist countries in small minds. Therefore, those workers aren't harassed."

My voice had gone flat. At the beginning of this conversation, I'd been like a dog pulling on the rope. But now I felt defeated.

"Exactly. It doesn't matter which mid-European country it is, or if it's Cuba. The consensus is, Communist is Communist. Everyone. Every day. It's not something you get over; you just are. Forever. And each is looking for a chance at terrorism. Ivan suffered the same harassment. After the first few incidents, he took the talk personally."

Neddel got up and put his plate in the sink. He reached for mine. I gave it to him and rose to get storage containers out for the leftovers.

"I guess I'm missing something," I said. "If Mrs. Henderson or her husband were worried his heritage was going to get him hurt, why would they stay here?"

"She grew up here, owns a fair amount of property, and has a good job. Ivan was working. Did good work and was respected for it. But the stigma was always there," Neddel said.

"Did he apply for citizenship? Denounce Mother Russia?"

"That's what's making Mrs. Henderson so nervous. Ivan had received notice of the date for his swearing-in ceremony, and left just before it. No note or anything. Just gone. Like you, he was proud of where he came from. And according to his wife, would defend his homeland."

"Phfft," I said.

"Doris, even though he came from the Ukraine, he was originally from

Romania. He was trying to find a place he belonged, and he was willing to work to be there."

I could hear Neddel's frustration with my attitude.

I bit my lip. I was acting just like the people who had harassed the Ukrainians. This wasn't me, it really wasn't, and yet I'd just done that. I was so ashamed. I looked at Neddel. He was an obelisk of solid ice.

This wasn't me; not the way I really felt or even lived. I'm not sure where it had bubbled up out of, my own frustration, or the fact that I was also trying to find a new place in life for myself. I didn't know. If I'd had a good, close friend, I'd have been dialing someone I trusted who could help me sort out my reaction.

"I'm sorry," I said. "Really. I don't know where that came from. It was uncalled for and not right."

"Ah-huh." Neddel wiped his hands off on a dishcloth. Then he turned and left.

I watched him drive off and was so close to tears, my fingernails cut into my palms. I wanted him to come back, to be like Ian, whom I could say anything to and who would help me sort out my thoughts and emotions. I missed that. I needed it.

The dust had settled, and I was still standing at the window. It was time to admit that I was getting really good at pissing him off. Melanie was right. Some other skirt was going to come along who wasn't afraid to show her emotions without getting nasty. She'd let him know how smart and desirable he was, and he'd leave me in the dust without a thought because she was kind, and I wasn't.

I put the leftovers in the fridge and the dishes in the sink. With Royally following, I went out to the barn.

With my butt parked in the lawn chair outside Duke's enclosure. The dog looked sad and kept looking back down the driveway as though he was waiting. Had I ruined his chances as well? My feet rested on Buttercup's side as she lay stretched out and snoozing. I dug into some serious self-analysis.

I'm not a fan of the process. Over the years, I'd figured out what my strengths were and my weaknesses. Yet how to keep myself out of hot water, or the frying pan, or buried deep in the poop-pit, all seemed to elude me. It took a while before I remembered how when one of us had done something bad, or was in crisis, my father would take us for a ride, park on the side of the road far from our comfort zone, and we'd talk. Just talk. Either about what was actually the problem or about the hole we had dug by not addressing our issue out front. That's what I needed to remove myself from every excuse I could reach and tell Neddel about my fears and insecurities.

"It's a good thing," I said to the pig as the big wood moths started coming out and hovering around the overhead lights, "that I know how to say I'm sorry. Though I suppose I should worry how many times that will carry any water. Let's go, Big Girl. Time for you to go to bed."

Once inside, I dialed the phone. I didn't even get voicemail. Neddel's cell was shut down. There was no way to make contact unless I drove over there. Just the thought of that scared me sick.

I shut off the lights, leaving the moths as disappointed in me as I was.

Chapter Eighteen

In the morning, I tried calling Neddel again. This time I got voicemail. I left a message asking him to call me back. After I hung up, I made myself promise not to call again for fifteen minutes, or actually every fifteen minutes until he picked up the call. I had to meet with Cliff, so after making sure I had my cellphone and would be able to easily get to it should Neddel call, I headed out.

My decision to work with Cliff at the Humane Society had been twofold. First, we'd be educating young people on the proper way to handle small animals, starting with pets, the critters most of them were likely to encounter. Cliff and Joanne Clarey from Tin Mountain Conservation hoped to grow that interest in animals of the woodlands and fields.

"Maybe a bird-watching club," Joanne had enthused.

We'd all laughed, a little giddy at the prospect of moving youths away from the televisions, iPads, and cellphones and out into the fresh air and world of nature.

Sometime during our coffee klatch, I considered Buttercup. She was a big girl now. And she could get a lot bigger if I didn't keep a tight rein on her feeding and make sure she got enough exercise. She liked people, but now that we weren't doing the parades and fairs on a regular basis, she didn't see as many. If I took her with me when I went to help Cliff and set up her small pen, she'd see the kids, and they'd see her. She was a pet, right?

I had broached the idea of taking Buttercup to the humane society outing, where they would be teaching camp kids the correct way to handle their pets, with Cliff a while back. At first, he'd been skeptical, but Joanne, who had known Buttercup since her bitsy piglet days, and I wore him down.

Being outside under the wedding tent was perfect. I had gotten there really early, the better for Buttercup to check everything out first. While I set up the low, small picket fence, she wandered around on the long lead. I'd picked a spot where she would be sort of there but not in full view. Her trailer was backed in close to where the fence would be as well. Royally had been left at home because I only had one set of hands, and in a crowd situation with people milling around, he could be assertive. Corgis were bred to herd for hundreds of years. It's his fun thing. His superpower. Even with me restraining him, sometimes the urge was too great.

"Um, Doris." Cliff watched me hook the lightweight fence sections together. "Is this going to hold that big pig?"

"The short answer is no," I said honestly. "Not if she wanted to charge it. But she's been trained since she was a baby to respect this fencing."

"What if she gets excited?" he asked.

"I'm going to hustle her into the trailer using a bowl full of snacks, close it up, and take her home. I'll come back for her gear. If I stand over here, I'm between her and everyone else. She's a pet, Cliff. Not all pets are small, and I'm sure you don't want to have a horse here."

I stretched a piece of tarp over one corner to make sure she had ample shade and set out her big water bowl. I'd done everything I could think of to make this work. Cliff kind of nodded. Joanne came out and dragged him off. I'm not sure if she really needed him or if it was for Buttercup's benefit, but I was grateful. He was making me nervous.

"We're going to take a walk up the power line and burn off some energy. I'll see you in a little while," I said, as they left and I reined in Buttercup.

The power line ran across US Route 113 and alongside the ten acres donated for the construction of the Humane Society building. There were houses on the other side, along VFW Street, but I wasn't going there. Twice a year, a bush hog tractor, a commercial mowing machine, clears a swath, so it's a great place to hike. It was all very intriguing to Buttercup and kept her running back and forth. She and I went up over small hills, around boulders, and across animal trails. At eight-forty-five, I put her back in the small pen with a supply of carrots and celery chunks to hold her. Buttercup immediately flopped down for a rest.

From my station in the tent, I had a full visual of the small pen. Everything looked fine. But when I turned to look out the main entrance, I had cause for concern.

"Excuse me," I said to the volunteer making last-minute adjustments to the pet equipment table. "What's going on over there?"

The woman turned around. Angie! Now I remembered where I'd seen her before.

"Hi, Doris," she smiled broadly.

"Hi yourself, Angie. No little guy today."

Now that I realized who she was, I felt foolish about the time we'd spent together, and I hadn't made the association. It probably also explained why she so freely shared information.

"No. I had already volunteered to be here. Eve switched her working days. Are you talking about the table with the white cloth? Those are the refreshments."

"Oh, I hadn't expected there to be food, especially outdoors.

"Seeing as this is day one, members of the Chamber of Commerce have been invited to check out the doings," Angie went on. "The Cupcakery volunteered coffee and baked snacks." She shrugged. "A little early in the day for cake, if you ask me. But Cliff said they'd only be set up for an hour."

"But not Stan the Hot Dog Man," I said.

She laughed. "If Stan were here, I'd have a hot dog. The buses are just unloading, so we've got a few minutes. Go get a cupcake."

I opted not to. Stan would have created a problem Buttercup could not ignore. But I wasn't sure how she'd feel about the sweet, sugary smell of baked goods. Just because I couldn't smell them from where I was didn't mean she couldn't.

I said goodbye to Angie and went back to my place behind the kitten playpen. Buttercup was still lying down.

Kids in summer camp t-shirts started entering the tent. A few carried muffin tops. We were about to begin.

Then, adults entered who I knew weren't volunteers or society employees. They had to be Chamber members. Most gingerly held a paper coffee cup and a napkin with a small snack. One of them was Racheal Gerrish. I changed position to block the small pen from sight.

It didn't matter if she recognized me. Buttercup might be a different story.

I had no real plan for introducing Buttercup during the program. This being the initial event, everyone kept right on script. The Chamber people clustered around the entrance for fifteen minutes or so, then began to leave. Even though I hoped she would be among the first to go, Racheal stuck around. Once, I saw her pass a business card to someone.

I couldn't believe it. She was stumping. Then I shrugged. Probably normal behavior for a Realtor.

Betty Louise Waterman gave me a wave. She owns Maid-for-You, a cleaning service. Betty Louise had on one of her signature powder blue T-shirts with the logo on the front and back. More advertising.

I laughed to myself. My small prejudice had raised its ugly head. What was okay for Betty Louise should be okay for Racheal Gerrish. There were others in the small crowd I knew. Actually, only a few I didn't. Eventually, all the Chamber members were gone. I spent the rest of our time passing out kittens and keeping an eye on the new handlers. One day, all these fur babies would be adopted. Today, they were just happy to be cuddled.

"Let her lean on your chest," I said softly to one small person. "That way, she feels safe. Can you hear her purring? She's happy."

The little girl gave me a missing-tooth smile.

Cliff had announced out front that the young animals were to be shared, and if the young visitors didn't want to handle one, they didn't need to.

The kittens and puppies were very popular. The ferret and the snake, not so much.

Angie explained leashes, collars, bedding, and clean water. She had charts with words and pictures that showed good and bad behavior. I snuck out to check on Buttercup. She was snoring. I had wanted a little interaction between her and the kids. Unfortunately, she slept through the whole event. It was only through the use of watermelon that I got her up and into the trailer.

"That worked well!" Cliff beamed.

"Is two hours long enough for the children to learn?" I asked. Secretly, I thought the animals were all ready for a nap.

"It'll have to be. That's all I put in my proposal. Two hours, two days a week, four weeks."

Joanne, my friend and Cliff's assistant, joined us.

"Where did you come from?" I asked. "I didn't see you this morning."

"I was covering the desk inside so Angie could be out here. This was fun, right?" She followed me over to the small pen. I started breaking down Buttercup's portable enclosure. As I lifted one piece out of the slide-in hinge attachment, she spoke again.

"Did the kids like Buttercup?"

"I don't think anybody saw her," I said. "We went for a good walk in advance so she'd be quieter. Then she ate her snacks and snoozed."

"Huh." Joanne laughed. "Well, don't feel slighted. I heard one of the visiting adults remark about her."

Hair rose on my arms.

"Who?" I coughed out. "Sorry…dust."

"Don't know."

"Man or a woman?" I asked, maybe a little sharply.

Joanne frowned. "Does it matter?"

I forced a little laugh. "No. But a couple of women were all dressed up, you know, in suits and heels. I figured one of them might have been offended to see what most folks consider farm stock."

"Yeah, I can see that." Joanne smiled again. "I especially noticed the woman in the retro red dress. You know, the kind Betty Crocker housewives all wore in the fifties? And listen to this, her heels were the *exact* same color. She was busy passing out her business cards. I think she's a realtor and thought this would be a place to find clients. I heard her tell Betty Louise that her husband was supposed to be here, but he had to go out of town on business."

I put the last section of the fence into the back of my Liberty. "She might have a house in your future. You never know," I said, then waved goodbye.

I was smoking under the collar, but for no good reason. I mean, she could have said something good, but I doubted it.

Instead of driving up US Route 113, where there would be less traffic, I took the White Mountain Highway. That meant I traveled right by the building taken over by the Gerrish Agency.

I drove past slowly. It was a no-passing zone, so the few cars behind me had to go with my whim as I checked out the vehicles in the parking lot. Both of the SUVs I'd seen at the Gerrish family house were there, which meant both Racheal and Richard Gerrish were in the office working.

As soon as I got home and had Buttercup unloaded, I headed for the telephone.

"The Gerrish Agency. How may I direct your call?" chirped the answering voice.

"Richard Gerrish, please?" I responded. *What would I say when he came to the phone?*

"I'm sorry, Mr. Gerrish is not in today. Would you like to speak with Mrs. Gerrish?"

"No. Hm, I thought I saw his car in the parking lot," I said without thinking.

There was a pause. The type where you don't even hear somebody breathing.

"I'm sorry. But he's not here. Let me put you through to…"

I cut in. "That's okay. I'll call back later. Thank you for your help." I hung up before Chirpy could respond.

"Oh, Melanie?" I called out, trotting down the hall.

I got the hold-it-a-minute finger. When her interaction with the client was finished, she took off her headset.

"S'up?"

"Who is the receptionist or secretary that answers the phone at The Gerrish Real Estate office?" I asked.

"How would I know?" My daughter frowned and replaced her headset.

"Can you find out?"

"I guess so. Good afternoon. This is Melanie. How can I help you?"

She was back in pharmaceutical question-and-answer mode. That's what she does: helps people with billing or medicinal drug questions.

Out in the yard, Buttercup cooled off in the wallow, a sand pit we sprayed with a lawn sprinkler set up on a post. Instead of mud, she lay in the wet sand, rooted around a little, and stayed comfortable in the heat. My husband, Ian, had come up with the idea and put it all together. It's a godsend during the hot months.

After I put the leads on Duke and Royally, the three of us went out onto the road for some exercise and basic behavior training.

Calwin Mountain Road gets zero to no traffic, if you exclude the few people who knew they could access the hiking trails at the end of the road. It was a good place to do sit-stop-and-go style training. There weren't a lot of distractions if I could get the chickens to stay at home. But animal trails cross, with birds and squirrels, so there were a few interruptions, which gave me a chance to stop and train without harping continually. Royally knew the work command, so he was all business.

I was pretty proud to watch Duke as he responded to Royally, the smaller dog. Royally was a little general. Duke was one of the troops. Now I understood why the female dog that had been seized with him had had such an impact on his behavior.

On the way back, I dropped off Royally and kept going up the road toward town.

"Maybe," I said aloud as we marched along, "we could stop and say hello to Eve. I know she's home because I saw Angie this morning."

When we drew abreast of the house, I saw a vehicle in the dooryard. I was pretty sure it was Missy's red Toyota. It didn't matter. I wasn't going to stop if somebody else was there.

But I hadn't considered Eve's Jack Russell. When we'd walked by, he'd been lying in the shade of the garage, but he jumped up now and ran halfway down the drive, yapping and carrying on. Duke snapped around. I could hear an ugly snarl starting deep in his chest. This was no time to be introducing him to a new dog. Specifically, one who was loose without at least somebody to try to call him back.

"Step up, Duke," I commanded, moving forward with a strong hand on his lead.

He held for a second, then moved back into position with a small rabbit hop. I kept on moving away from the area where the other dog was until we were far enough so his eyes weren't rolling back to look. Kneeling, I rubbed my hands all over him, saying what a good boy he was, and fed him a peanut butter treat. Yeah, I made them for the pig, but that's what I had in my pocket. He wiggled all over, so excited that he had done a good thing. And now somebody was telling him so, being nice to him, giving him treats.

I got all choked up. Every single time I ran into a situation like this, my heart broke for all the critters out there that never get a kind word, a soft touch, or any kind of gratitude. I just wanted to hug him, and he was willing to let me. Except a car was approaching. A red Toyota.

"Mrs. Flynn? What are you doing down in the dirt? Did you fall?"

Missy got out of the car and ran around the front. Duke, still excited from the praise, turned his yellow eyes on her and wiggled in her direction. She stopped short, fear in her eyes, hands raised. Duke stiffened. A little wave of his tail, but the rest of him was on alert.

"Missy," I said, using my happy voice. "Put down your hands, smile, and tell Duke what a good boy he was for walking right past Prince and not throwing a hissy."

Missy laughed. "You and the darn dogs. Yes, Duke. You are a good boy, but the lady that's walking you? She's a basket case."

He didn't understand the words, but OH MY GOD, here was a second person telling him he'd done right.

"Do you want a ride home?" Missy asked.

"No thanks, but I want to talk about Eve," I said.

"Ouch. Okay. I have another call to make." Missy headed back toward the driver's door. "How about if I FaceTime you tonight?"

"Okay," I said.

After she drove away, I turned the proud boxer-pitbull hero back toward the farm.

"Let's go, Duke. We need to find out what FaceTiming is."

Chapter Nineteen

Melanie had prepared me for my first-time-ever FaceTime call, so I was ready when Missy made contact.

"What do you want to know, Nosy Rosie?" Missy asked.

"I don't want to dig into Eve Saucier's private business, but I am concerned about the missing husband," I said.

"Boyfriend. Fiancée. Significant other," Missy corrected.

Melanie, who sat nearby and was supposedly so busy with her own stuff, cocked an eyebrow.

"She's about your age, right?" I asked Missy, trying to ignore my daughter.

"A couple of years older, but she's so green," Missy said.

"Green?"

"You know, innocent. This boyfriend, Dick, is six years older. He was attentive right up until the time his wife found out about Eve and Andy. Then, according to Eve, he got skittish."

"Because he was going to run away?" Melanie asked once again, face-planted on her own laptop.

"Not according to Eve," Missy said.

In the background, I could hear her young'uns laughing and carrying on. As she spoke to me through the screen, she was mixing up supper and perfectly capable of working around them.

"According to Eve, Dick was afraid of his wife." Missy's voice grew muffled as she pulled ingredients out of the refrigerator. "Oh, and that was one of the things she said Dick kept repeating. That she and Andy needed to stay off the wife's radar."

"Because he was worried the wife would come after Eve or Andy?" I asked.

Suddenly, Melanie was right under my elbow, bumping me aside.

"I thought you were working," I said to her.

"Shush, Mom," she said. "Missy, would the wife have been able to find Eve and Andy?"

"I don't think so," Missy said. "I mean, she knew Eve's name, but I got the impression Dick moved them up here, then went back to offload his wife. And then he would come back. Eve got all teary and told him this was supposed to be their happily ever after. He called daily. Then one day, he didn't. She never heard another word."

"So, she's up here with Andy. How were they getting by?" I asked.

"When Eve rented the house, Dick gave her money for six months' rent up front. Right from the start, Eve went to work."

"Because she thought, back at that point, there eventually would be problems?" I asked.

"I came right out and asked her that same question. She said, not really. She doesn't have much furniture or household items. She figured it'd take a while for Dick to get re-established up here. She was being prudent."

"It sounded like he was self-employed where they came from," I mused.

"I think the guy was just a jerk that got tired of playing house with both his wife and Eve, and bailed," Melanie said, over my shoulder.

I didn't want to admit I thought the same thing. Except I had an idea of who Dick was, and obviously, Eve hadn't told Missy.

"Missy, what are the chances of you seeing Andy's birth certificate?"

"Been there. Done that. No father is listed."

"Why not?" Melanie asked.

"Dick was married to somebody else. In a divorce situation, that would be cause for a big settlement or alimony payment," Missy said. "Eve could go in anytime during the first five years of her child's life and update or correct the birth certificate. They probably thought it was the best thing for them to do."

Suddenly, there was a crash and a wail behind Missy.

"Sorry, I gotta go," she said. "Supper is ready and the natives are getting restless."

I sat there for several minutes, thinking.

"Somehow, I know there's junk floating around in your head," Melanie said. "Do you want to talk about it before you blow the lid off your noggin?"

"I think I know who Eve's missing Dick is," I said.

"Oh, that sounded dirty," Melanie said.

"Yeah, it did. Unfortunately, both versions are probably correct."

"So are you going to tell me?" she asked.

"In a minute. Maybe." I rubbed my hands over my face, trying to figure out how I was going to verify what I was thinking.

"Are you going to tell Neddel?" Melanie was asking a question that she probably already knew the answer to.

The correct answer was yes. However, the naughty little girl inside my head was bent over, giggling hysterically at the idea of spilling my guts and telling the sheriff that I again had my nose in his business.

The ringing landline phone saved me from having to answer any of Melanie's questions.

"Hey, girlfriend!"

"What's with the southern drawl?" I laughed.

Rose Ann Lombard was the Medicolegal Death Investigator for the Office of the Chief Medical Examiner for the state. We'd met the day Buttercup unearthed human remains on the ridge above her home barn the previous year. Any death deemed suspicious or having occurred in a place or circumstance where no medical attention was available fell in Dr. Lombard's realm. She was one busy girl. And though short, blonde, and buxom, she was no Southern belle.

"Well, I'm in Meredith. That's south of you," she said.

"Twit," I answered at her insinuation that I didn't know my way around my home state.

"Listen," she said. "I'm headed west right now. I've got another call over near Dartmouth I need to respond to this evening."

We both groaned. That was the way of Rose Ann's job. She was no nine-to-fiver.

"But on Friday, I have to be in court in Ossipee in the afternoon. What are the chances we could get together for a cup of coffee? That is, if I don't have a client on the back burner."

"Actually," I said, with a sly little grin, "how about if you and I and our coffee adjourn to the Chocorua Mountain Road where you last encountered a freezer?"

"Well, you certainly know how to charm a girl," she said. "I was wondering when you'd ask where the freezer was discovered. During my conversation with Neddel, he was clear that you weren't invited. From the way he was talking, I thought it might have to do with your terrier senses and your need to ask too many questions."

I tried to laugh her remark off, but sounded a little forced.

"How about I text you the coordinates when I finish up in court? Does that work?" Rose Ann asked.

"See you then!" I said, still feeling slightly embarrassed.

But once the connection was broken, my brain was off on a different tangent. If we were going to have coffee on the side of a remote fire lane, we'd need banana bread to go with it. Fortunately, I always had a couple of frozen-in-their-skin bananas, provided Buttercup wasn't nosing around when I was ready to freeze.

Pasta boiled for my leftover steak tips turned into beef carbonara as I mashed a banana. We rarely have leftovers, so before I dished the banana snack out to Melanie and Zack, I'd have to slice a couple of pieces and find a safe place to stash them. Oh, wait a minute, I had my own freezer!

Chapter Twenty

Work the next day at the Agency for the Aged was pretty boring. Maryann warned me that Mr. Bennett had a tendency to just pop up out of nowhere, so I should be careful of what I said or texted. My file had more cases that day than I'd ever had. I bet that was due to me not having many on Tuesday. I'd be catching up for the rest of my career there. Yet I was still able to carve out a few minutes to stop in and visit Arnie Shaw, even though he wasn't on my list. I'd brought him a container of carbonara and a hunk of banana bread. While he chowed down, I made him a pitcher of iced tea and told him about my interview with the agency inspectors two days prior.

"I'm sure they'll be in contact, though I don't know when," I explained. "Arnie, don't be afraid to talk to these people. Tell them you want to stay here. But be clear about what you can or can't do. Also, you have the right to have an advocate with you when they show up. If they want to hold a phone interview, and you're worried you'll miss something due to your hearing, tell them no. Just tell them why. The agency is there to help and protect you."

I knew I was parroting what the agency would want me to say, but I had to believe that at some level it was the truth.

He laughed aloud. Little bits of pasta flew through the air. "You're so naïve. It's almost cute."

I tried not to react to what he said, to show that I was afraid he was right.

He went back to watching for the new dog in the neighborhood from his window spot, and I headed home. Tomorrow was going to be busy, and I needed to get ready.

Chapter Twenty-One

Our stint at the Humane Society went off without a hitch. There weren't any stray chamber members wandering around. Angie arrived a few minutes late, as she had come from babysitting Andy, but she was soon out there going over all the equipment new owners needed to care for their pets. She also added a hands-on doggie demonstration for a tick check, which I thought was wise.

I had kitten control, just like on the first day. We did some tick checking there, too. While little hands ran over even littler bodies, I held my breath. Not a single tick was found.

The last time we'd been under the tent in the morning. Mid-afternoon was a different story. It was hot. And Buttercup was up and restless.

When the volume rose among the children, she got noisy, too. It didn't take long for the kids to want to step out and see her. Though I didn't let her loose, I passed out roasted, saltless peanuts in the shell for the kids to throw into the pen before we returned to the pet training. Searching through the grass kept her busy until I was done.

My cellphone trilled.

"Hi, Rose Ann," I said, phone clamped between ear and shoulder. "I'm just picking up my gear. It was so late I didn't think you would call."

"Really?" she asked. "I thought I got out of court particularly early today. How about iced coffee?"

She told me she'd be waiting where Chocorua Mountain Road intersected with US Route 16.

Buttercup called.

"Nuts," I said, realizing I wasn't going to have time to take her home. "Looks like you get to go for a ride."

The horse trailer had open windows all around the top, which would ventilate the inside as we rolled down 16.

Negotiating the Dunkin's drive-thru was tricky. Because I hadn't brought the banana bread with me earlier, I got three donuts. I mean, it was only fair Buttercup get one as well.

Chocorua Mountain Road was actually a dirt access to hiking and fire roads higher up. I didn't dare leave the trailer, so Rose Ann and I rode up together Chocorua Mountain road toward where the freezer had been found with Buttercup tagging along.

"This is rough," Rose Ann said. "I mean, for Buttercup, don't you think?"

"No, she's pretty good. She generally rides lying down, which lowers her center of gravity.

The fire lane was a different story. I wouldn't be driving up that.

"How far up?" I asked.

I'd pulled in just far enough for the jeep to be off the access road.

Rose Ann blew out her cheeks. "Quarter of a mile. If you drive up, you'll have to back out."

"I'm good at backing, but that's a long way."

I dropped the tailgate of the trailer. Buttercup still had her halter on, so I attached her lead. Because she knows Rose Ann, Buttercup had her happy on. She made little squeals, grunts, and woofs. No doubt complaining about the trailer. She prefers to ride in the back of the Liberty. There's room if I take the seats out.

"Do you think you need the leash here? There's no one for miles," Rose Ann pointed out.

"True, but this is a new place. I don't want to take the chance she'll decide to explore."

The road was wide enough for a heavy pickup truck or a water tanker. But a full-sized piece of fire apparatus wasn't going to make it.

"You should have seen the medical examiner," Rose Ann said. "He nigh on to had a heart attack driving his shiny rig in here. Branches slapping and scraping along the sides. His shoulders were hugging on tight to his ears."

She stopped walking and pointed out the place to the right where the brush had been crushed or uprooted.

"There weren't any tracks by the time the freezer was discovered, but our best guess is that whoever came in here got this far. As you can see, the road takes a steep climb just there. They pulled up, offloaded the freezer on the low side, and backed out. So much for ever seeing them again. But the four-wheelers? Those guys told us exactly what they had done. This was virgin territory. They were still stoked about finding it."

She swung her arm from where we'd approached up toward the rise in the road toward the higher ridge line.

"They were headed up the road, saw the freezer, and drove onto the ridge. There they, in true male fashion, cannon-balled down, across the road, and up the side of the freezer. It was already tilted outwards. They hoped to get some air." She looked disgusted. "On the first pass, the weight of the four-wheeler and the impact pushed the freezer over the lip of the embankment."

I might have blinked a couple of times at the foolhardy antics of young males.

"That guy and his vehicle followed suit, landing mere feet away from the freezer." Now she looked happier. "He said he got a clear visual of what was spilling out, and the smell was beyond anything he could imagine."

While we were talking, Buttercup circled and sniffed. She got to the lip of the embankment and wanted to go down from where we stood.

"Where's the freezer?" I asked.

"Major crimes took it to Concord. They have a facility there where they do forensics. When they're through with it, the district attorney will decide if it needs to be kept or can be recycled."

"You mean to ReStore?" I asked with a smile.

"I doubt it."

Buttercup's front feet were over the lip. She was pulling hard.

"She wants to go see. So do I. I'll be back in a bit."

I gave the pig enough rein so she wouldn't drag me down too fast. It was only about twenty feet, but four hundred and fifty pounds headed down can pick up a lot of speed. And it was much steeper than I had realized.

"I'm coming too," Rose Ann said.

"You can't come; you're wearing a dress," I shouted as my feet slid out from under me.

I fell backwards and slid downwards on my backside, my trusty porcine yanking my shoulder out of its socket.

Rose Ann had been wrong. The roads had been a bumping, jolting ride, but this terrifying, unable-to-brake, slithering, toilet-flushing rush was where the rough actually was. My butt bounced off several rocks. Some I saw coming at me, a few were a total surprise. Twenty feet grew to thirty, stretched into way too far. I would have some lovely bruises. When we reached the gully, I saw that the freezer had gouged out a place on impact. Other areas showed smooth scoop scars left by a shovel. Of course, that was exactly where Buttercup wanted to go. Rose Ann was right behind me.

"What? You don't think I've never had to go to a site in a skirt?" she asked. "I want to point out that I was intelligent enough to trade my three-inch heels for half-boots. Usually, I put on a hazmat suit, but not this time." She pointed. "Gutty mess was right there. And there. Oh, and a big spot over there." She indicated the area that had been cleared up and taken away by the shovel crew.

"Hold on a second. Do you mean this guy was in bits?"

"Oh yeah. Several," Rose Ann said.

I reined Buttercup in. We looked around more and found a lot of animal signs.

The lingering stink must have brought critters for miles. It only took a few minutes to see everything we needed, as far as I was concerned. Buttercup was still checking around.

"How are you going to get her out of here?" Rose Ann asked.

"We'll use the heavy guns."

From my backpack, I took a plastic jar of peanut butter and a wooden spoon.

"Do not open this until you're maybe three-quarters of the way up. Drop a dollop on the ground and tell her what it is."

"You mean pean—?"

"QUIET! At the top, let her see you leave her another small taste."

Rose Ann nodded. "Shrewd."

"Yeah, we'll go with that."

While my friend worked her way up the bank, sliding and skidding, I got Buttercup to a place where I thought she'd be able to climb. There was no way Rose Ann was making a ladylike ascent. All I had to do was hold on to the lead, and Buttercup would help me up when she went, I thought.

Rose Ann stopped ten feet from the top. I watched as she struggled to get the plastic security seal off the mouth of the jar. She muttered out loud, but I'll bet she didn't realize it because she used some very unfeminine cuss words.

Buttercup wanted to go back to where the worst of the mess had saturated the ground, but her friend was up there talking, and she was interested in that as well. Then she got a good look at the colorful JIF label. She might be nearsighted, but she was not colorblind.

Having finally gotten the inner seal off, Rose Ann scooped out a couple of tablespoons of peanut butter and held the spoon aloft. She turned, ready to call Buttercup, but the pig was already moving upwards.

"GO!" I screamed, both hands wrapped around Buttercup's harness and my belly on her back.

Like I said, low center of gravity, close to the ground. The pig's hooves dug in. Squealing ferociously, she clambered up. Rose Ann had a sudden look of apprehension on her face. She dropped the wooden spoon and began her own frantic rush for the upper lip. When Buttercup and I came over the edge, my friend was on the other side of the road. The jar stood on a rock several feet away.

"I lost the spoon." Rose Ann's voice was shrill as her hands made shooing motions toward the rock.

"It's okay." I panted, holding the spoon up like a trophy. "I've got it."

Buttercup had paused only a moment, sucking the small dot of creamy goodness off the spoon and spitting it out. When she headed back up the slope, I had taken the initiative and grabbed the discarded implement.

We were all a mess, covered in dirt and twigs. Using the spoon, I hand-fed Buttercup, telling her what a good girl she was.

"Did you save your mama? Yes, you did. Yeah, no, I think that's enough." I held the jar out of range. "Too bad we lost the top."

Rose Ann reached a shaking hand into the skirt of her dress and pulled out the red plastic cover. Smiling broadly, I took it from her.

"And you're a good girl too!"

"Don't use your baby pig talk on me." Rose Ann finally laughed. "I couldn't believe how fast she came up that bank. The next time I have to go down over the side of a cliff to a site, I'm taking her so I don't have to ride back up in that heart-stopping sling."

We staggered back out to the truck, where our half-finished iced coffees were diluted by the melted ice. But the donuts still waited. Sort of. Buttercup had gone back in the trailer with hers and half of mine and Rose Ann's as well. She settled right down. The climb had taken a lot out of her.

"It's a good thing she's in such good shape." Rose Ann draped herself against the dash, so the limited blow from the air-conditioning could cool her.

I nodded, unable to open my mouth because I had just now remembered Doctor Hussey telling me about the pig's heart murmur. She was four, two years older than he had believed she'd live. And I had just put her through something that could have stopped her heart for good.

My stomach hurt. I was not a good mama. Rose Ann was still reeling from the rush. I don't think she realized I wasn't nodding in agreement so much as pressing my tongue against the roof of my mouth so I wouldn't throw up.

When we reached the spot where Rose Ann's SUV was parked, I opened the observation window on the side and took a good look at the pig. She appeared to be sleeping, lips curled up in a smile.

"I'm going to take a double shower," Rose Ann said as she got into her vehicle.

"So are the two of us." I waved goodbye.

I'd had all the excitement I could take for one day.

Chapter Twenty-Two

On the way home, my only thoughts were for that shower, a cup of tea, and a twenty-minute power nap. At the corner, just as I turned onto the Calwin Mountain Road, my eyes swept the lot behind the tall sign the Gerrish Agency had installed. There was the evil clown grin of Racheal Gerrish and a bold site map. I had actually avoided looking at the park for days. Oblivious to what I considered horrific news, a couple was sharing a snack. Two children and a dog played in the grass. That was the way things should be. Not a dozen houses with fences and no trespassing signs.

A car I didn't immediately recognize was parked in my driveway. Not a problem. Melanie knew a lot of people. Leaving Buttercup wriggling around in the wallow, I sailed through the kitchen door.

"Wait until I tell you where Rose Ann and I went," I called out, reaching for Buttercup's bowl.

When the pig realized I was going into the house, she followed me up onto the deck. Now she waited behind the metal mesh protector and the screen. Her grunting, woofing calls could be heard throughout the kitchen. Her supper was late, and regardless of how many snacks had been strewn before her, there had better be a darn good reason.

Melanie popped out of the living room door into the hall. Her face was pale. Even though her hands were knotted tightly in front of her, her fingers made a little shooing motion, like go away.

"What's going on?" I asked.

Right Brain whispered, *this doesn't look good.*

"Mom, you have a visitor." Melanie sounded strained.

Before she could say another word, a second person stepped out onto the shining hardwood floor.

"Oh, Doris," Racheal Gerrish purred. "Here at last. Wonderful."

"I'm sorry," Melanie whispered as she moved past me, taking Buttercup's bowl from my hands.

I left her to mix up pig chow and walked toward the door Racheal had disappeared back into. She stood near one of the tall front windows. The late afternoon sun shone in, adding a sparkling glow to her Jackie Kennedy two-piece suit. Exact, right down to the pillbox hat. Except Jackie had selected a lovely rose color, not this nauseating lime green. Hat, shoes, white gloves, all a perfect match. The only bits of non-green were the pale pink silk blouse, white gloves, and the chunky gold jewelry.

As I stepped closer, I considered that the glow might not be so much sparkle as slime.

"Hello, Racheal. I'm surprised to see you here." My mouth smiled. I'm not sure if my eyes got the memo.

"Are you?" Racheal didn't try at all. She was top-to-bottom serpent.

Before I could say a word, she held up her hand. Pearl button on the wrist-length glove, nice touch.

"Instead of texting you, or having my attorney call, I thought I would do you the courtesy of talking to you personally."

"Did you, now?" I motioned to the winged chair, but she ignored me. "What's going on?"

"I want you, and whoever your little vagabond friend is, to stop calling and harassing my husband." The words were tight-clipped.

This wasn't what I'd expected at all. I'd been sure she'd have some complaint about Buttercup.

"I beg your pardon?"

"When I was reviewing the incoming calls on my office phone, I saw one from you. My girl told me that you specifically asked for Richard and hung up when she offered you the chance to speak with me," Racheal explained.

"*Your* girl?" My eyebrows and ears went up.

"Terry or Tracy, whichever." She waved dismissively.

Her tone firmly set the bar for the rest of our conversation.

"If I had wanted to talk to you, I would have asked for you," I said. My temper was rising. But I was just smart enough to stick to my original story. "It was *Richard* who contacted us weeks ago, offering to help out with our Humane Society fundraiser. And *Richard,* who left his phone number. *Richard* offered a donation. Therefore, when we hadn't heard from him, I reached out to *Richard.*"

"Well, *Richard* is too busy to assist your efforts, whatever they are. Do not call again."

Racheal swept past me, heels coming down hard on the wood floor. She headed toward the exit closest to where her car was parked. That was the kitchen. I followed, but not in a hurried or foot-stomping manner. I reached the door as Racheal was fighting with the latch at the bottom of the ramp.

"MOM!" Melanie called out from over by the henhouse. "Buttercup is still in the yard!"

By this time, Racheal was crossing the gravel to her SUV. Buttercup, always ready to meet a guest, was bearing down at her from the barn. The lime-green pillar of righteous wrath spun around, holding out her arm at the approaching porker. Buttercup stopped dead, let out a terrified squeal, and raced for her home pen.

I gasped. "Did you just pepper-spray my pig?" I yelled.

It's a good thing the gate was open, because I would have ripped it off the hinges. Racheal ran for her car, which was pointed down the drive, and sped off. But I didn't chase her. I was running after the escaping pig.

We never use force with Buttercup. I might use my knees to direct her, my I-am-the-alpha voice, snacks to coerce, and the harness for control, but never a raised hand, a smacking stick, or God forbid something as dangerous as pepper spray.

I found her buried in the straw, rubbing her face. Her eyes were streaming. I tried to touch her, but she yanked away. With her head thrashing back and forth and her eyes shut, she was making enough noise that she couldn't tell it was me, and that I wanted to help her. I went to the small refrigerator and came back with a pint of fat blueberries and a Ziploc bag of carrot chunks.

Using a cloth and cool water, I repeatedly wiped down her face, shoving carrot sticks and blueberries in her mouth each time it opened. When Doctor Hussey arrived, he said what we were doing was all we could.

After Melanie had called the vet, she'd alerted Neddel as to what had occurred. When he showed up, he told me that Racheal had called him even before Melanie had. The realtor had reported that the pig had charged her for a second time.

"She wants Buttercup tested for rabies," Neddel said.

"What? How are you going to do that?"

I couldn't get up off the barn floor, because Buttercup's enormous head was lying across my lap. She didn't want to take a chance that some of the blueberries would be lost.

"Well, it starts with quarantining the animal for thirty days." He wasn't making eye contact.

"Then euthanize it," said Melanie.

"Before you remove the brain and send it to be tested," I finished.

"Doris," Neddel said.

"No!"

"Listen to me." He squatted down beside me. "We are not going to euthanize Buttercup. She didn't actually bite Racheal. But for a few days, can you keep her here? Maybe in the pen or the barn?"

My bottom lip quivered, and my vision blurred as tears rose. Buttercup, however, had had enough of the drama, and blueberries. With a twisting wiggle-squirm, she rolled over and away. She wanted to go to bed.

The rest of us had PB&J and coffee for supper, then Neddel left. This was his night on patrol. When he was gone, Melanie and Noah sat across the table from me.

"Okay, Mom," Melanie said. "Now that Mr. Straight-Line-and-Keep-It-Simple is gone, what the heck was Racheal Gerrish spouting off about?"

"Do you remember the other night when Missy called?" I asked. "We were talking about Eve's missing boyfriend, Dick."

I paused, but fluttered my eyebrows.

CHAPTER TWENTY-TWO

"No!" Awareness was all over Melanie's face. "You have to be kidding."

"What?" Noah asked. "What did I miss?"

"Eve, who lives next store with her son," I said. "She's waiting for her missing boyfriend to come back. He moved them here so they would have a home. She said that he's married and planned on leaving his wife. But he left to go take care of that mess and never came back. She hasn't seen him anywhere in the area. And I believe that boyfriend is Richard Gerrish, husband of Racheal Gerrish, who also hasn't been seen locally in a long while."

"No way," Noah said. "The Gerrish Agency is one of our biggest up-and-coming businesses."

I held up my hand. "Hold on, Noah. Eve's boyfriend's name is Dick. So far, that's all she's told us. If you take a look at Andy and that ad in the paper for the Gerrish Agency, there is a marked resemblance between that man and that small boy. The man's name is Richard."

"No." Noah was still shaking his head. "I remember when the Gerrishes first came up here over a year ago. He came into the bank." Noah rose and began circling the table as he spoke. "He had a business plan that he presented to the bank manager and the finance team. He had this idea that if a finance expert was present at big showings, the sales would go faster and smoother. That's why Christine Gillette attends so many of their showings, because he suggested it. If the house sells in, I don't know, thirty days maybe, the Gerrish Agency covers her hours." He stopped walking. "Recently, I heard Christine saying how it was mostly working out."

"Noah. When was the last time you saw Richard Gerrish himself?" I asked.

"I don't know. I don't have anything to do with that part of the business."

"Okay."

I got the old-fashioned telephone book out of the junk drawer. Christine and Matthew Gillette had a number listed in Tamworth. I dialed the telephone.

"Hi Christine, sorry to bother you. This is Doris Flynn. Uh-huh. Yeah. Fine. How are you? But listen, I'm trying to get hold of Richard Gerrish. He offered to help with the Humane Society fundraiser. I guess I wrote his number down wrong because I'm not getting through. Can you help me? Great! Yeah, I've got a pen. 447-0001. Perfect. Thank you. Yes, see you soon. Bye."

I returned to my seat at the table.

"This is the same number I called the other day. The office number. The woman who answered the phone said he wasn't there. But his car, which I've seen in their garage, was in the driveway. As was hers. Two cars, two people, right? I don't think so."

"It has to be," Noah said.

"Again, no." I took a deep breath. "I think the remains found in the freezer on Mount Chocorua are Richard Gerrish."

"That's wrong, Mom," Melanie said. "I heard today the preliminary identification is Ivan Henderson, Edith Henderson's husband, the foreign guy."

My jaw dropped.

Melanie was nodding. "I was blown away when I pulled the information up. I called Dolores and asked for his description, Henderson's. I told her that you wanted to know. Then I used my computer and a photo of Richard Gerrish to figure out his description. Same build, same estimated weight, hair and eye color, and two capped teeth."

I rubbed my face. How could that be?

"Take a step back," Melanie said to me. "Remember what I said about Eve's boyfriend, Dick? Maybe he really couldn't cope with the stress of having a wife and girlfriend and kid. Maybe he did just blast out of here."

I still didn't think so. I just didn't. It could have been that I didn't want Eve to have to suffer that tragedy. Left Brain didn't seem to be able to cope when Right Brain got all emotional.

Melanie wasn't done. "There is no way to figure that out from here. I mean, practically no one I know in this town other than Noah has met Richard. And to my knowledge, no one has met Dick either, right? Have you seen any pictures of Dick, or do you just have Andy's word that his father's picture was in the paper? Even Noah said that Christine hadn't seen him since the initial meeting at the bank. Every encounter we've seen between the Gerrish agency and the public has been with Racheal. But back where they came from in Nashua, I bet lots of people knew them. That's where we need to go to figure out what the Gerrish family dynamics were. How they got along at work and at home. Whether there was a chance Richard had previous affairs. Or if she did. I don't know what else. Maybe their financial situation?"

"I think you're right. The only way to get a clear picture of that is going to mean a trip to Nashua," I said. "That would be a long trip, even if only for one day. Just one of us will be able to go because someone has to stay here and supervise."

Sitting back with her legs crossed and her fingers drumming on the tabletop, Melanie smiled like the Cheshire Cat.

"And I know how we can do that." Her eyes drifted to Noah.

* * *

"You want me to take care of all these animals? And Buttercup? For two days?" Noah looked aghast.

"Noah, honey," Melanie said. "I just explained this. You and I are supposed to go to Boston tomorrow so I can meet with the new neurologist on Monday, right? Well, Mom can go with me instead, and you can stay here. As far as getting all the chores done, you'll have all day. You already took Monday off anyway. It isn't like you haven't helped out before, right?" She smiled again. "Mom and I can leave tomorrow morning. It's Sunday. So maybe people who used to live next to the Gerrishes in Nashua will be home. Monday, on our way back from the meeting with the doctor, we can stop in where the Gerrishes used to work."

"I don't think…" Noah's voice faded away. "Let me get this straight. You and your mother plan to do some highly illegal private investigative work in Nashua."

"Probably not highly," Melanie said.

I nodded in agreement.

"Or," Noah continued, "instead of your mother, you and I will be going from house to house in a private neighborhood, asking invasive questions about previous residents?"

"Pretty close." Melanie and I were both nodding now.

"The other option is, I can stay here and pig/dog/cat sit?"

I had never seen Noah so solemn. At least, not for a few months.

"You've taken care of them before," I pointed out. "You know where all the directions are posted, medications kept. And Buttercup trusts you. Neddel doesn't want her to leave the farm. As far as Duke is concerned, if you contact Neddel, I'm sure he'll help you out there."

"Are you taking whining Lilo with you?" he asked.

"Yes, to Lilo. No to Royally."

"Then I'll take door number three. What time do I need to be here tomorrow morning?" Noah asked.

After he left to pack his things and make sure he was ready for his new assignment, Melanie and I got down to business. While I went around making sure that the direction notices were up to date and medicines, snacks, food, and supplies were readily available, Melanie followed me with a notebook.

"These are the top five questions I think we need to ask people first," she said. "We may not get a chance to get past these. Do we have a cover story?"

"How about the truth? The man is missing, and we're helping with the search," I said.

"No one is actually searching," Melanie said.

"But Eve, at least, needs to know what happened to Dick. We'll take the jeep. I'll drive. Business casual, so not shorts and a t-shirt, okay?"

"I don't think that's a good idea, Mom. If word gets back to Racheal, she's going to come right back here." Melanie paced, fingers tapping her lips. "Okay, how about this? We tell people we're from the IRS and this is part of a hush-hush investigation."

My eyebrow rose. Melanie wore a broad smile.

"You're kidding, right?" I asked.

"Absolutely not! People love to dish dirt about their neighbors when the stakes are high. What gets up there faster than the IRS?"

I left Melanie behind to pack a bag and get some shuteye. The last thing I heard was her practicing her new opening line.

131

Chapter Twenty-Three

At seven the next morning, Melanie and I were ready to pull out. I had one last conversation with Noah.

"Okay, this is important," I said. "Under no circumstances are you to tell anyone what Melanie and I are doing."

Noah's jaw started a slow drop towards the floor.

"What about Sheriff Neddel?" he whispered.

"Specifically, Sheriff Neddel." I waited.

Noah's face took on a look of terror.

"It's easy, Noah. Think about it this way. What are Melanie and I doing tomorrow morning?"

"Visiting Melanie's neurologist."

"Perfect. That's all you have to remember if anyone asks. I called Neddel last night and told him I was going. He understood why it was important that I be with Melanie and said he'd be out sometime today to make sure everything was good here." I fastened my seatbelt. "If I were going to place a bet, I'd say he'll be pulling into the yard in about twenty minutes. Because right now he's at Bea's Diner having his breakfast."

Melanie said goodbye to her beau, and we were off, headed toward Nashua. During the ride, we perfected our questions and story for Richard and Racheal Gerrishs' neighbors, or any family we might uncover.

"I did some deep searching into Richard Gerrish after you went to bed. He has siblings out around Cincinnati."

"Well, we aren't driving there," I said.

"I didn't think so. From what I've read, they weren't close as a family. But maybe we should still reach out to them," Melanie said.

"Right," I said. "But let's focus on here right now. Start a journal page for Eve. List what we know, possible questions for her we should ask her if this trip fizzles out. Like, if she knows anything about Dick's family, or if she's met them. Remember to ask if there is anyone local to Nashua."

"Should I call and ask her that now, before we get there?"

I shook my head. "That would be inviting her to question what we're doing. If she were to tell me not to do this, I wouldn't be able to move ahead honestly."

"Okay," Melanie said. "What about doctors, or maybe a lawyer he might have mentioned?"

I nodded. "Good friends. Who did he play golf with?"

"Did he play golf?" Melanie asked. "I didn't find that when I was doing the deep dive."

"I don't know. But if I were selling real estate and new to the area, I'd go places where I might meet people who would be interested in what I offered. Golf courses, coffee shops where the locals hang out, bars. Those are the places off the top of my head."

"Churches, the Chamber, Rotary," Melanie added to the list.

It was a three-hour ride to Nashua. With most of the business district closed, we headed toward the residential area where Melanie's research had turned up a home address. My daughter dozed off while I drove. The radio played without my noticing. When the map app told me to take the next exit, I almost jumped out of my skin.

We were on the south side of Nashua. It wasn't pretty. The area surrounding the exit was filled with older strip malls and heavy equipment yards, so decrepit the buildings and signs were the same faded colors as their neighbors on the next lot.

I roused Melanie. We followed the directions, twisting and turning on dirty side streets, until we came to a three-story white clapboard apartment building. The sign said *Apple Tree Condominiums.*

"These are condos?" Melanie stared incredulously at the distressed structure. "Where are the apple trees?"

There was no yard. Just pavement almost all the way up to the building. The far end of the lot was blocked by two enormous green dumpsters. On either side, saplings and a wooden privacy fence were plastered with blown paper and plastic grocery bags.

"You're sure this is the right address?" I asked.

"Why, because this place has dump written all over it?" Melanie checked her computer printout. "Yup. Right place. Should be the second one in from the right, second floor."

"I'll go up to the apartment—oh, excuse me, condo—on the second floor. Then I'll try the third floor. You start with the apartments on the ground level. Hit them all if you can. Look for any type of sign or posting that will point us toward the building manager or superintendent."

I got out of the car feeling that I had overdressed. Instead of business casual, grunge might have been more appropriate. No one answered the door to the condo where Racheal and Richard had supposedly lived, but I was in luck across the hall. The woman had a toddler hanging onto one leg and an infant in her arms. She was thrilled to have adult interaction. I could see in her eyes that she wanted me to stay forever, or at least until somebody else came along.

My wish to remain in the corridor disappeared when the toddler made a break for it. Obviously, he also wanted out. He got tangled up in my legs, and his mother made a dive for him. With her free hand wrapped around his upper arm, she motioned with her head for me to step inside and close the door. I stood just inside the doorway.

"We've lived here almost three years," his mother explained. "I don't know any of these people at all. But I think the couple that lived there before probably moved out because they got divorced. Thank God they took their yapping dogs with them."

"What makes you think they got divorced?" I asked.

The little boy had brought me a selection of toys to look at.

"Not a single day went by that they weren't arguing. Early in the morning, in the evening, it didn't matter," the mother said. "They'd get started, then she'd just keep going. She screamed continually. It didn't seem to matter if they were inside the apartment, out in the hall, or even in the parking lot."

"But they were together, right?"

The woman looked out the front window. "Yeah. I guess. I mean, they lived together." She frowned. "They each had a car. I never saw them go anywhere together. If one of them went out, they went alone. Or both cars left. I don't know what they did for work, but they had to get dressed up. You know, like a suit. Oh, and she usually took her dog with her. If both of them were here, they would howl all day."

"Both of the people?" I was confused.

The woman laughed. "No, the dogs."

"They had more than one dog?"

"Two. Jack Russells. They're small and spotted."

"Yes, I know the breed. Huh." I edged out the door. "Well, thank you for your help, but I need to get going. You be a good boy," I told the child. "Mind your mama. Thanks again for your help, ma'am. Have a good day." And I was out.

I didn't get an answer at either of the third-floor apartments.

Melanie was still inside somewhere, so I went up a second set of stairs. Out of the eighteen apartments, five were occupied. Melanie had scored the most, talking with three tenants.

"You learned more than I did," Melanie said, latching her seatbelt. "I only got that they were loud. Oh, and there's a notice on the inside wall next to the door with the manager's contact info."

"Good catch. I missed that."

Melanie had printed photos from the computer. Using those, we circled the surrounding area visiting gas stations, pizza places, a coffee drive-thru, and a couple of quick-marts. Other than a few maybes, our mission was a washout. We found a Panera for lunch.

"We've got the rest of the afternoon," I said. "How about if we go back across Nashua to the real estate office where they used to work?"

"It's going to be closed," Melanie said.

I could tell she was already fading, but I didn't want to be doing door-to-door at five o'clock the next night.

"Probably, but we could check around the businesses the same way we did at the apartment building. You know, say hello and ask questions."

"Okay, but can I have Pepsi instead of water?" Melanie asked. "That would juice me up."

By the time we pulled into the closest strip mall to the Lang Agency office building, which was closed, Melanie was duly caffeinated. This area was a complete turnaround from where the Gerrishes had lived. Yeah, it was still urban and dusty, but most of the businesses were better kept. New, even. There was practically no trash blowing around, and the few residential buildings were better maintained.

"So, when they're ready to sell to the business world, they get a better price," I guessed.

Because there was an even split between cluster businesses and drive-in parking lots, we decided that I'd drop Melanie off. She was starting to show some of the MS symptoms, fatigue, and a little slow to respond. Then I'd hit a few of the ones that required jumping in and out of the car, and pick her up when I was done.

Three hours later, we were in the Aroma Joe's parking lot, sipping iced coffee and comparing notes.

"No one recognized Eve's picture. Only a few had seen Racheal. But holy cow, this was Richard's area," Melanie said. "I'm going to have to set up a graph for where he stopped in or ate."

"Fine. The facts are, those who remembered him said he was friendly, bought lottery tickets, liked coffee and deli sandwiches."

I started the car. It was time to head to Boston. It would be another hour and a half before we checked into the hotel, if the traffic was with us.

"No one remembered him coming in with a woman. Two that are close to the realty office said he came in with a guy, but they weren't a couple."

"Probably one of the Mr. and Mr. Langs," Melanie said. "By the way, you asked me about the secretary at The Gerrish Agency. She's nobody that me or my friends know. Zoe told me her aunt used to work in that office. When the new guy bought it, he told the employees they could stay, their choice. But the wife came in a few months later and fired them all. Zoe's aunt worked out the rest of the week, then Racheal made her transfer all her real estate customers over so the aunt had no connection with the public. She called the husband a coward because he never showed up again while they were there."

"Huh. I wonder how long ago that was," I said.

"Don't know." Melanie shrugged.

We picked up shrimp scampi to go before we reached the city and made it an early night. I totally forgot to call Neddel. From what Noah told Melanie when she called him, it was a good thing.

Chapter Twenty-Four

While we waited between the battery of tests the neurologist had scheduled us for, Melanie got a text from Noah.

"He says everything is going great. Neddel has been over a couple of times and took Duke for an overnighter." Melanie chuckled.

"I knew Neddel was getting attached," I said.

"Yeah, but Noah said Neddel knew you were in Nashua. He asked Noah some questions, and Noah freaked." Melanie looked at me with concern. "I don't want Neddel not to trust Noah."

"Me neither. I'll give Neddel a call on the way home. How did he know we were in Nashua if Noah didn't tell him?"

Still scrolling through her messages, Melanie shrugged. "I don't know. Maybe he's got the car bugged. Or has a tracker on your cellphone."

"He can't do that." I slapped my palm indignantly against the steering wheel.

"Seriously? Like you don't track my phone?"

"I put the tracker on your phone so that if you were gone for a long time, I could make sure you weren't somewhere having an MS event." I didn't enjoy discussing this. "For us, it's a safety thing. You track me. I track you. Neddel is different. We aren't in any kind of relationship. ANY kind,"

"Mm." Melanie went back to Facebook.

Melanie's visits with her doctors always involve a second person on her team to take notes. The amount of information can be overwhelming. If it's not good, her emotional response prevents her from remembering a lot of what's said. Today, even with the limited results available before all the testing came back, it was good. She had plateaued, at least for the time being.

To celebrate, we had raspberry-stuffed French toast and then got back on the highway.

* * *

The Perfect Place Realty had a flowery sort of presence. I wandered around the waiting room while the receptionist contacted Mr. Long, the owner.

"This feels more like a home decorator's office than a real estate agency," I whispered to Melanie out of the side of my mouth.

"It's all about staging," my daughter said. "Whoever did the décor here wanted you to feel like you were in the comfort of your own home, chatting with friends."

Mr. Long swept in. He blended perfectly with the décor.

"Good afternoon," I said. "I'm Doris Flynn. We," I indicated Melanie, but didn't offer the information that her last name was the same as mine, "are working alongside the sheriff's office to locate Richard Gerrish. We have this office as his last working address. Would you be willing to speak with us?"

There was a slight hesitation. Melanie stood up and brushed the wrinkles out of her trousers.

"No worries if you don't want to talk now." She spoke in a friendly tone. "Whatever it takes, we can wait. You know." She paused. "If warrants are needed. Then, eventually, subpoenas."

"What's wrong with Richard?" Mr. Long sounded slightly strangled.

"Nothing that we know of. Nor has he done anything illegal. I should have mentioned that earlier. He's just disappeared," I said.

Melanie gave me a sour look. We had decided not to say that, but I'd been watching Mr. Long's body language. He was a drama queen.

"Oh, my heavens!" he exclaimed. "Come this way. I'm the only one here today, but I assure you I can speak for both myself and my husband."

"Perfect," I replied.

It didn't take much prompting to get Mr. Long to open up.

He and his husband had opened the agency ten years prior. Four years later, after a few false starts with other employees, they had hired the Gerrishes.

"They were fabulous! A *perfect* fit!" Mr. Long was quite flamboyant. A little of him went a long way. "As a working team, they complemented each other *perfectly*. And our agency as well."

"As in?" I asked.

"Well. Hm. She was all about the business real estate market. Had an absolutely *fabulous* mind for remembering facts and numbers. She could explain flow charts so that any fool could understand them. Oh, and the way she dressed? All those vintage outfits? People remembered her. She was a standout at any gathering."

Melanie leaned forward, eyes aglitter. "I know, right? That Cinderella Blue bell skirt of hers is unreal."

I half-turned, eyes wide. Where had Melanie come up with this?

Mr. Long nodded with enthusiasm. "Richard did better in the residential field, convincing couples through his knowledge of school systems, property tax ratios, building equity, oh, and up-marketing. Very clever."

"So, the Gerrishes worked well here?" I asked. This wasn't getting us anywhere.

"Yes. Here at the office. But between us, as a couple, not so much." Mr. Long's fingers fluttered toward the outside world. "You never saw them go anywhere together. Unless it was related to selling property. They looked good on paper,"—he lowered his voice—"but they could barely stand to be in the same room together. A couple of times, I saw them having horrendous rows in the back parking lot. Tsk. Tsk."

"Do you know why?" I asked.

"No. But I could hazard a guess." He leaned forward. So did I. "Racheal wanted to sell the biggest, the best. She wanted to live like Hollywood, in a mansion in the hills with big parties and social standing. Richard would have been happier with a picket fence."

Mr. Long nodded, relaxing back in his seat. "We had a woman who worked with us from day to day. Eve. She wasn't married, but about four years ago, she had a baby. Oh my, he was A. DOR. ABLE. I don't think I ever heard Racheal say so much as congratulations, but Richard was all agog. He kept sneaking little things to Eve for the baby. His wife may not have noticed, but I did. I was doing the same thing."

Both my and Melanie's eyebrows rose.

"As a single mom, Eve was just making ends meet. Babies *need* so much. And the equipment is *so expensive*. I heard Richard say he'd get her some type of fancy car seat when the baby outgrew the infant one. I stepped in and said I'd pay for half. He was quite embarrassed to have been caught offering, but it worked out *fine*. Everything was fine until the day the daycare closed unexpectedly because of a water leak. Eve called the office, and I told her to bring the boy with her. He was three by then. Such a delight. And so cute!"

"I've seen him. He is. Doesn't carry her coloring, though." It was fish bait that Mr. Long didn't snap at.

"Everything went well. I played with Andrew. Richard played with Andrew. The kid was well-behaved. The day was going swimmingly until Racheal showed up around two. She'd been at a site meeting all day. She walked in the door, took one look at Andrew and Richard playing on the floor, and *blew* her stack! It was *epic!*"

Mr. Long fanned himself with a brochure.

"They were in Racheal's office, and she was *screaming*. She said awful things about Eve, who was in tears. My Ronald went in and ordered Racheal and Richard out of the building and off the property."

"Did they quit working here?" I asked.

"No. Racheal came back the next morning like nothing had happened. Richard worked remotely for about a week. But the worst part was that Eve, whom I told you had been with us since day *one*, gave her notice."

I noticed Mr. Lang's eyes were all shiny, and wondered if it was excitement or tears.

"We had a private chat, Eve, Ronald, and myself. She was *terrified* of Racheal. There was no talking her out of leaving. We gave her a generous severance package and told her she didn't need to come in anymore because we didn't want her traumatized."

Mr. Long pulled his handkerchief out of his breast pocket. I thought he was going to cry.

"Maybe a week or ten days later, I went to visit her at home. Her landlady told me that Eve had been offered a job far enough away that she'd had to move. I felt terrible. I hate to say it, but my opinion of Racheal suffered because of the incident."

"Is that why Racheal left?" I asked.

"No. But I think it was a serious wedge between her and Richard. A month after I found out that the sweet girl had moved, Richard asked for a private meeting. He told Ronald and me he could no longer work with Racheal, and he was leaving. Striking out on his own. Opening a new shop somewhere else. It was a blow."

I watched as Mr. Long's brain worked its way through whatever swirled in that chintz-covered space.

"Eve was gone. We hired Heather. Richard had given notice. That left Ronald, me, and Racheal. On Richard's last day, Racheal approached Ronald. She told him she was going with her husband. She believed they could still save their marriage. I didn't think so, but I was glad to see her *swishy* butt walk out the door. To my surprise, my husband told her she could leave right then, no need for notice. No severance was paid. That was it. She cleared out her office. We didn't see either of them again."

"Is there anything else?" I asked.

"Not that I can think of," Mr. Long said. "They were good at what they did, but together they were toxic."

"And Richard never even contacted you?"

"Never."

"You mentioned Heather started working here before they left. Is she still here? Could we speak with her?"

"Of course." Mr. Long went out and came back with the young woman we had seen when we entered.

"I don't know much," Heather said, after we explained what we needed. "There was a lot of confusion because the previous receptionist had left unexpectedly. I had to learn as I went. Mr. Gerrish was easy, and he'd do anything to help. Kind of a sad guy, but friendly. Mrs. Gerrish? She was a piece of work. I avoided her as much as possible. If she wanted something, I took care of it. I made sure she got all her messages, did research for her. Whatever. But she was not friendly. There was never any chit-chat. Though I did love her clothes."

We said thank you and left. Both Melanie and I shook our heads as we walked back to my car.

"What do you think?" I asked Melanie when we were back on I-93, headed north.

"That you've gone as far as you can up this tree. And you should bow out and let the authorities step in."

"Okay." I drove in silence for five minutes, then couldn't stand it any longer. "But there's a bunch of parallels in this between the Tale of Richard and the Dick Story that need to be considered."

"See, I was right. I told Noah, the older you get, the less time it takes you to circle back to a subject no one else wants to talk about."

Before I could reply, Melanie turned as far away from me as the seat belt would allow. Then she curled up around Lilo and fell asleep.

Suddenly, I realized that was where our afternoon should have started. With chagrin, I realized that our normal conversation on this return trip from Boston circled around Melanie. She hadn't said anything, but I was suddenly worried that she felt slighted.

Chapter Twenty-Five

Noah was stretched out in a lawn chair when Melanie and I pulled in. Everything looked pretty quiet.

"Catching a few rays?" I asked with a smile.

"Can't get the cats back into the cattery," he replied with a grimace.

"How is it you are keeping Buttercup and Royally so quiet?"

I knew food had to be part of the equation. Even though Royally rolled his eyes toward me and whined about his need to be where I was, he wouldn't leave Noah's side. There were also half a dozen clucking biddies close by. Noah held up a box of Goldfish. With his other hand, he pitched a few over his head and onto the lawn, which needed to be mowed.

Pig. Dog. Chickens. A maelstrom of flurry and feathers followed.

"That works," I said.

"Yeah, but I don't think it's safe for the chickens. Royally plays rough."

I watched as the corgi made a tight U-turn, slid beneath the belly of the rooting pig, and came up the snack winner on the other side. Blanche, the hen in command, made a jump, trying to snatch the crunchy cracker from his mouth. Royally snarled and snapped. The hen wasn't even fazed. I'm not sure if she had nerves of steel or lacked in the smarts department.

Noah took our bags and followed Melanie inside. I heard her say she needed a shower and tea. Hot tea with sugar and lemon, to be exact. Buttercup and I found Noah in the kitchen a few minutes later, considering the sugar bowl.

"How much sugar?" he asked.

Reaching for the honey bear, I told him that I'd take care of it.

"She's overtired," I said. "So am I. We'll both have a cup, spend a few minutes sitting down and veggie, then we'll be ready to go again. If you didn't eat all the cookies, why don't you get some out?"

"She said it went well when she called me earlier," Noah said.

"It did, honey." I put my hand on his arm. "But these appointments are always draining. And it was a long ride. Tell me how it went for you?"

Noah brightened, but before he could speak, someone else did from behind me.

"Look whose home," Neddel said from the doorway.

My shoulders tensed.

"Aren't you glad to see me?" Neddel asked.

"Of course." I stepped forward and kissed his cheek. "I just came through the door, and I need a couple of minutes to get caught up, that's all. Would you like tea? Coffee?"

I didn't dare look at Noah, and I was terrified he'd ask if we had learned anything about Richard while we were in Nashua.

Buttercup went by me, dragging the old lady Siamese by the tail.

"Crap!" Neddel drew a sharp breath. "Is the cat dead?"

"No, that's Tiny. She came from a house where they had goldens. I take it this is how they played with her. Tiny has been here a long time. I don't know how the pig and the cat communicate, but they both seem to be okay with this behavior. Buttercup. Give her to me. Sit."

I took the pig-slobber-covered cat into the cattery and put her in her crate with a healthy pinch of catnip. Every resident cage filled as I went from door to door with the package. My own house cats were trying to get into the act, too, so I left three pinches spread out on the floor.

As for the rest of the critters, Lilo got only the smallest milk bone treats, but Buttercup, Royally, and Duke each got one of the big boys.

"Everybody out," I said, holding the screen door open.

With my own tea in hand, I sat at the table.

"How did it go with Melanie?" Neddel asked.

I explained what the doctors had said, and then, because Neddel hadn't been around when Melanie was first diagnosed, what it meant.

"Did you do any shopping, maybe stop off to eat somewhere?"

There was a look in his eye that his casual slouch in my kitchen chair didn't hide. I wasn't fooled for a minute. He knew what I'd been up to.

"You might want to talk about it, but can you tell me about the body in the freezer?" I asked. "Melanie told me an announcement was made on Saturday that it was Ivan Henderson."

"Presumed to be," Neddel corrected. "Pathology came back with several matching markers, but we haven't gotten the DNA results yet. That could take a couple of weeks."

"Hm." I frowned. "I thought it was quicker than that."

"No. A fast test is seventy-two hours, but you have to have a pristine sample. And the lab has to have no cases backlogged. The tests aren't performed locally. All human specimen testing is done at the New Hampshire State Police Crime Lab and the University of New Hampshire Forensic Anthropology Identification and Recovery lab." He got up, poured an iced tea from the pitcher in the refrigerator, and took a peek out the door.

"The remains found in the freezer were degraded. An additive was added prior to, or at the time of placement, and before the remains were frozen. Undoubtedly by the killer. Then the whole mess was left for a while before it was all frozen."

"Eew, are you kidding me?"

My stomach flopped. The thought of what that marinating mess would have looked like, smelt like, blossomed into a technicolor poster in my brain.

"No. We don't know where the freezer was kept. There was evidence around the bottom that it had gotten wet more than a few times. To be honest, I'm not sure why the owner decided to turn it back on. Maybe because of the smell? Who knows? But they did. According to Doctor Lombard, at some time after the body had disintegrated, it was frozen, not before."

"Talk about overkill," Noah said.

Neddel and I both snapped around.

"I'm going to go order pizza. Are you guys in?"

"Sure," I said, before turning back to Neddel. "I don't understand how a body in a freezer decomposes to mush in less than a year. Wouldn't the air seal protect the remains?"

"No, specifically if it was placed inside as a fresh kill," Neddel said.

Noah coughed. "I don't think I want to eat with you guys."

Neddel waved him away, and Noah disappeared quickly. "I asked Doctor Lombard the same thing. Her reply was that it couldn't. Not only that, but she pointed out the body had been dismembered, and not professionally."

"NOAH?" I ran to the door and called out. "Pepperoni, onions, and green peppers, okay?" I sat back down. "If I understand you right, this body was dismembered, put someplace where it would melt with the addition of an additive. Then put it in the freezer and frozen. Then it defrosted? Am I getting this right?"

"Basically, the additive was probably added at the time it was dismembered and put in the freezer. Then one day, someone turned the unit on."

"Well, like I said, that's disgusting. How did you decide it was Henderson?"

"I didn't. The lab came back with the match using coloring, a hair sample that survived, and a few teeth that looked like they'd been capped."

"Looked like?"

"The caps had melted."

That surprised me. What corrosive would be strong enough to melt enamel caps? I needed time to think about all this. However, as soon as I stopped asking questions, Neddel came up with a few of his own.

"Why were you in Nashua?"

Time for the big reveal.

"I think Eve Saucier's boyfriend Dick and Racheal Gerrish's husband Richard are the same person. Also, there's a good chance Dick is the father of Eve's son. At one point, Eve and the Gerrishes were all working in Nashua. Racheal saw the boy, Andrew, and Richard together. There's a strong resemblance between those two. She got Eve fired from her job, and I think Richard moved Eve here."

"To get rid of her or make her safe?" Neddel asked.

"Eve and Dick worked together. His wife also worked there. He told her he was in the middle of divorce proceedings, and when he was free, they would live here together. Dick gave notice at his job, probably said see you later to Racheal, and got ready to come up here. But Racheal didn't let go. At the last minute, she packed up and came with him. The question was, did she know Eve was already here? When they first arrived, where did Racheal and Richard live? Melanie and I saw where they lived in Nashua, and the house here isn't much, but it's a step up. Mr. Long said they both were top-grade real estate sellers. Which means there was money, right? How does that fit in?"

I got up to let Royally and Duke back in the house. Duke went directly to Neddel, shoulders hunched in submission, tail wagging madly. He was in love.

"Regardless of what happened when they all arrived here, Dick took off. He didn't go back to Nashua, as far as Melanie and I could tell, or at least not to where he had been. Melanie said he had family in Ohio. But he could have gone anywhere, right? Anyway, he's just gone. I was hoping I could find him for Eve, that's all. He had a good job, and the misters liked him. It wasn't inconceivable that he would go back there."

"You're right. The deal for me, Doris, is that somebody has to report him missing. Eve hasn't, and I don't know why not. Racheal hasn't. Again, why not? If their life together was as bad as I've heard, when he told her he was leaving, she probably didn't care where he went. Or she might believe he'll come crawling back. Or he'll come back to Eve, and she's watching."

My mouth went dry. "I think I assumed Racheal didn't know where Eve was, but that was naïve of me. The evening Racheal was here and told me not to call looking for Richard again, she said something about my vagabond friend. I thought she meant Melanie, but it could have been just as easily been Eve. The poor girl told me she had called the Gerrishs' real estate office a couple of times, looking for Dick. So, she knew that's where he was supposed to be. Racheal told me she monitors all the calls that come into the office. My guess is she has control issues. And caller ID. What if she knew Eve called once and was watching for a second call? How can she not know where Eve is? And therefore, confronted her directly? Is she afraid that if she does, Eve will give up all pretense and notify your office that Dick is missing?"

I raised my head. Neddel sat across the table, knees and arms crossed. He shook his head.

"Time to drop it, Doris," he said. "You aren't the only one who has come to these same conclusions. If you keep poking around, eventually you're going to step on toes and possibly ruin an investigation."

I sat across the table from him for several minutes, just looking at him. He didn't turn away, and neither did I. It was on the tip of my tongue to jump on a hot wire and push Neddel, but Left Brain cautioned against it.

"Actually, it's time to put the pig to bed before the pizza gets here," I said.

Walking out to the barn with Duke running along beside us, I brought up a subject that I didn't want to.

"Neddel, Duke has to go back into the kennel. He is the property of the Humane Society, and technically, my responsibility. There are rules. I don't find homes for these dogs; they do. He has to be cleared by their agency before he can be put up for adoption."

"How long will it take for him to be cleared for adoption?" He squatted, hands caressing the dog's head.

"I can do my bit and send in the results I have for his re-homing when I get home from work. My records are caught up, so it'll be quick. Oh, and I haven't tested him with cats. How did you know he would be okay in the house with them?"

"I didn't," he said. "I just accepted that he'd listen when I told him no."

I reached out to give Neddel a shove. Sometimes he was just so cocky that it was cute. I had to smile, but this was the perfect time to give a lesson, just like handling one of the dogs. If the occasion presents itself, jump on it.

"You just gave me the step back. Right? Basically, you told me that I didn't know what I was doing, right there in my house. Same goes for you, mister. That isn't how we do this. There isn't any assumption when these dogs come to me."

"No, maybe not. But I trust him. I trust him enough to bring him into my home. I'm going to have him trained so that he can be my partner."

"He's a smart dog, but is that a thing?" I asked. "A dog partner that's not an actual K9, with all the special stuff those dogs go through?"

"Yes. The warden service is going to start a basic class during the evenings in Twin Mountain the week after next. I'm signing us up, so you better turn your paperwork in. While we move along, I'll see about the K9 attribute parts. Even if he's never recognized, he's a good dog."

He gave me a little squeeze. Duke ran back to us. If there were going to be hugging, he wanted in.

Chapter Twenty-Six

In the night, I dreamt about a little child with a folded newspaper ad in his pocket. Beside him, a woman in a Betty Crocker dress from the 1950s stood beneath the WELCOME TO THE WHITE MOUNTAINS, BIENVENUE sign. She had a fistful of pages and offered them to all the cars that sped past. Then, in Schuler Park, at the tiny baseball diamond, a pig lay on third base, asleep in the sun.

When I first woke up, I lay chuckling at the vagaries of the human mind. I could understand the child and the woman, but what was going on with the pig? Then I realized I needed to haul my butt out of bed. There were animals that needed to be tended before I left for work.

"I kind of like seeing people and being out in the world again," I told Buttercup. "But by the same token, I miss making my own schedule."

My plan had been to arrive early enough so I would be there when both Maryann and Hector clocked in.

"Hey, I brought coffee cake," I said as my co-workers showed up.

In the event they were heavy eaters, I had a smaller container for Heidi.

"Did you hear?" Maryann asked in a low voice. "She's not coming back, Mrs. Henderson."

I felt sad.

"Poor woman," I said. "Maybe she was just too distraught to handle the stress of the job."

"You misunderstand me. She's not coming back because she's under investigation."

The surprise must have shown on my face.

"She's the wife," Hector said matter-of-factly.

He slid another big hunk of coffee cake onto a napkin. Once wrapped, it disappeared into his pocket.

I opened my computer. Maryann had told me back when I first started that my position got all the outliers, or the people who showed up on the radar without a regular appointment.

"None of the clients we do home visits for, except the brand-new ones, are scheduled, but there's a pattern. After a while, you know who's coming up," she'd explained.

Sometime in the last few days, I'd decided that if I was expected to drive thirty miles between clients, I'd use the phone periodically. While I pulled files, I called the couple who were the furthest out from the center of town.

Waiting for the call to be answered, I gathered what I would need for the day. There was nobody around, and I worked with the phone tucked between my ear and shoulder. As I crossed from the hardcopy file cabinets back to my desk, I thought I saw a flash of color beyond the office door.

Right across the hall was the restroom. I got creeped out because I really thought I was the only one in the area. My effort to ignore that split-second peek barely got me to where I could put down the files. I ended the call and crept out into the hall.

Further down, a doorway separated our group from the cubicles of the in-house caseworkers. A key card was needed to get through, and there was a hydraulic hinge, so it didn't work quickly. As a general rule, our group went out into the main area, but they didn't come in. If there was someone creeping around back here, I wanted to know who they were.

I pulled the restroom door open just enough to squeeze inside. Way down at the end of the narrow room, in the furthest stall, I saw the toes of a woman's shoes. I also heard sniveling. Like, trying-to-stop-crying, nose-blowing noises.

I moved over to the sink and waited. Four minutes later, the stall door swung inward. Heidi stepped out.

"Eek!"

On seeing me, she'd squeaked like a mouse I might have just stepped on.

Her face was red. She wiped at her cheeks with both hands, trying to remove the evidence of tears.

"That was a very girly squeal," I said with a smile.

She rushed over to the sink and splashed water on her face.

"He's terrible." She sniffed. "Way worse than Mrs. Henderson."

"Who?" I asked.

"Mr. Bennett," Heidi answered.

"How can that be?"

"Oh, she was impossible to work with, but he's worse." Heidi had a little bag with her and dumped makeup out onto the counter. "He doesn't know the rules. He makes them up as he goes along. I heard him tell the director he had a list of people who were wasting time, and he was going to tighten that up. I don't know anyone here who can find a minute to waste."

"Slow down, Heidi. You'll send your blood pressure up to the ceiling."

She leaned on both hands, taking and releasing deep breaths.

"I'm in here crying right now because, on top of everything else, he's always talking badly about everyone he walks by. I mean *everyone*." Heidi looked me right in the eye. "It doesn't matter if it's a client or an employee. He was walking through the lobby, talking on his cellphone and dishing on Mrs. Henderson."

"Who was he talking to?" I asked.

"No idea. He was out in the open then. Now he's in his office with the door shut. I think he's on the phone. But he doesn't realize that anyone within twenty feet of that door can hear him. Doris, he bad-mouthed clients while they were standing right there."

I was aghast. "How many people are you talking about?"

"Half a dozen or so." Heidi patted on concealer. "They got these embarrassed looks and hurried as far across the room as they could get. One woman who comes in often, always with a complaint. When she turned toward me, she had one nasty look on her face."

"That's bad."

"You're telling me." Heidi packed up her bag. "She's the type to go higher up the food chain and raise a stink that would hurt the agency terribly."

I ran back to my desk and returned after grabbing a file. "Let's go."

Heidi was ready to insert her keycard into the separating door.

"Where are you going?" she asked.

"To burn the horns off a bully." I adjusted my no-nonsense look and shooed her along in front of me.

There was a queue in front of her desk of people who had arrived after she'd fled. As soon as Heidi focused on the first person in line, I crossed over to Mr. Bennett's office and rapped on the door. Without waiting for an answer, I cracked the door open and slipped inside.

The director was reading the daily paper and looked up. I didn't wait to be acknowledged but moved swiftly to the desk.

"Good morning, Mr. Bennett." I smiled, placing the file on top of his paper. "I'm Doris Flynn. I'm sure you remember me; we were introduced the first day you were here." I talked fast enough so that he couldn't cut in. With any luck, I wouldn't run out of air. I also kept my volume down. "I have a file I need you to okay for me to skip today. The client has scheduled hospital testing. I'm not trying to be rude, but Heidi is swamped right now. I knew you didn't have anyone in here because, as I'm sure you're aware, the walls are made of cheesecloth. You can't whisper without being heard. Anyone standing within twenty feet of where you're sitting...Can. Hear. Every. Word. You. Say."

I let my eyes go blank.

"I wasn't speaking..." he began.

Then comprehension crossed his face. His mouth remained open slightly.

"There are clients who come in here who are looking for nothing more than an excuse to complain. To the state, the media, their lawyer," I said in a lower voice.

I didn't look at him, but out the window behind his seat. He had a good view of the wasteland. Since I'd been working here, I'd come in every day apprehensive and left feeling cowed. Inside my inner consciousness said, *no more.*

"You're very perceptive, Ms. Flynn." He handed me back the unopened file. "I'm sure you know best how to handle this client's needs."

CHAPTER TWENTY-SIX

"Perfect. Have a good day." I smiled and left.

This time, I opened the door wide enough so that he could see Heidi, who was multitasking her way through the clients crowded around her desk. She never saw me leave.

He's going to fire you, Left Brain whispered to me.

"There are a lot of other jobs out there," I muttered to myself.

All day, it seemed every time I left the cool, air-conditioned comfort of my vehicle, I returned to a blistering oven. Keeping mentally on task was hard. I forced Eve and Racheal out of my mind, but then Mr. Bennett took up that space. From him, my thoughts segued to Mrs. Henderson, Ivan Henderson, the freezer in the woods, and wondering what Rose Ann Lombard found out on her jaunt up Ossipee Mountain.

On my return trip from my last client call, I got stopped at the light at the end of the Kancamagus Highway again. My itchy fingers and nosy brain wanted me to make the turn. I wanted to. I really did. But in the end, I didn't.

Before my own brain could argue that I should have taken that left, I said aloud, "There's nothing more for me to see just driving past."

The light changed. Fifty feet down the road, I came up with a different idea. After I dropped off my files, I flew down Route 16 toward home.

"I'm taking Buttercup for some enrichment training," I called out to Melanie. I was changed, hitched to the trailer, loaded, and out of the yard without having heard a peep from her.

"I know it's hot in there, baby girl," I said to the rearview mirror, knowing Buttercup in the enclosed trailer couldn't hear. "But I think this will be fun, sort of."

Beyond the old salt-shed-turned-car-repair-shop was a picnic table pull-off and rest stop. The U-shaped drive was long enough for three cars. Hedged between a couple of moldering picnic tables was a wooden billboard for the map of the surrounding trails. While Buttercup sucked down a bottle of water, I wrapped her harness around her and attached both the long and the short lead. There was a plethora of evidence that this space had been used mostly by people who had dogs that needed a quick place to go. Not being a hound, Buttercup was able to ignore the deserted dung.

The forest was cool. We followed a path that took us to the Saco River. Though it was running fast, the water level was way down due to all the hot weather we'd had. Right here, this branch of the watercourse was shallow. I spent a little while sitting on a wide, flat boulder waiting for the pig to get bored. Eventually, she gave up turning over rocks looking for edibles and snorted her opinion at the lack of goodies.

We returned to the path, which we wandered down to a place behind the salt shed. The bank was a tall sand washout with no path leading up. What a disappointment. We returned the way we'd come.

Before we got back to the parking area, I led the pig across the paved road to the paths on that side, towards the mom and pop mini-mart. I was limited as to where I could leave Buttercup, and she wouldn't get into any trouble. Definitely not near the single gas and diesel pump.

With a certain amount of trepidation, I tied her to the iron pipe handrail on the steps.

"Stay," I said, and dropped a couple of peanuts on the ground to sweeten the deal.

Inside the store, I grabbed a bottle of water and a fruit and nut granola bar.

"Hot day to be hiking," the woman behind the register said.

"Yeah. Down by the Saco, it's not bad, but the deer flies are fierce." I took a sip of water. Outside, I could see the top of Buttercup's back as she snuffled around a little.

"I drove over hoping to find the guy across the street open," I went on casually. "He's worked on my car before, and it's old." I laughed. "Time for another layout of funds."

"You'd best be looking elsewhere," the mom owner said. "He's been gone all winter. I read in the paper earlier this week that he won't be coming back."

"Really? He set up shop somewhere else?" I tried to sound disappointed.

"No, honey, he's dead. His carcass was found in a freezer south of here."

She might have had a little grin happening. If the tips of fangs showed, I was out of there.

"You're kidding, right? That's a terrible joke." *And Halloween isn't for months,* I added to myself.

A man walked up from the back of the store. The pop. I stepped back slightly.

"She's not kidding," he said. "Guy was quiet. I heard he did good work. Came in here a few times and was hard to understand. Foreigner, you know? But okay. Is that your pig out front?"

"Yes, sir, it is."

The mom almost broke her neck as she whipped around to look out the fly-spotted picture window.

"This is a quiet place to take her for a walk," I explained.

He nodded and took a pack of cigarettes out of the rack. He didn't seem concerned about Buttercup, but the woman had that weird thing happening on her face again as she went from incredulous to horrified to, I don't know, disgusted. Ignoring the laws of the state, the pop lit up.

"Gossip is his wife did him in."

He seemed to enjoy talking about it. I egged him on.

"He wasn't a small guy," I said. "How could his wife have bested him? OMG! Poison?"

"Who knows," Pop said. "It's a fair guess you never saw his wife." He hacked out a laugh. "She was four, five inches taller than he was. Weight-wise, I bet she had sixty pounds on him."

"That's true." Mom jumped into the conversation. "Not to mention she had an ugly side. Just like her old man. Crazy mean."

A vehicle pulled up to the pumps. I could see the old timer in the driver's seat looking at Buttercup. Time to go.

"Have a good day." I hustled outside.

The pig and I went back into the woods where we'd come out. Ten minutes after loading up, we were home. I had more research I needed Melanie to do.

* * *

"You know I have a job? And a life?" My daughter waved the shopping list of questions I'd written out in my face. "Also, I don't have any way to check either the Hendersons' or the Gerrishes' financial records."

"Tomorrow morning, I'll drop the small trailer at the feed store. I can email my list to them this evening. I'll see what I can find out in town while I wait for it to be loaded." I ignored Melanie, who I knew was basically as nosy as I was. "I'm thinking we should invite Eve and Andy over for supper. She works on weekends. So, it'll have to be during the week."

"She has today and tomorrow off."

I looked up, and Melanie shrugged.

"I asked Missy. You know what a bleeding heart she is. Anyway, she thought it would be nice if those of us around Eve's age got to be friendly. Inviting her here will be better than throwing her out into a gaggle of girls all at one time."

"Good thinking. I'll take Duke for a walk down there after supper. He's been out on the run for a while. Maybe he's worked some of his energy off."

"I think he misses Neddel, Mom," Melanie said. "I went out and sat in the barn for a while. He just moped around the entire time."

That let me know Melanie was aware that something had happened between Neddel and me. It also reminded me Duke was pretty much ready for adoption, and I needed to get his paperwork sent in soon.

I tried Neddel's cellphone again. The voicemail message had been changed. Now it provided the telephone number for the sheriff's office and specifically directed the caller there.

"Right," I said to Royally. "And when Dolores answers the phone, I'll just tell her that I was rude and abusive to the sheriff, and I'd like to leave an apology. When she and her lady friends start burning up the gossip hotline, Patty Monson will love hearing that. She'll be baking him something more substantial than cookies."

Chapter Twenty-Seven

By breakfast, I'd pretty much decided that whatever Neddel and I had had, it was all done now. But there was still Duke.

At the end of the campers' visit to the Humane Society the next morning, Cliff and I moved kittens and puppies back into the animal shelter. Then we started to pick up the gear and posters laid out before the campers had arrived. I broached the subject of Duke.

"It's a Bethel dog?" he asked.

"Yes, that's where the paperwork goes. I emailed my summary report last night." I hefted a box of brochures and coloring books. "The dog is really doing well. He's not an alpha. His problem before was a hyper-aggressive kennel mate."

"Does the sheriff know this?" Cliff asked. "You're sure he can handle this dog?"

"Cliff. These two are soulmates. Right from the first moment, they were attuned. Neddel has taken Duke out a couple of times to handle him. They even had an overnight visit. When the sheriff brings him back, Duke is absolutely despondent. He even knows the sound of Neddel's vehicle. A mile down the road, he can hear it coming and starts sounding off."

"What about corrective training?"

"Neddel mentioned a few days ago that he wanted to sign them up for the seven-week course that's starting in Twin Mountain next Tuesday."

Cliff stopped and grinned at me. "Man wants a dog. Dog needs a man. That's what we're all about. I'll call Bethel, get them to send me the release."

I grinned back. "Perfect, I'll tell Neddel."

Eventually, I was the only one in the wedding reception tent. All I had to do was dismantle Buttercup's little pen, and I could go home. This was the first comfortable day in over a week. There was a nice breeze. It was sunny, but not the brain-frying glare we'd put up with all week.

Buttercup rustled around. She seemed to have energy to burn.

"How about a little excursion?" I asked her. "There's something I want to check out, and you might as well go as well."

Buttercup didn't disagree, so I hooked on her long lead and crossed the perimeter into the clear-cut area on the power line. We hadn't gone far up the rambling, small hills and modules before we veered off to the other side. The tree cover was heavy enough that I wasn't really 100 percent sure what I was looking at. We came out in the wrong backyard. This one had an above-ground pool. Buttercup gave a happy grunt, her tail wagging furiously.

"Nope. Not your pool. Not to mention, Chubbalinski, even if you figured out how to get in there, you wouldn't be able to get out."

Buttercup gave a tug and a grunt.

"Sorry, I don't see a snorkel in your size."

I used my knees to direct her back out to the clear-cut. Our second foray into suburbia brought us behind Arnie's building on VFW Street. We were cooking with gas now, by golly. Staying on a deer path just inside the woods line, we slipped through to the backyards on Woodland Grove Road.

"You know someone will eventually look out their kitchen window and see us," I told the pig. "You'd better be ready to find a truffle fast."

I hadn't put fly dope on either of us, and we both twitched and shook to drive the deer and black flies away. Stepping out into the sun was a relief. Biting flies fry quickly in direct sunlight. The smart ones went back into the woods to look for different prey.

It being a workday, I had figured Racheal Gerrish would be manning the desk at her real estate office or lying her butt off to some poor schmuck that didn't know Conway Bog wasn't a highly prized building area. Therefore, I and the not easily hidden, four hundred and fifty pound porcine strode across the back lawn headed toward the deck, bold as brass.

After securing the long lead to the railing where Buttercup could root among the overgrown weeds in the flower border, I climbed the steps. I had a strong inclination to peek over my shoulder, but that would have advertised my trespasser's guilt to anybody watching. I wasn't worried if that person was Arnie.

My intention was merely to peek in the window. But my advance was halted right outside the screen door, because the inside door was unexpectedly wide open. And I found myself looking at the raised rump of a kneeling woman. I could hear muttering that might have been cussing, or really bad singing.

What happened next was a surprise to both of us, because I'd thought I'd been as silent as rising fog. The woman jerked upright, looked back, and screamed. Then she flipped as neatly as Buttercup did onto her backside. I might have let out a *small* yelp as well.

"Oh my God, Doris! Are you trying to give me the big one?" The woman's voice was a tad shrill.

"Betty Louise," I started, then bit my tongue before I said something like, "I didn't expect to see you here, or what are you doing? Which was what I really wanted to know.

"Well, don't just stand out there. Come on in," Betty Louise said, turning back to her work. "Mrs. Gerrish, the lady of the house, isn't here, so it's safe."

"Why? Is she dangerous?" I stepped inside, but stayed where I had a full visual of Buttercup in the backyard.

"Phfft. Not really. She's new, not somebody you've come across, probably. Only been here a couple of months." Betty Louise huffed for breath as she vigorously scrubbed the tile.

"Are you trying to wear a hole through to China?" I asked.

"No, she wants these rust stains cleaned off. But I gotta tell ya, I don't think that's gonna happen. That old freezer must have been sitting here for a hundred years."

I almost choked when she said there'd been a freezer where she was kneeling.

"Are you looking for me or Mrs. Gerrish?" Betty Louise glanced back at me.

"You, actually," I squeaked. "I don't know Mrs. Gerrish at all. Really, not at all. I'm, ah, hoping you could fit me in for a few hours every couple of weeks."

Lord knows how I'd pay for that.

"I'd like to, honestly. But I'm full up with clients right now. Sorry." She swiped the back of her arm that wasn't covered by a rubber glove across her forehead. "How did you find me here?"

I guessed and said, "I saw your van out front."

"Ha. Ha. Yeah, I guess that would be a dead giveaway. Once again, sorry I can't help you out."

"That's too bad. Listen, before I move along, do you think I could use the bathroom?" I asked. "If I have to squat in the woods, the deer flies will do considerable damage."

She pointed the way, and I used the half-bath off the kitchen. Everywhere I looked, there was something that said woman, but no hints that a man lived there. I looked inside the medicine cabinet, had a peek into the hall and living room, and returned to the hall where Betty Louise had gone back to cleaning. I hesitated just long enough to take a discreet photo of the area she was scrubbing with my cellphone before I said goodbye and left.

Buttercup was no longer in the flower bed. She was thrashing around near the edge of the paved walk. A stone had been overturned, and she'd found a rag of some sort which she was bent on destroying.

I flipped the paving stone back into place, reached into her mouth, and yanked the rag out.

We were now in open view of the houses on either side. None too gently, I hustled the pig back to the deer path. She was making a lot of disgruntled noise, grunting and woofing. Not to mention her back was all hunched up. She didn't want to go, and I was afraid she was being loud enough so the neighbors were going to know.

My phone rang.

"Hey, Mom. Where are you? I'm down by the truck."

CHAPTER TWENTY-SEVEN

"Almost there. Hold on."

I huffed and puffed, both from the heat and from the exertion of trying to keep Buttercup moving forward. I broke the connection, cutting Melanie off. Now that I had Buttercup moving quickly, I had to stay on top of where she was going. If she got diverted, it might take me a while to get us headed back to the power line and eventually to where Melanie was.

Melanie had the small pen broken down and in the back of the jeep. The tailgate was down on the back of the horse trailer.

"Pig. Pig." Melanie called, then tossed a handful of nuts up into the trailer.

"What are you doing here?" I asked, pushing the tailgate up and locking it into position.

"I had to go to the pharmacy. I'll take the truck; you take my car." Melanie was sweating from the exertion of hefting pen pieces. "That old guy you've been talking about? Arnie something? He called a while ago, and he's all wound up. He wants you over at his place pronto."

"Did you tell him that I'm not working today?" I asked.

"Then you shouldn't have made friends with him. Because he said he needs help."

"Oh crap, I hope he didn't fall down again," I said.

"Phfft." Melanie tossed her keys to me. "There you go, Mother Teresa."

* * *

I drove around to Arnie's house. If he'd been good enough to call Melanie, then chances were he wasn't on the floor somewhere. I sat in the lot for a minute and called Long River Chinese Restaurant. I hated to pay extra for delivery, but I figured soothing Arnie would be as easy as getting Buttercup and Royally to behave. All I had to do was offer sustenance.

When I pulled my credit card out of my pocket, the rag Buttercup had found fell onto the seat. Melanie had a small trash receptacle just behind the console. I shoved it in there.

Walking in, I was ready to be smacked in the face with the stale smell of old man and rotty food. Instead, I encountered the nose-stinging scents of

163

Pledge and Clorox.

"I didn't know all those windows opened, Arnie," I said.

"And who's going to close them, I ask ya?" he demanded.

"I'm sure you're perfectly capable."

The stacks of dirty clothing were gone from the sofa, so I sat there.

"I take it you got housekeeping in here?"

"Four hours today, then two hours every Tuesday. Old biddy had the nerve to tell me it'll take two months to get down to where everything is caught up," he groused.

I didn't doubt that for a minute.

"I'm sorry that upset you, Arnie. But it looks nice in here." I smiled pleasantly.

"Didn't come cheap. The laundry room costs. She had to use my credit card to put money on the washing machine access card."

He was still blustering, but I could see a little happy in his eyes.

"Is that why you wanted me to stop over? I'm not working today," I said.

"I know, but I got a big envelope of paperwork from your job. I don't understand it. You told me I could get somebody to help. I called this morning, but nobody called me back."

Typical. No patience, I thought.

"Here's the deal, Arnie. I'll help you with what you got today. But in the future, you need to wait for scheduling."

He pointed out the fat manila envelope and said the housekeeper told him to order groceries from Hannaford's and have them delivered.

"Who ever heard of such a thing?" he asked. "She threw away about everything in the refrigerator. What am I supposed to eat?"

"Fortunately for you, today I ordered Chinese. It should be here in about twenty minutes."

I emptied the envelope as we waited for our lunch. The first page of the document offered housing options. Arnie was adamant about staying in the apartment.

"Then you'll have to come up with a plan," I said.

My phone dinged. DoorDash was out front, so I put the pages aside.

"You know that blue house where the little dog, the Jack Russell, lives?" I asked.

Arnie opened up the container of Moo Goo Gai Pan.

"This has got rice. I like noodles better," he said in a querulous tone.

I lifted my butt off the chair. Reaching across the table, I said, "No problem. You don't have to eat it."

The old man pulled the takeout container out of my reach.

"I never said I wasn't going to eat it. Only that I like noodles."

"I'll remember that."

The order had come with chopsticks. To my surprise, Arnie snapped them apart and deftly picked a snow pea out of the container.

"What's the yammer about the dog?" he asked.

"Not the dogs exactly, but the people," I said.

"Are you cross-eyed or what? There is only one dog. And there is only one person. That weird, yelping woman."

I knew then it was Racheal and Richard's house. I'd been told by the Longs and their across-the-hall neighbor that they had two dogs. After Arnie had inhaled a couple of big bites and was focused on the entrée and the boneless pork ribs, I spoke up.

"Arnie. I don't know why you think she's weird, or where the yelping comes in, but I do know she has a husband. I haven't seen him around, but I see his car down on the job."

He was drinking from a two-liter bottle of Coke, not a glass.

"You seen the way she dresses? In her grandma's clothes? I'd call that weird. She don't say nothing below a scream. Yells at the dog. Yells at the cleaning lady. Yells just to hear herself." He laughed at his own joke.

"Okay, well, that's covered." I picked at my subgum chow mein. "Are you sure you haven't seen her husband there? He's tall, light-colored hair. That's his black Denali SUV."

For the first time, Arnie moved the container more than five inches from his mouth.

"You might think I'm a nosy old pip, and you could be right," he said. "But I got good vision. In the couple of months that she's been there, I have never seen a man. Except the movers, and they wore matching coveralls. And those are both her vehicles. She's the only one that drives them. She doesn't seem to prefer one over the other. Some days she takes them both out, like exercising a couple of hounds."

He went back to eating.

"She's got a cleaning lady? I wish I did. I wonder who she uses," I mused.

"You know Betty Louise? She used to be a Bell, but I think she got married. Anyway, she cleans houses so she can pocket the cash and not tell Uncle Sam. Ha. Ha. She's a smart cookie."

His answer verified that he could indeed see exactly what was happening over on Woodland Grove Road.

I let him finish his meal while I filled out the paperwork the Agency for the Aged had sent him. When Arnie dozed off, I picked up the leavings and put the leftovers in the refrigerator.

Looking back before I closed the door, I saw an old man with a full belly napping in the sun. And he was surrounded by an apartment which, if not completely cleared out, had just undergone some serious cleaning. It made me feel good that I'd had a small role in getting that done.

Chapter Twenty-Eight

When I'd walked Duke down past Eve's house the night before, it had taken me a fair amount of cajoling to get her to agree to come for supper.

"It's just us," I'd said. "Nothing fancy. You live in the neighborhood now, so consider it a two-family meet-and-greet."

"It's nice of you to offer," Eve said.

She was still a little tense, but I could see she was right there on the edge about accepting my invitation. It was time to make this work for me. I added a tiny slope to my shoulders.

"To be perfectly honest, I have a second reason. I recently had to go back to work, which means Melanie is home alone all day long. With her MS, I worry. It's not that far for an ambulance, but they aren't, you know, right near here."

"How about if I make a coconut cake for dessert?" Eve asked.

"Really? Holy cow. Okay. Call before you leave, because there is no way Buttercup will ignore a coconut cake if she's out free-ranging in the yard."

* * *

It was a gorgeous coconut cake. Three layers of lemon goodness with lemon and coconut between. The whole thing was sheathed in a thick layer of lemon frosting and totally disguised by coconut.

"Eve! I could have eaten just a big hunk of this, and bypassed the lasagna." I licked my fork.

Melanie cut in on my coconut euphoria.

"Hey, I made the lasagna," she pouted.

Looking at my daughter, my eyelids drooping with the need and greed, my fingers inched toward the cake plate again. "I never said I did. I was just remarking on how this is absolutely the best coconut cake that I've ever had. Bar none."

"Grandma would roll over in her grave," Melanie admonished.

"After a taste of this, she'd be tunneling out." I drew my hand back. No doubt about it, I was too full for one more bite.

Neddel and Josh had been told to stay away, but Missy and her two youngsters joined us. If we were a small group, all moms and kids, Eve would be more relaxed. Andy, Sam, and to a lesser extent, Julie, were spread across the kitchen floor, varooming Sam's Matchbox collection. All the dogs and the pig were fenced out. The cats had decided by common consensus— other than Pumpkin, one of my ginger cats—to excuse themselves. Pumpkin appeared to like small people. He continually circled Julie, offering headbutts and a fluffy tail. He was an old guy, way beyond adoption age. I could hear him purr every time she cooed.

We'd spoken of many things local: schools, playgroups, and the best deals for permanent residents, but I had a need for information.

"That's okay, Eve, leave the dishes. I've got all evening," I said.

"Okay, but you've got that deer-in-the-headlights look. The one where I might be the deer, and you're the headlights," Eve said. "It's making me nervous."

Melanie and Missy laughed.

"See," Missy said. "Somebody else is wise to you."

I ignored my daughter's friend.

"I like you, Eve. I have since the first time I met you. And I think Andy is absolutely adorable," I said.

"But?" Eve stiffened.

"There's not really a but. Just want to help you out."

Eve started to speak. I'm sure she was going to tell me she was fine, but I didn't wait for the words.

"You've spoken of Dick. He was here, and now he's gone. Obviously, you don't know where, and that's none of our business. But Eve, until he comes back, there are people who can help you."

I could only hope she wouldn't take Andy and stomp out the door.

Her facial muscles got hard. "I've pretty much decided that if he's gone of his own volition and isn't interested in us, I don't need to find him."

"He has a responsibility."

Eve's cheeks took on a high flush.

"Tell me, is Dick's full name Richard Gerrish?" I asked.

Her bottom lip quivered. "How did you know?"

Melanie reached out to take Eve's hand. "We want to help you. And be your friends. You may not want Dick around anymore, but Eve, you can't do this alone. You have no family here. If you don't want to tell us stuff, don't. It doesn't matter. Out here on this dead-end road, we're our own tiny neighborhood."

Eve sipped her iced tea.

"What's wrong with your car?" Missy asked.

"I don't know." Eve took another sip, then sighed. "I'd had boyfriends before Dick, but never a married man. He was so gentle. His wife, however, was a spitting moray eel."

I couldn't help smiling at the image.

"He wanted out of his marriage. He'd said so, but she had her fingers snarled up in everything that they had or did. Not only that, but where we worked, she did business property sales. Between them, they brought in big commissions. Residentials were good, but not in the same league. Anyway, when I found out I was pregnant, the Mr. Longs were thrilled. They were so good to me. So, I didn't leave. Andy was a toddler when I had to bring him to work one day. He and Dick were building with blocks when Racheal walked in unexpectedly."

She gazed down at her son.

"I was thinking how similar they were. Same eyes, same smile. Racheal saw it too. She knew. She hadn't wanted children, a family, but she couldn't understand why Dick would. I never told Mr. Long, but after he sent the

Gerrishes away that afternoon, Racheal called me. She was very clear about how she could ruin Dick; take everything he had ever earned. Then she said that me being a single parent with a small child meant I was going to have to trust other people. I wasn't going to be able to go it without friends. She could hurt me there as well. I totally freaked out."

"I—we all—can understand that," I said.

I caught Missy looking at the children. Eve's fear was universal.

"Dick talked about leaving, opening his own agency. He'd been here and loved the area. When I called him, all hysterical, he decided it was time to make the move. Through his contacts, he found the house I'm in. Slam, bam, thank you, man. Ten days and I was here." She smiled sadly.

"But he went back to Nashua?" Melanie asked.

"To button up his affairs, file for divorce, give his notice, all that stuff. He had a small amount of money put away for us. He left that with me. But most of what he had was tied up with Racheal, and he wanted his share. For a while, he came back and forth to us every week as he set up an office here and got ready for the final move. Then one night, he showed up, and he was distraught. Racheal had left her job. At the last possible second, she had told him she was going to move up here with him.

Dick said he tried to dissuade her, but she ran right over him. She'd even found a place for them to live in Tamworth. He didn't know what to do. We tried to keep going with our lives, but then one day, he just didn't come back." Big tears made their way slowly down Eve's cheeks. "I loved him. I thought he loved me and Andy as well. It doesn't matter now. I have Andy. We are a family."

"Mama?" Andy held up a dump truck with fat tires. "I need one of these."

"You sure do," Missy said to distract him. "Hold on, I'll write down where I bought that one."

Andy followed Missy to the telephone notepad.

"Did Racheal know you lived in the valley when they moved here?" I asked.

"I don't think so, but I'm sure she knew I wasn't far away," Eve said.

"Does she know where you are now?"

"I don't know. We don't travel in the same circles. I try to keep a low profile."

Andy solemnly handed his mother Missy's note.

"Time to go home, big guy," Eve said.

The little boy held out the truck to Sam. Missy opened her mouth, I'm sure to tell Andy he could keep that one, but Eve shook her head. They said goodbye and were just out the door when I made a shooing motion to the other two young women.

"Go along. Walk her home. Make sure she's okay. Sam, Julie, and I will make sure all the cats have on their pajamas."

"Really?" Sam came off the floor like a rocket.

"This way," I said, taking Julie's hand, "to the cat bedroom."

We checked food dishes and water bowls, counted cats, made sure paws were washed, and finally closed the doors to the crates. I wasn't sure what else to do with them, but Sam filled in the space. It seems they had a cat at home, Mr. Fussy. While I picked up the kitchen and did dishes, Sam and I had a heart-to-heart talk about Mr. Fussy's inability to catch a mouse that was plaguing Sam's mother.

When Missy came in, I told her to cut Mr. Fussy's food in half.

"Sam says he's fat, and he won't chase the bell on a string. If he's not hungry or too big to play, he's not interested in chasing a mouse."

I left the girls and went outside, where Buttercup still lounged on the lawn. Mosquitoes buzzed around her ears, sending them flapping.

Talking with Eve had made me sad.

"This was supposed to be a good evening." I sank down to the ground beside the pig. "I think I might have ruined that."

The grass was long enough for me to pluck a blade and tickle Buttercup's nose. To make me stop, she rolled backwards and effectively pinned me down.

"How can I figure out if Racheal knows where Eve is? Or where she and Richard lived in Tamworth?"

Buttercup woofed. Rubbing her head against me was a hint to give her a scratch.

"You're supposed to be helping me figure this out," I said.

In the drive, Missy buckled her children in the car. After a couple of soft grunts, Buttercup wiggled and squirmed until she was in position to jump to her feet. It was time to say goodnight and go to bed.

I spent a few minutes with Duke. He'd been left to himself for most of the evening because I wasn't sure about exposing him to the excitement of three small children. He lay on his belly facing up the road, ears at attention. He was waiting, and I knew it.

I took him out of his enclosure and got the dog brush. As I worked, I explained how sorry I was that Neddel and I were falling away from each other, especially now that it looked like Duke was going to have a forever home, but that I had a plan.

"As soon as the word comes down, Duke, I'm going to walk into Neddel's office like I have every right, and tell him you're ready. I'm not going to leave until he swears in blood that he's coming for you. No dog Patty Monson could find for him would be as good as you."

In the house, Pumpkin, exhausted from his playdate with the children, curled up on my bed for a well-earned nap.

Chapter Twenty-Nine

When I came back from picking up my trailer at the feed store, I saw a couple of vehicles in Eve's yard. One had the Diesel Works logo on the driver's door. Andy was squatting down in the driveway beside a pair of legs, which I presumed were attached to a torso beneath Eve's car. Eve stood on the stoop. I'm sure she watched her little boy, so he wasn't in the way or in danger. The hood was up on the car. I got only a quick look, but it seemed more than one person was under there.

"Melanie," I called out as I went inside, "who's over at Eve's house?"

If they were young people, Melanie would know. She had her finger on the pulse of the valley.

"Brian, Travis, Noah, he only had to work a half day. And I think Jesse." Melanie had an assembly line of six-inch Italian sandwiches on the kitchen counter. And a string of dogs and cats watching from the linoleum.

"Jesse?"

"She's a gear-head, Mom. Seriously, she may work in an office like Noah, but she knows more about cars than he does."

Missy's husband, Brian Shaw, worked over at Diesel Works as a heavy equipment mechanic. Like Travis, who did repair work at a local garage, he was all about engines, transmissions, and all the other components that kept a motorized machine moving. Noah, of course, worked at the bank.

"Maybe Noah is trying to learn." That was good, right? I was giving him the benefit of the doubt.

"Phfft. He's over there being window dressing. He still has his tie on."

She pulled a couple of big Tupperware containers from under the cabinet. "Hook up the pig. Supper's ready to take down there."

If I told a stranger that the pig was going to pull a cart full of food a quarter mile down the road and not try to scarf it up, no one would believe me. The trick was for me to walk in front with a metal dog dish in my hand, filled with pig chow mixed with peanut butter. Worked every time. It also made her walk fast. Buttercup could run in short sprints. She was amazingly fast, considering her weight. The cart, with Melanie in the seat, slowed her down.

I got the pig hooked up to the goat cart. Then, Melanie and I carried out the coolers of sandwiches, chips, and drinks. Melanie climbed into the seat. I reached for the pig bowl on top of the car. Buttercup couldn't reach it up there. Because Prince was an unknown, we left Royally and Lilo at home with their own suppers in front of them.

"Chow's on!" I called out as we turned onto the drive.

It was a surprise to see Neddel. He hadn't been there when I'd gone past on the way to my house. I missed a step when I recognized him. It was too late to turn the pig and cart around, so I kept going but angled away from where he stood. Before I could get the harness unhooked, he'd walked over, put his hands on my shoulders, and given me a little peck on the cheek. I was struck dumb. But as he explained, as I stood there with my jaw all the way down to my waist, repair work needed cool heads and several opinions. I had no idea what was going on, at least, between him and I.

"We're going to need parts," Brian said, about halfway done with his first sandwich.

I took a peek up the drive. Eve and Melanie were laughing at Prince's efforts to get a bit of a sandwich. Buttercup, released from the cart, had finished her meal and was enjoying a rub on the unfamiliar lawn.

"To the tune of?" I asked.

Brian looked at Travis.

"Carburetors aren't cheap," he said. "Even rebuilt ones. I can salvage the rest of the parts at the junkyard in Redstone."

Both guys looked at Neddel.

Why? I wondered.

"Do it," he said. Grabbing a second sandwich, he added to me, "I'll meet you and the pig up at the house."

While I hooked Buttercup up, Melanie told me that Jesse would give her a ride back, or she'd walk. Neddel and Duke were already out in the yard when I got there. On the deck, Royally and Lilo raised a ruckus.

"I didn't know Duke could catch a Frisbee," I said.

Buttercup's disc wiggled with excitement. She loved the Frisbee. Of course, she was known for chewing them up when done playing.

"He knew how to chase a ball," Neddel said. "We just stepped up his abilities."

He followed me into the barn and hung the lightweight cart where it was stored on the wall.

I couldn't wait any longer.

"Neddel, why did it seem Brian was asking you about the carburetor?" I asked.

"The VFW has a slush fund for small local emergencies," he said. "Brian and I are both members. I'm the treasurer."

"What? How could I have not known that?"

"I don't hang around down at the post. I'm just a member. It's a civic thing. You're on the soup kitchen board, right? Same thing."

Yeah, I was. But no, it didn't seem the same. I was still hashing that bit of trivia around with Left Brain reeling in surprise, when Neddel spoke again.

"Melanie told me you'd had Eve over for dinner."

"Yup." I took a handful of rags and Buttercup's curry comb into the home pen.

"What did you all talk about?"

He leaned on the side of the pen. He looked so handsome my chest ached. Duke stood on his hind legs, shoulder to shoulder with his human buddy. We needed to talk about him and me. Yet, my lips wouldn't pry apart. He just kept watching me as I worked. After a few minutes of silence, I folded.

"We started off with local information, school stuff. Andy goes to kindergarten this year. Then, sometime after the coconut cake, we talked about Dick."

"Cake?" he asked, then recovered and said, "What about Dick?"

"There's a piece still in the refrigerator. Go ahead inside. I'm almost done. If we're going to talk about Dick, we need to sit down."

I wish I could have dragged out swabbing down the pig longer, but I knew the sheriff side of Neddel was just going to wait until I showed up, or come back out and haul me inside. On the kitchen table, the cake plate was already empty. He had tea, and all three dogs lay on their bellies, eyes on him, ready for the strike if he spat a coconut-laden mouthful out.

"First," he said.

I stiffened my spine, ready for the lecture.

"Cliff called me from the Humane Society. Bethel faxed over Duke's paperwork. He has to have a physical tomorrow, then I can take him home."

"I have to work tomorrow," I said.

I was surprised he'd beaten me to the punch, and maybe a little letdown that I hadn't been the one to tell him. But the way things were going with us, I wasn't sure how short of sending a letter that was going to happen.

"That's okay. I want to take him to the vet myself so I can see how he does with somebody new handling him."

I nodded.

"That brings us back to my conversation with Melanie."

"Neddel…" I began.

"Hold on. I've been thinking. The last conversation we had, you brought up some good points about Richard Gerrish."

The door opened, and Melanie and Noah came in. The attention of all the dogs was diverted from Neddel when my daughter flipped the lid on the cooler, and the odor of cold meat crossed the room. There was a chorus of whines, including one from the deck. Noah dug out the milk bones.

"Any grinders left in there?" Neddel asked.

"Nope, and nary a potato chip either," Melanie said.

"Neddel, you just ate two grinders and that huge piece of cake," I pointed out.

"All the cake?" Melanie asked. "Oops, sorry, Noah."

Without accepting responsibility, Neddel continued, "Melanie said you had a notebook that I might want to look at. Why don't you get that out so I can see what you've got in it?"

"What is it with you and Melanie talking about me behind my back?" I asked.

They both shrugged.

"Okay." I considered where to start. "She and I got the same stories from a couple of people as to why Eve and Dick came here. We know why and how it happened. Our timeline takes us up to the day Racheal gave her notice at The Perfect Place Realty office. I thought they'd moved right into the blue house on Woodland Grove Road, but then we heard Racheal had rented a house in Tamworth. We don't know where or how long they were there. Noah said he remembers Dick coming into the bank."

"About that," Noah cut in.

I held up the wait-a-minute finger.

"I've also been told by somebody who has been watching the blue house on a daily basis since before the Gerrishes moved in that there has never been a man living there since the property changed hands. And there is only one dog. We heard there were two. Both Jack Russells."

Melanie spoke up. Unlike Noah, she didn't wait for permission to speak.

"I remembered Mr. Long saying the Gerrishes had Jack Russells, plural. A lot of people are dedicated to breeds. I asked Eve today where she had gotten Prince and if she'd been told he would be tolerant of other dogs or cats. She told me Dick had left Prince with her. And yes, he was good with dogs, but she didn't know about cats. And he's devoted to Andy."

A furrow developed between Neddel's brows.

"He's got a chip. It'll be easy to check," Melanie said.

Noah was bursting at the seams now.

"Christine Gillette is the bank officer working with the Gerrishes. I asked her a while ago how it was going. The other day, I asked if Richard Gerrish was easier to work with than his wife, because I heard he was a tyrant."

We all looked at Noah. He had matured a lot in the last eighteen months and met our gazes with a calm, controlled attitude.

"Christine told me she's never worked with Richard. This is the second time she has admitted that. She met him the one time they had met at the bank to hammer out the details of how they were going to handle house closings. The bank manager was there, but Racheal wasn't. She might not have been part of the equation then, you know, like if he was trying to set something up for his own separate business. I didn't ask. That was last spring, so at least a year ago. Whenever she goes to an event, Racheal is the realtor who is there. Christine says there always seems to be a reason Richard is absent. Usually because he's working in the office in Nashua."

"If Richard had an office in Nashua," I said, "Mr. Long would have known. I'm sure he would have mentioned it. We specifically asked him if he'd seen Richard, and Mr. Long told us no. Richard belonged to the Hidden Links Golf Club, but on their member website, he is no longer listed. If he's somewhere else, I don't think it's Nashua."

"But Racheal said the first day we met her down at the end of the road when she was touting the house lots that she and Richard were partners and he was in Nashua that day," Melanie said.

"I know." I looked at Neddel. "Another thing I heard from Arnie is that, even though there are two cars in the garage, it's Racheal that drives them both. On some days, she even takes them both out herself. From Arnie's apartment, you can't actually see into the garage, so he wouldn't know if there were one or two vehicles there. But I've been past their agency when both cars were in the lot. I called, and the receptionist told me he wasn't there that day. Huh? Is Racheal driving one car over early, walking home, and then showing up in the other?"

Eyebrows rose all around the table.

"It's not far, so that's possible, I suppose," Neddel said. "Doris, can you remember the dates you went by and saw Richard's car there?"

"No, sorry, I can't," I answered.

He rose to his feet. "First, I'll verify that one of those cars is registered to Richard. If so, I'm going to start riding by to watch for it. And if I see it, I'm stopping. I'll make a few calls down to Nashua, too."

I nodded. So did Melanie and Noah.

CHAPTER TWENTY-NINE

"You." Neddel pointed to me. "Will do nothing until further notice. Please?"

My head jerked to a stop.

Wait a minute, I thought.

For a few minutes, it seemed he'd been happy about what I was doing, but now he was going all super-nova, hard-nosed cop on me.

"Neddel?" I said.

But he already had his cellphone out and was punching buttons.

"Duke. Car," Neddel ordered.

The dog beelined for the door. Neddel said a distracted goodnight, and the two of them were gone.

Even though no one else knew, for a moment, I was mortified. I thought we were going to behave like adults, and he'd just flipped me off like I was of no consequence.

"Of all the…"

"Easy, Mom," Melanie said.

Noah misread what had just happened. "Did I do wrong?" he asked.

"No, sweetie, you did exactly right." I headed out the door, Royally at my heels. "I'll hose down Duke's enclosure and disinfect it. He won't be back tonight, and tomorrow he becomes Neddel's dog."

In the barn, I packed Duke's personal things. His bed, blanket, and toys without thought that Neddel had probably bought all new. I gathered all the records I had for him, which I would drop off the next day with Cliff. That's where Neddel would have to go to fill out the adoption paperwork after Duke's checkup. Even though Duke was still my responsibility, he had moved on. Someone had opened their arms and heart, and he'd found a forever home. I couldn't deny him that. I couldn't call Neddel and demand he bring the dog back. But then, I couldn't call and say congratulations either.

I fretted and fumed as I went along. I was angry with Neddel, though other than he'd been quick to leave, there was nothing I could put my finger on. Worse than that, I was furious with myself. I had allowed someone to usurp Ian, letting my emotions guide me.

You're an absolute idiot! I swore to myself. Anger held the tears back, but barely.

With Duke gone, Buttercup could go into the enclosure and check it out. She'd been there before, but she was nosy. Royally didn't like to go inside the pen. I think he was scared that he'd get locked in. When I first got him, he'd spent most of his two years shut up in a small crate. He lay on the floor of the barn watching, waiting for me to come out and shut the door. Probably with no issues if Buttercup could get closed inside. But he didn't go away. When I looked at him, I could see the love in his eyes and the ache because he knew I was hurting. Then tears fell, a few that dribbled over my cheeks. I lifted Royally, reaching back to close the pen as if shutting Neddel away.

Finally, the caged run was ready for the next canine client assigned to me.

Chapter Thirty

With every day that passed, it became more difficult for me to apologize to Neddel. We were friendly, but not like before. He didn't drop in as often, but then I knew he and Duke were taking classes three nights a week in Twin Mountain.

That was also the excuse I gave Melanie when she asked where he was. I got really busy when her questioning started. I missed him, and I told her I did. But he was busy. That's how it was with cops.

When I decided to move away from the more antiquated way of interviewing my assigned clients, i.e., face-to-face conversation, and use technology—the phone—I got liberated. And I mean that in the worst possible way.

First, because if I knocked off the forever it took me to get from one place to the next, it meant that I had more time for actual conversations with people who had a wide variety of needs. If a client was new to me, I made the trip to their home, met them, checked out their digs, and explained I would do a follow-up call. Not a single one broke out into hysterical sobs and chest-beating about how they could not exist if I didn't randomly pop in and interrupt their lives. The upside to that is they weren't calling the agency and accidentally telling somebody I wasn't following the Masterplan.

Did I feel guilty? Sure, I did. I had a secret list of the people I'd called so my next visit would be in person. But I sure saved a bunch of calls, not driving an hour away to a house where the client was gone for the day.

This new version of house visits got me past the five or six questions I was supposed to ask—and because I had more time, into the nuances of their daily life. Many who had family to assist or were mentally right in the minute were aware of all the programs the agency offered. Several, however, scraped by with no idea that help was right at their fingertips. A few, like Angus, believed that if they reached out, they would suffer in the long run.

I justified my change in routine by concluding that if challenged about calling as opposed to dropping in, I would point out that Mr. Bennett had told me to respond in what I considered the best manner to the clients. And that's what I felt I was doing; well, in my own mind I was.

Second, being in the office, I spent my lunch period wandering around the huge building where I made it my business to check every nook and cranny. It didn't help me answer the niggling little worry about what had happened to Dick, or Mr. Henderson, but I got away from my desk, and I uncovered a few little nuggets of information that might help those folks who were only lonely. There were visiting angels out there. One just needed to find them.

My grandmother used to say that for every good deed, there's an evil twin. Like Tom, who had been my guide on day one, I became well-versed in things I shouldn't have known. Like where money budgeted for support services might actually be going.

The possible end of my career came into view barely a week after my new job style started. Mr. Bennett sent me an invitation to his office. Since the day I'd walked in and offered my unsolicited opinion, I had avoided the man.

"Ms. Flynn," he said. No pretense at a smile, or invitation to have a seat. "It's time for one of the little chores managers are handed. Your six-month evaluation."

I quickly did the math. I hadn't been on the job for six months.

"Okay." I smiled and helped myself to a seat.

His eyelids did the tiniest flutter.

Oh-oh, I thought.

My smile had risen with ease. Now I had to hold it in place with a force field.

"Really only a few things. You seem to be prompt, for the most part. No complaints from other staff or clients."

Whew. I had the overwhelming desire to check the time on my cellphone. How long did this type of evaluation take? Five minutes? Ten?

"I've found, however, that the array of services your clients request has jumped considerably."

He kind of sniffed, like Neddel did when Royally might have tooted nearby.

"Is that a bad thing?" I asked with concern. "I thought that's what we do here. Make sure the elderly and infirm receive the best possible care for their quality of life."

I might have been directly quoting the mission statement posted in the main lobby.

"Yes, of course. But as I am sure you are aware, everything must balance within the budget while all receive equal treatment."

"Absolutely," I responded.

We observed a moment of silence.

"Is that all, Mr. Bennett? I still have clients to contact today." I positioned my feet under me. If he said yes, I would rocket out of there.

"Not quite," he said. "There is also the issue of your being in unauthorized areas of the building."

I swallowed hard. What was considered unauthorized? And how did he know I was there?

Think fast, Left Brain screamed. *In about five seconds, he's going to consider that you shouldn't even be in the building, never mind wandering around.*

Right Brain raised its own squeal. *Where's the bathroom? I've got to pee!*

My words came out a trifle strangled. "Restless leg syndrome."

He actually looked surprised. "I beg your pardon?"

I tried not to cough, but it was right there. A roadblock in my throat.

"Excuse me, sorry. I suffer from restless leg syndrome. When I spend too much time sitting, like driving or working at a desk, my legs get all jittery. Or I have muscle cramps. The best thing to do is walk it off. It never occurred to me I would be someplace where I shouldn't be. I'll be more careful."

Just for good measure, I threw one leg out ahead of me and bobbed the knee of the other, causing a rapid tapping on the floor.

"Sorry," I repeated. "Stress is bad."

Mr. Bennett didn't say a word. He just motioned me out of the office.

On my way back to my area, I paused at Heidi's desk.

"I need a map or a chart or a list of the areas in the building that I am restricted from," I said.

I'd pretty much figured out where I was on my own, but to CMB, cover my butt, in the event Mr. Bennett turned my wandering into an issue, I'd lay down the theory I was confused.

She looked up at me with a deep frown.

"What are you talking about?"

"Are there places in this building I am not supposed to go to?" I asked.

"Phfft. I don't know about you, but I am very busy." Heidi keyed her headset. "Good afternoon, New Hampshire Agency for the Aged. How may I help you?"

I had been dismissed.

As I crossed the building, a couple of uncomfortable thoughts entered my head. If Mr. Bennett knew I was someplace other than my area in the building, how? Was he also prowling? Heidi mentioned once that he was all over the place.

You'd better hope he doesn't come into your work area when you're supposed to be on the road, and find you on the phone, Left Brain warned.

I lost a step at that thought. Then, too, Heidi's abrupt attitude surprised me, and I didn't feel this was a good time to ask why she was so short. Instead, I gathered my files for the few clients I still needed to talk to that day and left. I'd do a drop-in or call from home; I wasn't sure which yet. Then I'd type up my reports on my own laptop. I got to the stop sign at the end of East Main Street, and in a flamboyant move, slapped the left turn directional on. It felt like I'd just flipped Mr. Bennett off, and I didn't care.

I traveled up Route 16 to the Kancamagus Highway and took another turn. I was on the way to make an extra home visit.

Standing in front of Mrs. Henderson's front door, I wondered what I would say. I could hear a big—like really big—dog barking.

The woman who opened the door could have been Mrs. Henderson's mother. She looked like the same person, but this lady seemed old, kind of folded from the sides towards the middle. No neat suit or string of pearls. Just a garment I couldn't identify, covered over with a long, shapeless, and ratty sweater. She had one hand on the collar of a mastiff. The top of his head was at her waist.

"Doris!" Mrs. Henderson said, obviously surprised. "Can I help you?"

Now was the moment. I didn't think. I let the bulldozer in my brain take over and took a step forward.

"Hello, Mrs. Henderson." I kept moving, inching past her and into the house. "I dropped in to check on you." The mastiff raised its head. "Well, you certainly are a big guy."

Mrs. Henderson had been looking over the yard behind me in a confused manner. Maybe she'd been inside so long, she'd forgotten what it looked like.

"I probably should have called to see if you needed me to pick up anything on my way," I said. "But I didn't expect to be out here today. Should I call Melanie? That's my daughter. She'll run out for you."

I was babbling and couldn't shut it off.

"No, I'm good. Ah, would you like coffee?" Mrs. Henderson asked.

"Ha, I never turn down coffee." I took another step. The dog, thinking we were going to go further, moved across the room. "Are we going this way, big guy? Look how smart you are."

"His name is Julius," Mrs. Henderson said as she followed the dog and me.

He took us through a second living room and into the big family kitchen. I walked behind him, but not so quickly that I couldn't look around as I went. When I chanced to peek over my shoulder, I found Mrs. Henderson several steps back with a vagueness in her eyes. She pulled the sweater-coat tighter around herself like it was mid-January, not the sullen, heavy heat of August. But by the time we reached the center of the kitchen, Mrs. Henderson had recovered. Sort of.

"Sit there." She pointed to the chair on the far side of the maple table. Extra chairs lined the wall behind me. There was also a full two-tier hutch and a half-size buffet. The style was Mediterranean and at least fifty years old. My designated seat wasn't either of the ones that had a placemat with ducks wearing blue ribbons or chairs that showed the scuff marks of regularly used furniture.

"You know," I said, after an awkward silence that felt a week long, "I've lived in the valley for twenty-five years. I'm almost a local."

Nothing.

"I've driven up this road a gazillion times. Seen this place, but never gave a serious thought to what happens when a business like a hotel or a motel folds. I mean, the building is still here, but what happens to the owners? This place is pretty big, you know? Did your family just find a place in town? I'm sorry; I'm not trying to be insensitive. It's just look at you. From motel owner to the office director for a senior services agency."

Suddenly, I was gulping air. What had I just said? Heidi had let me know she didn't think Mrs. Henderson was coming back, and here I was going on like she was just on vacation. My face was burning.

"Doris." Mrs. Henderson pulled a jar of Sanka out of the cupboard and turned on the hot water tap. "You might be very good at walking dogs and helping elderly clients, but you're a lousy actor."

She didn't go near the seat where her coffee cup was already in place. Instead, she leaned against the counter, looking very unnatural doing so. It was evident we weren't going to have a friendly chat. She knew I had an ulterior motive. Mrs. Henderson had made the internal decision not to give up anything voluntarily.

"Why are you here, Doris?" she asked. "Let me guess. The group of you are dying of curiosity, and you drew the short straw."

"Actually, no." Cheerfulness hadn't worked. What was next? "No one knows I'm here. I didn't come on a good Samaritan call. I know we haven't worked together all that long, but you and some of the others have. If you're having a rough time, those people should be reaching out, and I can't see that they have. I find it deplorable that people have become so inarticulate that they can't spit out a few words of comfort or an offer of help to those they see every day. If you don't want to talk to me, so be it. I'm not here for a Doris bashing."

I didn't lift my butt, though that was logically my next move.

Mrs. Henderson was silent, lips pressed together. Then she said, "I have no intention of bashing you, Doris. Nor would I have expected anybody from the agency except maybe Heidi to have reached out."

She seemed to wilt just a tad.

Maybe, I thought, *none of her friends had stopped in either.*

Does she have friends? Right Brain asked.

"I'm fine. I have to admit it's been a hard few months. I contacted the sheriff's office about Ivan's disappearance because I didn't know what had happened to him. I was worried. It never occurred to me that if an unnamed body showed up in the woods, I might be treated as a criminal. Or the authorities would consider me their prime suspect."

"I hate to say it, Mrs. Henderson, but from what I understand, that's the way it works with all spousal cases."

This wasn't going even remotely the way I had expected. The water was still running in the sink. Steam rose, hot enough to make coffee. Mrs. Henderson had gone unfocused again. The jar of Sanka was clutched in her hand, pressed against her chest. She looked lost.

And I wasn't alone in that thought. Julius had flopped down on a dog bed the size of a twin-bed mattress. He got to his feet, the ones with the lion claws. I watched him rub against the woman's hip like a cat, making little whine noises. Annoying, but they got her attention.

"I know, baby," she said to the dog. To me, she added, "I'll be right back."

After she shut off the water, she left the kitchen, closing the door behind herself and Julius. I had no idea where they went, so I took a chance and scouted around a little. Right beside the Barcalounger was a chest-style stereo, circa 1960s. The lid was closed, but on top there was a stack of vinyl albums in their paper sleeves. I checked the top few and couldn't help but notice the ceramic coffee mug with the mustache handle and ancient coffee dregs inside.

I heard Julius give a little bark. Mrs. Henderson must have let him outside, and now he wanted back in. I rushed back to my seat. When she reentered, my former boss had run a comb through her short hair. It wasn't much, but better.

She put the jar of Sanka back in the cupboard and dropped a pod into the Keurig. "What do you take in your coffee?" she asked.

Our conversation wasn't exactly friendly, but it wasn't strained either. She told me that she had never worked in the motel when she was growing up, though this was where her family had lived.

"It went belly-up after my mother died, except for the ski jump on the south side. I was still in college. At that time, I wanted to be a teacher. My father couldn't cope alone. He just closed the doors." She shrugged away the memory. "For a while, we rented the rooms by the week. People lived there all summer. A few in the winter, but it was too cold. Pipes froze, things like that. When my father's health failed, I moved back here from Concord. Even then, I was working a government job. So, I transferred divisions and took a lateral job. I moved back in here. Dad died. I stayed. End of story."

"With family, you do what you have to," I said. "My husband passed away unexpectedly. My daughter has medical issues."

I hadn't planned to, but I related how Melanie had ended up back at the farm and my concerns about her.

"She's an adult and understands how the disease progresses. I just worry. It's hard to explain."

"You don't need to. I know how you feel. Ivan was foreign-born. He wanted a green-card bride. I knew that. At first, I laughed at the idea. Over time, he and I came to realize we had similar problems. We were both outcasts, different from others we knew, both physically and in what we expected of the world. I'm not some cute little homemaker. I wanted to work in the business field. My job was a challenge. I believe that I did it well."

"Obviously," I said. "Look how far you've gone."

"Ivan had to wear a back brace," Mrs. Henderson went on. "He wasn't strong like his friends. He liked classical music, particularly the violin. In his village, there was a strong division between fiddles and mandolins and Stradivarius."

Mrs. Henderson swirled the coffee left in her mug. Julius's ears perked up.

"We were good together because we were misfits. He was a handicapped foreigner, and I was this oversized, masculine woman. Then the harassment started. In his mind, it was the same as back in his village, where he was physically abused all the time. I think he ran in fear. He was so close to citizenship. And he left."

The telephone rang. We both jumped. Worse than that, the interruption brought Mrs. Henderson back to the moment.

"Look at the time." She was all business now, rinsing her cup out. "I'm sure you have more important things to do than sit here and chat. Thank you for coming, but I assure you that I am fine."

"Okay," I said.

I tried to stall, but she was really good at hustling me out the door. On the way through town, I marveled at the duplicity of human nature. Like a Cheerio box filled with potting soil, if you didn't open the box, you couldn't really know what you had.

I approached Calwin Mountain Road and waited to cross the traffic. During those few seconds, right after I saw the billboard that offered the house lots, I saw the D6 bulldozer. It was parked just inside the parking area and slightly behind the billboard, but conspicuously in view of travelers. Like a hint that the build would start any day.

The driver of the car behind me touched the horn. Startled, I made the turn and continued to the safety of my own driveway. A little hot flash episode heated me from bottom to top.

When I pulled in, the critter envoy clustered around my vehicle. We all trooped into the kitchen where they got cookies, carrots, and a coo and pat from their animal mom. I settled for a fistful of chocolate chips and another cup of coffee, which I didn't need. My ears started to buzz. I needed sixteen ounces of water and time to walk the caffeine rush off.

The arrival of the D6 meant construction was inevitable. I knew a plan was needed to halt that operation, but was unable to organize my thoughts.

"Let's go, Buttercup."

I jangled her leash. I couldn't get away from Royally and decided to use the cart.

"You can ride," I explained to Royally as I belted the harness around Buttercup's middle. "That way, I won't have to chase you all over the neighborhood."

Buttercup trotted up the road, while in the driver's seat, Royally's tongue lolled out. I wanted to check out the D6 and was so intent on that idea that we went right past Eve's house without noticing. Like I've said, Buttercup could move along at a good rate of speed.

Right beside the first bench, we turned off the road. There were no other people there at that moment, though I noticed the trash bin was full.

"Phfft. Probably tourists cleaning out their cars," I said to the critters.

The cart bumped across the ground. Buttercup kept an even pace. That was a good thing. It showed stamina. I avoided the sign but circled the D6.

I hadn't noticed the magnetic sign attached to the seat plate before. It identified the machine as the property of Coleman Rental. Further back in the lot, red stakes formed a random pattern in the ground. They'd replaced the thin ribboned ones Racheal had set out at the first open house.

"Hm," I said.

Buttercup looked up at the sound of my voice. Was I going to give her a snack? No? Then we might as well go home. Ignoring the small rocks that caused the cart, and Royally, to bounce, she crossed back to the road. She knew the way.

"It doesn't look to me like they have a plan with the lots," I said aloud. "Or that the lots are very big. Maybe whoever drove them into the ground did so for the same reason the dozer is there. You know, like a marketing ploy."

I was talking to the pig's rump. She was all done. No snacks, no casual stroll. Royally asked to get down. That meant I had to stop Buttercup or do a really fast maneuver in front of the rolling wheel. I elected to leave the dog in the cart. He wouldn't jump out. He'd done that once and run afoul of the same wheel.

Using my cellphone, I called Coleman Rental.

"Hi." I used my chirpy voice. "You people have a D6 bulldozer down at the end of Calwin Mountain Road. I'd like to find out about renting it."

The guy guffawed. "I'm sorry, ma'am. It doesn't work."

"I beg your pardon?" I was confused. "How did it get there?"

"Well, it chugs," he explained. "We can get it on and off the trailer, but it doesn't actually work. Contractors rent it for advertising reasons, or people rent it as a lawn ornament at Christmas. You know, to hang lights on it."

"So, a contractor put it in that little picnic area?"

I hoped I sounded like I didn't know anything about the parking spot. On the other end of the line, I heard the tap-tap of fingers on a keyboard.

"According to this"—more tapping—"it's a real estate developer, not a contractor. But if you need to actually dig, you need something besides that old girl."

"No, I'm good, thanks. I only need a five-minute-push sort of thing."

I laughed and got off the phone before I said something even more asinine.

* * *

Later, Noah pulled into the driveway. It wasn't five yet, so he must have been the early-in guy at the bank that morning.

"Hi Noah." I held out the plate of brownies Melanie had made. "Brownie? Can I use your cellphone for a minute?"

He traded the black device for the rich, gooey sweet.

"The Gerrish Agency," a young woman announced.

"Hi, I have a question. Perhaps you can answer it. Is this Tracy?"

"Yes," she said. "But you need to talk—"

I didn't give her a chance to finish. "We were at the open house for The Bright Water Development and filled out the preliminary paperwork. Today I drove past and saw a bulldozer on the property. Does this mean the wastewater plant is going in back there?"

"Wastewater?" She sounded rather choked. Not even interested in exactly who I was.

"Yeah. You know, septic tanks and all that?"

"Oh, my god!" Tracey said. "I've got to find Mrs. Gerrish."

I broke the connection. I looked up, ready to hand Noah back his phone, and found both he and Melanie staring at me with open mouths.

"Mom!" My daughter sounded as strangled as Racheal Gerrish's receptionist. "What are you doing?"

I slid the phone across the table toward Noah. "Spreading hate and discontent."

"Why?" she asked.

"Because I can."

The cellphone trilled.

"Don't answer that, Noah," I ordered.

He yanked his hand away from the device. The ringing stopped. Noah, Melanie, and the plate of brownies disappeared into Melanie's room with the door closed.

I felt guilty for about fifteen seconds. The phone rang twice more in the next half hour. Finally, I shut it off, knowing I had done a bad thing.

"It doesn't matter," I told Buttercup as I closed myself into the garden patch and left her outside. "Well, maybe. But this time we're going to chalk it up to karma."

I spent the whole supper hour weeding and throwing handfuls of good stuff over the fence to Buttercup and the Blanche Chicken Gang. I don't know if they heard my muttering. I was lost in thought for a while, moving from berating myself about baiting Racheal to worrying about Mrs. Henderson.

"Heidi said Mrs. Henderson went out at lunchtime every day for what Heidi thought was a meetup with Mr. Henderson," I told the crickets that tried to run away. "From the way Heidi talked about it, I was sure it wasn't something that stopped weeks or months before Mrs. Henderson was put on leave. You know what I mean? Like her husband was home, and she had to slap his bologna and cheese sandwich together. But Neddel said Ivan disappeared months ago. Was she going home to sit by the phone and wait, or just because of her dog, Julius?"

I had to use the wheelbarrow to help me move from one place to another. Royally stood, tail wagging.

"As a shade-tree mechanic, you know, practically working privately out of his own garage, Ivan might not have had a tax number, right? So, if he asked to be paid in cash, or accepted personal checks that he cashed without depositing, he could have had a stash of money somewhere that

Mrs. Henderson didn't know about. I didn't see a credit card machine at the repair shop or a sign that said, 'Visa welcomed here.'"

I sat back on my heels. Sweaty, dusty, and frustrated.

"Did he have the guts to string her along for years, knowing this is what would happen?"

"If you're out here in the dirt talking to yourself, then it's a sure bet supper is still waiting," said a deep voice from outside the fence.

My head shot up.

"Neddel!" I squeaked.

Finding him standing there in jeans and a muscle-revealing t-shirt stunned me.

"Ah-huh. I hear we need to have a talk."

Chapter Thirty-One

If I had thought Neddel would be angry when he found out I visited Edith Henderson, I was wrong. He didn't seem to care at all.

"How did you know I went there?" I asked.

"She called me." He rummaged through the refrigerator while I made up cat dinners. "She wanted to let me know that people were coming to her house. Even though your visit was harmless, she was worried others wouldn't be so."

He laid the fixings for ham and cheese sandwiches on the table. Noah and Melanie appeared out of thin air, magically drawn by the siren's call of chow. Neither spoke. The three of us didn't make eye contact.

"Did she let you in the house?" he asked. "Because when I was over there, even when I asked if I could step inside, we stayed out on the doorstep. She didn't even acknowledge the request."

"Yes. Maybe a little hesitantly. That seemed more to do with her dog than anything else."

I spread mustard as I tried to gather my thoughts. Neddel waited, bag of chips in hand.

Finally, with a knot in my gut, I said, "I've been inside Racheal Gerrish's house…"

Now, I got a reaction.

Neddel's right eyebrow jumped up to his hairline.

"I didn't get to the bedroom level, but I was in the kitchen and living room. There is exactly one wedding-style photograph of Racheal and Richard. It's on the mantel. His side is camouflaged by an overfull pot of plastic pothos plants. I didn't see a damn thing that indicated a man lived there. No shoes by the door, coat on the hook, guy magazines, maybe a tie left on the bathroom counter. Absolutely nada."

"What? You didn't look in the closets?" His tone hinted at sarcasm.

"Of course not. Though I did open the medicine cabinet."

His left eyebrow joined its brother. All of a sudden, I felt exhausted. "Just listen to me, okay? You can judge me all the way back to your house if you decide to walk away, but just for this minute, please?"

I received a vague nod in response. Then, suddenly, some wire in my brain crossed a different wire. I took a quick look around. Melanie, Noah, and Lilo were gone. My throat closed up, but I swallowed past it. I took half a step closer to Neddel and touched him with the very edge of my fingertips.

"Neddel. I...I was so wrong. Not just the day I was stupid about the foreign people being here, but so many times before."

He opened his mouth.

"No, please just listen. I'm not sure how long I'm going to last."

The thought flitted through my head that if I laughed, this wouldn't all sound so serious. But I couldn't have done that even if I'd tried.

"You've always been so good to me. And Melanie. You're so understanding even when I know you think I'm being stupid, and I've been so mean. I've abused your friendship, demanding information I'm sure you aren't supposed to share. Playing come-hither, then smacking you away."

He grinned slightly, which led Left Brain to consider if Neddel was wondering what I was talking about and when the come-hither had happened. I was trying to figure out the words to say that I cared for him, maybe more than I realized. But that wasn't working either.

"I know you have other...I don't know, friends. Like Patty Monson. I understand why."

He cut me off.

"The Brown Widow?" he asked.

"What?" I asked, confused.

"That's what Dolores calls her. I asked what it meant. It seems Patty Monson likes to attend weddings, her own." His grin grew. "She meets 'em, weds 'em, drains 'em, and dumps 'em."

"Really? I know that's how she works, but I never heard it called that."

Neddel's hands cupped my shoulders, lightly rubbing. His palms were so warm.

"Can I kiss you, Doris?"

His words were barely a whisper. He'd kissed me before without asking. This felt so intimate. I could barely nod in response. Those warm palms drew me to him, close against his chest. His kiss was long and deep, sweet and yet searing. When he pulled away, I was bereft. I could have kept on much longer.

"I know every time we're together, you're thinking about Ian. I can feel it in your body. Everyone grieves in their own way. For their own time," he said. "One day you'll stop grieving. I know that. I see it in your eyes, feel it when we touch, that you long to share, but you aren't quite there yet. You will be. But for right now…we'll have a cup of coffee and you can tell me what else you know. Okay?"

I couldn't answer him. We walked back to the house. He held my hand as we went, touched my back as I went through the door. Neddel stood beside me as I poured coffee and fixed his the way he liked it. He was so close I could almost feel him breathing. We sat at the tables with our knuckles and knees touching.

I did want him. I knew it. I just could not tell him. When I tried, I felt a sob build way down in my belly, and I refused to allow it to rise. It was a long few minutes before I started talking again.

"Somebody who was, ah, working at the property let me into the house. Emergency bathroom problem. Anyway, I was inside for only a short time. I wasn't interested in anything Racheal had wanted, touched, or owned. I wanted to know about her husband. But I didn't find a single hint that he's been there in, I don't know, forever. Okay?"

"Okay," Neddel agreed.

"With thirty-five thousand year-round residents in this valley, there could be any number of men who have disappeared. But there are only two I know of. In the realm of my world, there is a fifty-fifty chance he is one of them.

You have a body. Just one. Even the small bits of identifiable matter could be either guy. I'd expected Ivan Henderson to be like his wife. Big, broad, and, because *he* is Romanian, probably dark and swarthy. But he's more like his Hungarian cousins, medium size, mid coloring, and son of a gun, he had a couple of capped teeth. There are framed photographs of him everywhere in their house. I do question the American stylization of his last name."

If I had mentioned anything Neddel had not already known, he didn't give out a clue.

"Many foreigners tweak their names when they come here," Neddel said. "Specifically, if they came from a situation where they were a scapegoat."

"That's true."

I was chewing my lip, not looking at Neddel. Edith Henderson hadn't said anything like that to me. But it could be true; she might have told somebody else that. I opened my mouth ready to ask, but Neddel had another question.

"So, you happened to be in Racheal's yard when you became indisposed," Neddel said. "What excuse did you use with Mrs. Henderson? Oh, I was going up the Kanc, and suddenly, OMG, I had to pee!"

"You're being an ass." Now I could smile.

"Sorry, go ahead."

"Even though she was a hard boss, she wasn't unfair," I said. "She's also from here. A lot of the clients know that, even if they don't know her personally. Mr. Bennett is a recent relocation from the southern end of the state, like last week. He's been commuting up here from Rochester daily. Gossip at work is that he just rented one of those townhouses behind the Zen Spa. And no, I don't know anything else about him. Except that the man gives a whole new meaning to the term 'dark of the moon.'"

Neddel nodded. Very slightly.

"The people I worked with spent all their time keeping off Mrs. Henderson's naughty list," I went on. "Now they're looking for places to hide in the superstructure. Mr. Bennett is rude, crude, and socially abusive. And he's an equal-opportunity discriminator. It doesn't matter your sex, age, or if you work for the agency or are a person it's supposed to serve. He'll flatten you in a second and not care who knows."

"That's pretty harsh," Neddel said. "You haven't worked there all that long. Are you sure you've been there long enough to understand how management has to work? Really. I'm asking because that sort of thing could get you in court."

"I may be a short-timer, but I'm good at reading people. He fits the ticket perfectly."

"How did the opinion of your fellow employees,"—he held up a hand to silence me—"and the minimal amount of interaction you've had with your new supervisor, take you to Mrs. Henderson's house?"

"People talk. There was the question of whether Mrs. Henderson would return. Or, if Bennett planned to be around for a while, whether they should explore other employment options."

"Let's sit in the living room," I said. "It'll be more comfortable."

When Neddel nodded in agreement, I took my coffee and walked toward the living room. As I passed Melanie's closed door, I heard the masculine bass of the Indiana Jones theme. She and Noah were bingeing.

I tucked myself into the corner of the sofa closest to the tall front window. Neddel sat beside me. Much to Royally's disgust, Neddel and I occupied one cushion. There wasn't room for a thirty-pound corgi.

"You've told me about Racheal's house," Neddel said. "I can't believe I'm saying this because it's not your job, but mine. Tell me about your visit with Mrs. Henderson. Consider the small facts."

I looked up into his beautiful blue eyes, the dark ring around the iris making my thighs tighten. He wanted to know. Right now, he wasn't going to tell me to back off. I exhaled for the first time in weeks. I felt validated.

"I didn't call. I didn't buy flowers, bake a cake, or anything like that. Instead, I walked up to the door and knocked. A dog started to bark. I could tell from the boom-boom-boom, he was a big guy. I felt slightly intimidated. When she answered the door, I told her there were employees, myself included, from the agency who were worried about her. And she let me in."

I told him about my conversation with Mrs. Henderson. Then, I pulled up the small things I'd noticed.

"There are a lot of new tools in Mr. Henderson's shop, and not a single personal touch. However, in the office is a place where a file cabinet used to stand, and not long ago."

"Go on," Neddel said.

"Later, when I went to her house, I thought it was weird. The living room is split by a half-counter. I think it's because at one time, the part right in front of the entry was the registration office for the motel. Just inside the front door is a two-drawer metal filing cabinet. It looks like it came in the front door and was set down and left. It's totally out of place. I bet it came from the old salt shed turned repair garage."

Neddel's eyes narrowed.

"I've been inside the garage," he said. "I saw where the file cabinet had been, but when I asked Mrs. Henderson if something had been removed from the office, and she was standing right beside me, she denied it."

"Maybe she didn't move, but he did before he disappeared. She might not consider that as being what you mean," I said.

Neddel scowled.

"No, don't look at me like that," I said. "She's worried about him being gone and what's happened since. If the cabinet was moved prior, then it's not connected. She knows where it is. You're asking her if she can spot something that's missing."

"You keep telling me she's a smart woman," he said.

My head bobbed up and down. "Yes. But in this instance, she's also emotionally invested. We walked through her house to the kitchen. It's an old place, but clean. Kind of sparse. However, throughout the rooms I traveled, there was evidence a man was supposed to be there. Things that weren't evident at Racheal's house. Boots on the drain mat. A heavy, oily coat on the hook looked to be a size medium. The types of things you would expect a mechanic to wear. And there were pictures. Not wedding pictures, but one that was taken near Dinah's Bath. Man and dog. Man with a huge grin seated behind a roasted turkey. He looked happy. In all of them, he looked happy. Even the one where he and the dog were asleep in the Barcalounger."

"Is it possible Mrs. Henderson has a new boyfriend?" Neddel asked.

"I doubt it. She used to be formidable, but now you can tell she's not sleeping. Or eating either. I don't know where that sweater came from, but it was a horror show. I would say no."

"So she's grieving," Neddel said.

"Yes, but waiting for him to come back. When the news came out that those remains were at least assumed to be his, she separated herself from the rest of the world."

"What else did you notice?"

"One of them likes opera. Or, to be exact, string music. There were vinyls, 33s, stacked on an old-fashioned stereo right next to a huge, dirty coffee mug. The dregs have been there so long they've started to curl off the porcelain."

"You actually looked in the cup?" Neddel sounded impressed. "I did the same thing."

"Probably for the same reason." I felt myself getting all girly with glee. "So now you tell me whatever you can. It's only fair, don't you think?"

Duke had stayed calm near the door since we'd sat down. He seemed to understand we were having a moment and wanted to be part of it. He came over, jostling for space with Royally. There was a small show of force on the corgi's part. A little growl. Duke went around to the other side of the coffee table and walked right over the top of me. He settled himself on Neddel's feet, leaning on the man's legs. He had been the lesser in the canine power battle, but he was the winner here. Neddel laid his fingertips on the dog's snout. Duke closed his eyes and held perfectly still. It was clear they had bonded.

"When we went up on Chocorua Mountain the first time," Neddel began, "it was almost dark. We had to work fast. Doctor Lombard was there, working under the big lights. But things had quieted down some. She wanted the freezer taken, and the guys from the forestry department were getting ready to wrap it and move it. They'd just been waiting for her word."

I noticed his left foot was tapping on the floor.

"On the ground, almost lost in the mud, was this two-inch piece of shiny metal. When the photographer was done, we bagged it. It was easy to tell the metal was the bit end of a straight-edge screwdriver. The next day, it was identified as having been in the locking mechanism of the freezer, most likely to keep anybody who stumbled on the freezer out. No key was found. That's a piece of information we're holding back, Doris. Okay?"

"Absolutely," I said.

"The sections of the remains were in black trash bags. Forensics ascertained that, even though they were frozen in the bags, wherever the body was for the weeks before they went into the freezer, they weren't in those bags."

I pulled away and looked at him, startled. "How could they know that?"

"I really can't explain it, but it has something to do with residue on the exteriors of the bags," Neddel said. "We also did some digging into the Hendersons' finances. Edith Greene had a healthy nest egg. The property is worth money. She lived frugally, but after she got married, there were purchases made. The truck in the driveway, the tools, she bought them all. She also paid the credit card bill for all the parts Ivan Henderson ordered for his garage. It gets a little fishy. We didn't find any parts around in the garage, invoices from repair work, or anything that tells us he made money. Not even to equal what his wife paid out for tools and parts."

"So maybe my idea that he worked for cash is correct," I said. "And he could have kept it a secret from her."

"That's true. When the forensic financial officer spread everything on the table and explained it to Mrs. Henderson, she kept saying that it wasn't possible. I pointed out he could have hidden the money from her, decided he'd had enough, and left. She insisted he would have taken the truck. But why would he? He knows how easy it would be to track that one. He had to disappear and take nothing. Just walk away into the fog. Our only suspect is his wife."

"Because?" I asked.

"When we started asking questions, we ended up uncovering the church group that sponsored bringing Ivan Xehac here. We learned that he took an American bride, Edith Greene. Every person that we interviewed, except for a couple of elderly romantics, said it was a marriage of convenience."

"Like a green-card marriage?" I asked.

"Exactly."

I finished my coffee but sat there rubbing the cup between my palms until Neddel tugged it free and put it on the coffee table.

"What are you thinking?" he asked.

"Richard Gerrish is gone as well," I said. "I'm sure that he and Racheal weren't in a green card marriage. But what about money? If they had a fair amount put by, and he said he was leaving, she most likely didn't want to lose it. Can you check their financials?"

"There's a jump," Neddel said. "Remember, no one has reported Richard Gerrish missing. But to check their financial records on just a whim? No."

Neddel pulled back slightly. "You asked me about Ivan's registration and why he didn't take his truck. But because he wasn't a citizen, and maybe also because he knew he'd be leaving and not taking it with him, the vehicle registration has Edith Henderson's name on it."

I was watching Neddel and just barely aware that the dogs were as well.

"While I was at it, and because you brought up the point that Racheal might be shuffling both vehicles around, I took a look at their registrations as well. The Gerrishes each registered their own vehicles. The kicker is that Mrs. Gerrish's is paid for, and she has the title. Mr. Gerrish still has a couple of years' worth of payments left."

"He could have left it behind so that she'd get stuck with them, right?" I asked.

"Exactly."

For a little while, we were both silent. Then I turned on the TV. The show *Tracker* was on. I think the actor is hot, but besides that, I actually enjoy the program. Neddel usually spends most of the show explaining why the scenario is improbable and the actions incorrect. The only way to keep him quiet was to watch *The Big Blue World* documentary.

The only time I stirred was to make sure all the animals were tucked in. Neddel reclined against the back of the sofa, eyes half closed. I wasn't sure if he was deep in thought or zoned out. It was late when he yawned.

"I gotta go," he said.

I had been on the edge of this for a while, since our one-and-only night together back when we were still reeling from the identity of the body found on the ridge.

"You could stay," I said softly, half in hope he wouldn't hear me.

"Okay," he said, just as quietly. Then he shut the TV off.

I spent twenty minutes in the bathroom, seated on the edge of the tub as I tried to think of a good reason to renege on my offer and send him along.

Nada.

The dogs were out in the hall. The door to my room was closed. When I let myself in, only moon glow lit the room. It was enough to highlight the form beneath the covers.

When I slid in on my side, Neddel reached out.

"Are you okay?" he asked.

"Yes," I said.

And I think that, finally, I was.

Chapter Thirty-Two

Unable to sleep any longer, I crept out while the only hint of dawn was a glow along the top of the tree line. As I quietly let myself into the vegetable patch, I wondered if even the residents of Lubec, Maine, way out on the edge of nowhere on the coast, were able to see more than the advance guard for the Orb of Life.

To my ears, I moved silently, but others heard. From his kennel, Duke stepped out, the heavy flap of the dog door plopping back into place. Buttercup grunted and groaned as she roused herself from her beauty sleep. And lastly, there was the butt-butt-coo of Bernice. She, like Duke, already had her eyes upon me.

There was no dew, which meant I would have to run a water line out for the garden sprinklers. But not yet. I knelt in the dust, tiny pebbles pressed into the thin sheath of flesh over my kneecaps. A daddy long-legs spider skittered away. I saw the flutter of a squash leaf, a signal that a much smaller animal was also among the vines. With a practiced eye, I pulled weeds, separating the toxic ones—buttercups, nettles, and thistle—from the ones the chickens and my own Buttercup could eat.

"I should get a goat," I told myself in a hushed tone. "A pygmy fainting goat. I've always wanted one. Then there would be no waste at all."

The vision of Neddel, asleep among my sheets, flitted across my vision. I blushed hotly and forced the image away, picturing instead tiny, perfectly formed baby goats bouncing across my lawn.

With my back to the barn, I could see across the withered orchard toward the river. Above it, a faint bit of confused fog rose, then spread and disappeared so quickly it seemed like an apparition.

Buttercup, finally on her feet, woofed out a question. Was I there? Would I come and open her door? But I didn't move. At the sound of her call, the heads of nearby grazing deer rose. Big ears like antennas in space twisted, honing in on her location. Only the flutter of those velvety soft appendages and their semi-circle twist as the deer chewed their mouthfuls of grass alerted watchers they were there. Slowly, with the inherent grace Mother Nature gave to all animals, with the exception of ninety-eight percent of the human population, the mothers and still-spotted young moseyed back toward the forest.

I continued to pluck weeds until an entire row was devoid of a single leaf not bound for my own table. Then I tossed the safe ones into the chicken coop and released the gate.

Blanche had done her job. The others had been roused. All except those still waiting to release their own orbs rushed outside.

With Duke on his lead and Buttercup, Royally, and Old Tom behind us, we all crossed to the orchard. It was a good place to sit and think. To wonder what my place in this world actually would be. Was I headed toward a relationship with Neddel? If so, what of Ian? How would I know?

The smooth side of a warm mug rubbed my arm. I turned in surprise and accepted the offering.

"This," Neddel said, as he sat down beside me, "is the way to welcome a new day."

His nearness was not something I shied away from. Not at that moment. I realized it was okay for me to know this man, to even like him. Maybe he would be a fixture in my future. Only time, and my ability to grow, would tell.

The day fully broke. The silence had grown overlong. Buttercup wanted to go home for breakfast, and the dogs seconded the motion. Neddel carried the mugs while I lugged Old Tom. It wasn't very often that he wanted to be babied, but he was having a moment.

Neddel laughed at him. "You know, with all that long, fluffy gray fur, I keep wondering if he isn't actually a girl."

"Watch your mouth! According to the folks up on Cathedral Ledge, where I picked him up, he was responsible for every kitten in a two-mile radius."

"I don't think he could walk two miles." Neddel was still grinning.

I offered only a small smile. Old Tom had been with me for seven years. Life was fleeting. I could feel his bones under the thick fur coat, and it worried me. Why was there no fat? Was he already fading?

I had to fight the urge to run into the house and call the vet to schedule a checkup. At the exact moment I felt a tiny tightening in the base of my throat, that old cuss twisted, planted a claw, and sprang from my arms to race Royally to the back door.

"Ouch," I said, as a droplet of blood oozed out of my forearm.

"I told you to let him walk," Neddel said.

I wanted to punch him, but the laughing glitter in his eyes sapped all the strength out of me.

"What?" he asked.

"Eggs? Scrambled or fried?"

I was such an idiot.

Chapter Thirty-Three

Later in the day, Melanie skipped down the hall with Lilo hot on her heels. Here, on the kitchen side of the gate, Royally and Buttercup waited for their girl to arrive, ears up and tails wagging. Neddel was seated at the kitchen table. His attempt to install security latches on the old windows had failed. With a stream of under-breath cussing that made my sides ache as I attempted not to laugh in his face, he finally read the directions.

Melanie scrambled over the gate. Royally was the bigger problem, as he was right under her feet. A fall would be bad for both of them, so I scooped the dog up and out of the way.

That left more room for Buttercup. Her rump was all a-wiggle. She loved Melanie, who I'm sure she thought was a littermate. Pushing Lilo aside, my daughter reached down and ran her manicured fingernails along Buttercup's backbone, spreading the butt-wiggle up the length of the pig's body, creating a category one tremble.

"Who's a good girl?" Melanie cooed. "Who is it? Who?"

As my daughter continued with the baby talk and fingernail scratching, the pig groaned aloud.

Rurr, rurr, rurr. Then a little grunt.

Neddel's head turned. His eyes narrowed. "Is she growling at Melanie?"

"No," I said. "She's purring."

More than once, I'd said something about one of the critters, and Neddel had given me a look that begged to know if I'd lost my mind. Today was no exception.

"Doris," he said. "Pig."

I shrugged, accustomed to his skepticism, but Melanie spoke up. "Buttercup doesn't know that. She thinks she's a cat."

"No," he answered. "She's quite aware of what she is."

I bit the inside of my lip. For the last few weeks, since Buttercup had come to my defense when I'd been attacked, I'd come to believe Neddel was more tolerant of the pig. Now I wondered.

Melanie straightened. Her smile had slipped a little, and there may have been tension in her shoulders that hadn't been there before she'd come over the gate.

"You don't understand," she said. "Buttercup came here alone and confused. She was a baby. The mama cats took over. They taught her where to eat and find water. They house-broke her. When Mom put her in the crate at night, she had to leave the top hatch open so the cats could get in. They purr. Buttercup is doing the best she can to imitate that."

"Phfft." Neddel went back to studying the lock installation directions.

Melanie wasn't done. "You're being an arrogant jerk."

Neddel didn't rise the bait, but there was a twitch on the bottom side of his jaw.

Surprised, I looked up from the cutting board. Not only did Melanie have that go-ahead-fool-pick-a-fight stance, but the two dogs and pig had tightened around her. Lilo watched her mama, waiting to be told what to do. But Royally and Buttercup seemed to know where the problem was. They had their eye on Neddel, who I don't think was aware.

"Come on, baby," I said softly to Melanie, who I felt needed a few moments to wind down. "Let's go outside."

I hoped the pig and the corgi would go with me, but they stayed where they were. If Melanie calmed, her animal entourage would too.

"Relax, Melanie," Neddel said. "It's no big deal. She's just a pig, that's all."

He hadn't looked up until just then, but he figured out right quick what was going on.

"Listen, I'm not trying to demean Buttercup. But she's a pet. You know, like a parakeet."

"Right," Melanie said. "Like Duke. Just a dog. No brains. Just woof-woof, tell me what to do."

Neddel frowned. "Duke is different. Dogs are smart. He can use logic."

Melanie opened her mouth, but I held up my hand.

"Neddel," I said. "Pigs are actually more intelligent than dogs. I wouldn't pit one against the other, but you should know, Buttercup helped me teach Duke. I mean, so did Royally, but Buttercup helped him learn not to be aggressive."

Neddel had realized this conversation wasn't going to go well for him, but he didn't know how to end it. Before I could go further, Melanie stepped in.

"Buttercup." When she had the pig's attention, Melanie used her alpha voice. "Go get Duke. Fetch."

Buttercup looked up at Melanie. Her tail did a slow wag. She didn't understand. We were in the house. The room wasn't that big. Couldn't Melanie see the big dog?

"Buttercup, fetch Duke," Melanie ordered.

Obediently, the pig shuffled around the table to where the dog lay. Using her snout under his butt, she got him to his feet. I wouldn't say she herded him, but he allowed himself to be directed to Melanie. She took the box of dog treats out of the cupboard and, with words of praise, gave the pig and all three of the dogs a snack.

"I'm not saying," Melanie's words were directed to Neddel, "that if I told Duke to fetch Buttercup, he wouldn't eventually figure it out. But watch." She paused for a two-beat, then commanded, "Sit. See? They're all doing the same thing."

Sure enough, even the big black and white butt went down to the floor for a chance at a second snack. Neddel shifted his gaze to me. I hadn't thought about what my face was doing, but there might have been some displeasure there.

"I'm sorry, Melanie." Neddel's voice was tight. "I'm still not used to the idea of a pig as anything more than a farm animal. I do well for a bit, and then I fall back on old prejudices. I'd like to apologize all the way around."

"Even to Buttercup?" she asked.

I rolled my eyes. Now she was pushing it.

"Yes, even Buttercup," he said.

Melanie turned back to the pig, scratching her head with one hand and Duke's with the other. "See, I told you being an equality libber would pay off."

My daughter headed outside with Lilo, which had been her original destination. Royally and Buttercup clamored to go. After all, she'd just passed out treats. Duke was unable to follow without adult supervision. He still liked to wander.

"You did very well there, at the end," I said to Neddel quietly to let him know he hadn't damaged his budding relationship with Melanie

"Woof, woof," Neddel responded and went back to working on the latches.

I followed along. The first ones he did went to Melanie's door and the one to her office. That way, he'd be out of her space if she had to work. The living room had three windows. Two in front and one on the side, plus a heavy oak door.

"We'll put a deadbolt here." He nodded toward the porch door.

I couldn't wait any longer.

"Neddel, I think you should contact the people who owned Racheal Gerrish's house before her. When they moved, they left behind a freezer in the mudroom. It couldn't have been very big, but the marks show that it was rectangular, so not a small square one," I said.

"You saw this freezer?" he asked.

"No, remember I told you that I went into her house one day to talk to someone working there? I used the bathroom, too. The person had used Comet and steel wool to scrub the stains out of the tile. She said the unit must have been there for years and leaked oil onto the floor. She's an expert in cleaning. I would believe her."

"So, the freezer is gone, but you don't know where it is?"

Though I thought his tone was slightly condescending, I had a point to make, and I couldn't stop pushing at it.

"No. But while you're at it, you should ask Edith Henderson if she has a freezer," I heard my own irritation.

He looked away, then turned back. He has a tell: His tongue runs around the inside of his lower teeth. I waited to see if he'd share his thoughts.

Neddel's lips pursed. He squinted. Even though I couldn't read his thoughts, I could tell his mind was traveling a crooked road. When he said my name, I was startled.

"I'm sorry." I shook my head. "I must have been zoned out. Say again?"

"I said, I did ask that question."

My heart sped up.

"When we had Edith Henderson come in during the early part of the investigation, but after we'd found the freezer in Chocorua, I asked her if she had one. She said no, but she was clearly nervous. We got a search warrant to look inside her garage and house to check for any signs of foul play. But I kept my eye open for a space that might have held a freezer."

I blinked hard before blurting out, "When I was going through all this earlier, why didn't you say something?"

"Because you were so cute going all Sherlocky there."

He reached over and chucked me under the chin. I was mortified for a moment, but demanding validation in the next.

"Did you see the file cabinet in the garage?" I asked.

"No. But as you said, there was a two-drawer file cabinet smack dab in the middle of the living room."

"What was in it?"

"The top drawer was totally empty," Neddel said. "The bottom drawer held a file filled with old repair receipts, warranties, and the titles to some of the cars back in the woods. Nothing current. There's a basement under the main structure. Down there, we found an open space where a freezer could have fit. Right next to a bulkhead stairwell that showed some fairly recent damage on the steps."

"Holy jumped-up criminys!" I exclaimed.

"Faced with that evidence, Mrs. Henderson said there had been a freezer down there that hadn't worked in years. I knew it existed because the warranty was in the old file. She told us that, months before he left, she and Ivan had muscled it out and onto his pickup truck. Her reason was they were cleaning the building out for possible sale."

"It didn't look like that to me when I was there," I said.

"Maybe not, but the basement was pretty empty," Neddel said. "She couldn't tell me much about it except that it was old, from when her father was still alive. Also, that it didn't work, was white and a chest style. The warranty told me it was sixteen cubic feet, Sears and Roebuck brand. But nothing else."

"That's what you found, wasn't it?" I asked.

I opened my mouth to point out appliances had warranties you could register. There was probably a central place with all that information. But Neddel was looking pretty smug, I decided to check into that myself before bringing it. If I were wrong, I didn't need to add another black mark to my scorecard.

"Pretty close." He got up and poured himself another glass of tea. "The rub on this is using the approximate date she gave us; we established Ivan was seen several times after that."

"Who told you that they'd seen him?" I asked.

"We found eyewitnesses from across the street from his shop. And I told you that we took all the records from the garage. It was kind of a hodgepodge, but he had ordered parts, accepted and deposited a few checks. It's solid."

The information must have tasted sour because Neddel's face twisted up.

"Setting up a timeline from Ivan is difficult. He didn't go anywhere other than the parts store. He'd even stopped going to church. The woman at the store was the best source of information. Her husband said most of what he knew; she told him. The few regular customers we spoke to said he was there, and then he wasn't. No one could give us a when."

"So, what did the Hendersons do with the freezer?" My mouth was an acre of Sahara Desert.

"Edith Henderson said she didn't know."

I blinked twice. *How was that? It had taken the two of them to get it up the stairs and into the pickup. Wouldn't it have taken two to get it out?*

Neddel must have read my mind. "I know. Especially when she said it was a struggle to get it out of the basement. And the damage to the stairs and marks on the bulkhead are testimony to that. But according to Edith, Ivan told her getting it out of the truck would be easy. He'd just push it. She assumed he had gone to the dump and disposed of it."

"If he did, then he got a receipt for payment. The dump charges for stuff like that."

I waited while Neddel took a sip of tea. It was infuriating when he slowed down the action. I wanted to know right now. It might be a good habit for a cop, but I have to tell you, in the household scenario, it stank.

"The receipt system at the landfill is automated," Neddel said. "Dolores personally went through all the receipts, going back two years. We found several freezers. Unfortunately, no names, license plate numbers of drop off vehicles, or specific descriptions other than refrigerator/freezer are on the forms."

I collapsed against the chair back. "Seriously? What about…"

"And," he cut me off, "when we showed the witnesses Ivan's picture, we got a couple of responses like, 'yeah, I've seen him here before,' but no one could attach him or his pickup to a freezer." Neddel held up his hand. "There won't be any fingerprinting or other analyses done because that whole section of the landfill—all those fridges, freezers, air conditioners, anything that might have a hazmat issue—are loaded monthly and hauled off to be crushed. If it didn't happen yesterday, it's gone."

Chapter Thirty-Four

I made supper. Outside, the evening glowed with the pre-twilight sun. While Melanie and I picked up the kitchen and washed out the cat dishes, Neddel took the paper and went out to the living room. When I followed, I covertly watched him, seated in Ian's chair with the newspaper and a cup of coffee.

Ian?

It's okay, sweetheart. Truly.

His voice spoke in my mind. I choked up, tears burning my eyes. How many years would I be like this? Ready to find someone new one minute, living in the past the next. How could I move on? Forcing myself to sit and open my laptop, I typed randomly, hoping to be swept away.

"What are you doing, Doris?" Neddel asked.

"Ah, checking on Buttercup's harness," I said.

But the screen in front of me said I had accessed the nh.gov page. Specifically, the United States Citizenship and Immigration Service. I relaxed as the questions my fingers typed in were answered.

Where in the State of New Hampshire do individuals swear in as naturalized citizens?

The Oath of Allegiance is offered at the Warren Rudman US Courthouse, 55 Pleasant St, Concord, NH.

How often does this ceremony take place?

Monthly.

Is a calendar of dates available?

Please reference USCIS.gov website for list.

Does an individual have to be scheduled?

All scheduling is done by the USCIS.

Does an individual need to be accompanied by a sponsor or family?

All participants can attend alone or with guests.

"You're clucking like a chicken, Doris. What gives?" Neddel laid his paper aside and rose, cup in hand.

I immediately closed the laptop. My gut knew I needed to get out of the room before I started babbling and told Neddel what I was doing.

"I need to measure Buttercup. Her harness is getting too tight and needs a spanner put in," I said.

"Okay," he said. "Let's do it."

Right then, I was deep in pig poop.

"Melanie can help." I searched for another excuse. *ANYTHING*. Nothing popped up.

Neddel laughed. "You're all about me and the pig getting used to each other."

I followed him outside after I gathered what we would need. Melanie was lying in a lawn chair on the deck, surrounded by fur and fowl. We'd have to do this on the deck because it was dark enough now that we needed the outside light to be on.

"Whatcha doing?" she asked.

"Fitting Buttercup for new duds," Neddel said.

Melanie looked over the top of her sunglasses. "Ah-huh. And you're going to help?"

Neddel shrugged. "How hard can it be?"

"Easy as pie," she said sweetly.

She'd pushed her glasses up, but I was sure she was watching.

"Sit right here," I said to Neddel. "Hold the dishtowel over your knee like this."

"What's this for?"

"Pig slime," Melanie said. "She gets excited."

"What? Wait!"

Too late. Buttercup and I stood right in front of him. I held the cloth measuring tape in my hand after passing Melanie the notepad and pen.

"Ready?" I asked.

Buttercup had done this before, so she had an idea of what to expect. Neddel? Not so much.

"Buttercup. Nose here." I put my finger on Neddel's knee, then prodded her with my knees.

She sniffed his foot, looked up at him, sniffed again, and made her teenager noise that meant, *nope. Not me.*

From my pocket, I pulled out a few peanuts in the shell. "Hold these," I told Neddel. "No, higher than that. I don't want her to have them until I'm done."

He complied. I put my finger against his knee.

"Buttercup. Nose. Here," I said again.

She took two little steps forward and put her disc against his kneecap. His torso leaned back slightly.

"Is this safe?" he asked.

"She won't bite you," I said. "And I'm pretty sure she won't jump on you."

All three of the dogs had come over. Buttercup's disc wiggled around on the dishtowel. The dogs' noses got in on the snuffling, and the towel started to get damp.

I worked quickly, calling out measurements to Melanie. We were almost through when Royally crowded Duke. He sidestepped into Buttercup, who threw her shoulder out to push him off, causing him to step down off the deck and into the chicken crowd. That created a mess of noise, all of which culminated in Neddel giving a nervous cough.

"Ah, Doris? Are you sure she can't jump up on me?" he asked.

"I didn't say she couldn't jump up on you," I said, stepping back. "I said I didn't think she would."

There was a strangled gurgle from Neddel, and a giggle from Melanie.

"All right. All of you, down."

I threw a big handful of peanuts out over the lawn, and the critters were off. It was every chicken for itself as they tried not to get trampled. Buttercup ran off with everyone else, but by the time Neddel had peeled the soaking wet dishtowel off his trousered leg, she was back. Buttercup stood at attention right in front of Neddel. He watched her warily.

"She wants your nuts," Melanie said.

Neddel shot her a withering look, but dropped the peanuts still clutched in his fist to the ground.

"Okay, you too. I have things to do, so I'm not getting into this."

Notebook in hand, I walked back inside.

* * *

Later, I decided to find out why Melanie was being so hard on the sheriff.

"Sometimes it seems you really don't like Neddel," I said. "Is there a particular reason for that?"

I had just come back into the house after seeing him off. Melanie was seated in the maple rocker facing Ian's chair, feet up on Buttercup's snoozing back. Lilo was trying to crawl over Pumpkin so she could be the closest to Melanie.

"He has a first name," she said.

"Everett."

"Yes, Everett. It's quite appropriate, don't you think? Everett, like the Energizer Bunny? Everready or Everlast, whichever. Always so serious. Unwavering, I guess."

Her hands were waving around in an airy way, or maybe to defuse, but her eyes were watching the big overstuffed chair.

"You know," I said, sliding into a seat on the sofa, "I like Neddel. Everett. I do. But I loved your father. I wasn't ready to lose him." I realized I was also looking at Ian's chair. "He's always right there in my mind. Or standing at the very edge of my vision. I don't want him to go, but I'm afraid he might because of Neddel."

With Lilo in one arm and Pumpkin in the other, Melanie somehow made it over Buttercup and huddled up beside me on the sofa cushion. There was a canine-porcine scramble on the floor to follow her. She didn't speak. We didn't cry. Both of us held on to each other. It was a balm we both needed.

"Mom?"

"Yes?"

"Do you think you'll ever call him by his first name?"

"I doubt it," I said.

"Even if you get to be, you know, *friends*, like on a regular basis?"

I gave her a shove, but she yo-yo'd back.

"On another note…" I told her what I'd seen on the computer about the USCIS.

"What are you going to do with that info?" she asked.

"Our time is finished at the Humane Society. So tomorrow, I'll drive to Concord and ask some questions. Neddel is busy almost every night taking Duke to night school, so he won't be around. I'll get the chores done early and drive down. I should be back by supper."

"Okay. Next question. Were you trying to scare Neddel with Buttercup?"

I had to laugh aloud. "No. I didn't want to tell him what I was doing on the computer. He wanted to know. It's odd, don't you think, that he seems to be willing to listen to what I find out when I'm snooping around, but he keeps insisting that regardless of how I feel about Eve, I should keep my nose out of it. That goes double for Edith Henderson. I told him I was checking on a new piece for Buttercup's harness. It snowballed from there. I offered to get you to help me, but he said he could handle it."

"He may be good at intimidating criminals," Melanie said. "But he's not good at facing off against the pig."

I scratched the side of Buttercup's face with my foot.

"Not many people are," I replied.

* * *

The next morning, we were up early. Even though I tried to be quick, Melanie came dragging into the kitchen before I had my to-go cup ready.

"Pig's done. Dogs, cats, all fed," I said. "You just need to let them all and the chickens out."

"Nice," Melanie said. "I have a short list for BJ's when you go through

Tilton."

I tried not to groan aloud. I hate to shop. Melanie yawned and headed back down the hall while I gathered up the things I wanted to take with me. It would've been a lot simpler if Royally hadn't been dancing around my feet. He wanted to go, but once in the city, I'd be forced to leave him in the car.

Once I got into Concord and through the congestion of the Ralph Pill Mill intersection, the courthouse was easy to find. Against my own ethical code, I opted for pay-to-park half a block away. Once inside the building, I found my way to the information kiosk and up to the chambers where the Oath of Allegiance gatherings took place.

It was actually a large courtroom. There was business happening there when I arrived, so I went looking for the Clerk of Courts.

"Whew," I said, laying my small satchel of tools on the counter. "It's been a while since I was in a court building. I think back then, there was a ninety-year-old security guard with a big flashlight. This is the first time I've ever been through a metal scanner!"

The young man smiled at me. "I guess you don't fly much then, do you?"

"Never. Perhaps you can help me? I need some information about a man who was scheduled to take the Oath of Allegiance here for citizenship."

"We don't have anything to do with that," he said. "You need to contact U.S. Citizenship and Immigration Services." He plucked a pamphlet out of the several in a display and pushed it across the desk.

I pushed it back. "Yes, I know. I am looking for a specific individual." I pulled Ivan's photograph from my satchel. "I was hoping to find out if anyone recognized his being here."

Immediately, an older woman zoomed up to the counter. She wasn't as tall as the guy, but definitely outranked him. He fell back as fast as the redcoats did in Lexington.

"Are you with the police?" she demanded, then snidely added. "Or a private investigator?"

I placed my driver's license on the counter. "No ma'am. My name is Doris Flynn. I'm neither of those. I'm a private citizen with an elderly friend who is searching for her husband. She believes he came to harm on his trip to

Concord. I'm trying to establish if he got this far."

The woman, perhaps forty though she looked much older, motioned the young man to assist the next person in line.

"See that half-door? Go over there."

I was in front of the Dutch door for only a few minutes before the top half opened. On my side was the lobby. On the woman's side was a corridor. Beyond her, a security guard hovered. If he were trying to be discreet, he needed more practice.

"I'm Irene Ganley. This is not something that we normally would do. Can you explain to me exactly the reason for your visit?"

"I have a friend of advanced years who married a foreign man—"

Irene cut in, "A green-card bride?"

"Edith doesn't consider herself that. He had a good job. His own business. They seemed happy. Then there was some uproar in the area about foreigners coming in and taking the work. He was threatened," I said.

"Did he go to the police?" she asked, then quickly said. "No, I bet he didn't. If he were from a third-world country, he would be afraid to do that."

"Exactly. Anyway, he had an appointment to be sworn in. I'm not sure why he came alone, but he did." *Just a little deviation from fact*, I thought. *Not a lie, really.* "He never returned. The police won't help. So, we—her friends—are just checking. You know, we called the hospitals, checked police reports regarding accidents, that sort of thing. I thought if I could establish where he was seen last, it might be easier. I'm not asking for anything that might be considered sensitive stuff. Just whether he got this far."

Irene handed me back my license. "What was the date of his appointment?"

When I told her, she registered surprise.

"That was a while ago."

"I know. Edith didn't even go to the police for weeks. When we realized she hadn't come out of her house practically at all, I went over to ask her why. She's afraid. She doesn't know what happened. To be honest, she's not very worldly and doesn't understand that she can advocate for herself. She believes it's up to the authorities."

"Pathetic," Irene said.

Her unsympathetic attitude was starting to fry my bacon, but I tromped on that.

"Ms. Ganley, not all women are as strong as we are. I believe it behooves us to help those who aren't, and perhaps in time they will blossom."

"Mm," she hummed. "What's his name? Can I see the photo?"

The door closed in my face, which left me a little worried. The picture was gone. I waited for ten minutes. When Irene didn't return, I edged over to where I could see beyond the service counter. She wasn't there. I returned to my post. Ten more minutes. I was about ready to find the young guy and ask about Irene when somebody tapped me on the shoulder. It would have been a mess if I'd faceplanted against the wall, but I almost did.

Irene Ganley stood behind me. She waved me to follow. We headed down the long hall towards the broad white granite stairs leading up.

"No one in my area recognizes the picture," Irene said. "And without a court order, you aren't going to see the security tapes. I asked the people who work in the courtroom. Again. Nada. There's one other possibility."

She stopped walking so abruptly that I was two steps past her before I came to a halt.

"Actually, two. Okay. So, when people come in for their appointments, they have to provide identification and the notice. Heather, who checks them in, is working upstairs in her office. We're going there. She might remember this man. Also, there's a start-up photography girl who sets up in the lobby on USCIS day to take pictures of the happy new citizens. She also does passport photos, stuff like that. She gets to be in the building because she's on a grant program. Don't ask me to explain it. Anyway, her business name is *Your Best Side*. She's down in the Ralph Pill Mall. Do you know where that is?"

"I do, actually," I said, just as Irene rapped once on the door, threw it open, and shoved me in.

"Here she is," Irene said. Then, she was gone.

I looked at the woman, whom I presumed to be Heather.

"Holy cow! She's a whirlwind!" I exclaimed.

"She is that," Heather said. "Now explain about this guy."

I told my story again.

"Please bear in mind, Mrs. Flynn, that legally I can't check my records and tell you if somebody signed in or not."

"Okay."

"But I'm not averse to looking at a photograph in the event I just happen to recognize the person."

"Okay," I said again.

Heather held Ivan's picture. On her desk, the computer monitor displayed a list of names. If I were a betting person, I would say she'd already checked the roster for the day of Ivan's appointment and knew the answer. She handed me back the picture.

"I'm ninety-eight percent sure I recognize this man as having taken part in one of the allegiance ceremonies."

"Thanks. Can you answer one more question? On the date I gave you, how many people were scheduled to be here?" I asked.

She turned back to the computer. She hadn't pushed any buttons that would cause information to update, and there hadn't been any flash of light to indicate the screen had changed. I'd been right.

"On that day, seventy-six. It appears the ceremony for the previous month was cancelled, probably due to weather."

At the Ralph Pill Mall, I found parking right in front of the photography shop. A little girl about nine years old sat behind the counter.

"May I help you?" she asked.

"Are you in charge?" I smiled.

"Mom is in the darkroom. Hold on."

The door to what I would have assumed was the bathroom was closed. A red lightbulb was lit above it. The child knocked to alert the person inside that they were needed. Then she came back to the counter.

"It'll be a minute. My name is Carson. Would you like a coffee?"

"That would be lovely."

By the time Sarah Reddig emerged, her daughter and I were seated and laughing about school stories.

Like Irene, Sarah wasn't sure about the ethical ramifications of what I asked.

"As I said, I don't need or want any information other than if this man made it through the two-and-a-half-hour drive to Concord and got this far. That's all."

"Would you mind if I asked my lawyer first?"

"I don't mind."

She was already on the phone. When she hung up, she said, "Ms. Flynn, this will take me an hour or so. I have to finish the project I have going on in the darkroom so it doesn't get ruined before I go through my files. Can you come back, say, in two hours?"

"Absolutely. I'll go over to Panera. Can I bring you back something?"

Carson's face lit up, but her mom said, no thank you. I drove over to Panera, had lunch, and walked through the L.L. Bean Factory Outlet. When I got back to *Your Best Side*, Sarah and Carson were seated behind the counter with an array of photographs laid out in front of them.

"Look what happened!" I said with a laugh. "I was leaving Panera, and these leftover cookies were calling out, 'Take me, take me!' What could I do?" I put the small bag down beside Carson.

Sarah laughed. "Mrs. Flynn is a wicked, wicked person, isn't she, Carson?"

The little girl was all grins and nods.

"Normally, I keep everything digital. These are commemorative pictures. You know, to celebrate the day. I take them for everyone who wants them, then when they order pictures, I make them up. But these sets are ordered on the day, and I charged a deposit, so I have them ready. There are always a few who never return to pick them up," Sarah explained. "I believe this is the man you asked about. If so, then yes, he was at the ceremony."

Among all the photos of people in whom I had no interest were four shots of Ivan Henderson. Two by himself, holding his certificate, and two with a woman who looked to be of the same heritage. She sported a wedding ring, and from the way they were intertwined, I'd say she wasn't his sister.

"Thank you," I said.

"Can I assume that if the authorities get involved with this, there will be others who want to see these pics?"

"I'm afraid so," I said.

Sarah sighed. "Thank you for your honesty. And the cookies. Good luck."

Chapter Thirty-Five

The ride home from Concord took forever. My heart was heavy. This wasn't what I'd expected.

"I can't tell Mrs. Henderson," I said aloud. "Neddel should probably know, but I'd rather send him a letter from Alaska than tell him face to face."

I was rolling down the exit ramp in Meredith when the voice who lives in my dashboard told me I had a call.

"Hi, Melanie."

I knew she was about to ask me what I'd found out, or maybe how come I was still so far away. But she had a different reason for the dial-up.

"Ah, Mom? Racheal Gerrish is here."

"What?" I almost had to pull over to the side of the road.

"Yeah. She's outside in her car. She won't get out because Buttercup is right there. And I don't know what's wrong with her, but I think she's going to eat the car."

"Don't go near Racheal," I said. "Buttercup is still angry about the pepper spray."

"I didn't go down. I stood on the deck. She pulled all the way up to the ramp and blew the horn until I went outside," Melanie said.

"Don't hang up the phone. Go out and tell her I'm on I-93. I'll stop at her office when I get back into town. Not her house. Her office."

I turned the volume up so that I would be able to hear what was going on around Melanie and heard the screen door slam. Melanie called, "Pig. Pig." Then I could hear her talking, but not exactly what she said.

"Are you still there, Mom?"

"Yes. Is she gone? I can't believe she drove on the lawn."

"I'm just glad I got Buttercup and Royally up on the deck before she backed out. I don't think they like her. Listen, stop at McDonald's or someplace so your blood sugar is stable before you talk to her," Melanie instructed. "If you don't, you'll go all flipping supernova. And let me know before you walk into the building, got it? I'll have Noah standing by."

"Poor Noah," I said, then cut the connection. *That's a good idea, Melly-girl.*

* * *

There was only one car in the parking lot at the real estate office. It wasn't the one I'd seen Racheal driving. Instead, it was Richard's vehicle.

The door to the office was unlocked. The place lit up like Macy's on parade day, and there wasn't a single soul inside. I looked everywhere. The hair rose on my back. When I stepped out onto the porch, Racheal was casually leaning on the railing.

"Doris." She smiled. There might have been a pointy canine tooth gleaming against the bright red lipstick. "So glad you could stop by."

"At your request, Racheal." I smiled back and wished I didn't have such nice, even teeth. "What can I do for you?"

"Well, it's like this. I bought a house here in town a few months ago."

"That's nice."

She levered up. Some of the playfulness was gone.

"I know you are aware of where I live. As a matter of fact, you and that monster hog have been there a few times. Probably spoken with the gardener."

I didn't bite. I wasn't going to throw Betty Louise under the bus. If she knew about Buttercup, then she knew I hadn't driven to her house, so I couldn't have been in the driveway. Her conclusion would have been that, logically, I had used the game trails. Which meant she'd found me using game cams! What an idiot I was!

"What is it you want, Racheal, that would force you to drive all the way out on Calwin Mountain Road?" I asked.

"I don't know why you're snooping around. Asking questions that make my clients nervous. I've asked Richard about you. He doesn't even know who you are. Stay away from us. Our house. And stop chasing my husband. Do you understand?"

She brushed past me and went inside, slamming the door. I could only gape after her. What was all that nonsense? A total waste of time.

She knew I'd been to her house. She'd warned me off. And she had specifically brought up Richard. How she knew I was asking questions about him was a different issue.

I pulled out of the lot and into the Schoolhouse Motel, where I had seen Noah's vehicle idling earlier. I shut off the engine, killing the lights.

On the White Mountain Highway, Richard's vehicle zoomed by with Racheal driving.

"Are you all set, Mrs. Flynn?" Noah asked.

"Yes. This was just a useless commercial break in my life," I said. "I'm going home."

"Can you give this to Melanie for me?" He handed me a single page.

"Melanie wanted to check out the possibility you put out that Racheal Gerrish was moving both cars between the house and office. She sent me out to time how long it would take to get from Racheal Gerrish's house to the office. The top number is how long it took me to drive from here to the Gerrish house," he said. "The second number is walking between the two on the road. The third number is if I take the riverbank shortcut."

"I didn't ask Melanie for this," I said. "But it was a smart idea."

"I know, but you talked about how both cars were there, but only Racheal was living in the house. This shows that she could drive here, walk home, and come back with a second car in half an hour. If she did all of that before six-thirty in the morning or after eight at night, she'd be like a ninja. Almost invisible."

Then Noah was gone. I started my car, but it took me a few minutes to drive away because I was still perplexed about the empty real estate office. Then I realized that I'd been inside, touching doorknobs, or who knows what else? Getting my fingerprints everywhere. Gooseflesh ran up my arms. Instead of going home, I went to VFW Street.

"Hi, Arnie," I said. "What's happening?"

"I already had supper. My friend Georgie brought me one of them steak and cheese subs from First Stop."

"With the onions, peppers, and mushrooms?" I asked. "I love those. But actually, I'm just checking in on you."

"That's it?"

"Pretty much. To be honest, I have a question about one of your neighbors. The blue house lady with the little dog."

"He's not a bad dog," Arnie said. "I've seen him out with the gardener and Betty Louise when she's at work there, and he's good. Poor little mite just gets all twitchy when the owner lady handles him."

I wonder why.

"I heard she's been driving the big SUV around," I said. "Do you know what happened to the sporty one?"

I was taking a chance. If Racheal drove Richard's Denali in broad daylight, there had to be a reason.

Arnie laughed uproariously. "Heck, I sure do. Carvana picked it up a few days back. You know, I've seen the commercials, but I thought it was a big-city deal. Nope. They were right here in our little town."

I think my jaw dropped. Who would have believed Carvana would come here to pick up a vehicle, and what local would bother calling them when Roadside Motors right down the road bought anything with wheels? Unless, of course, you didn't want your vehicle to be sitting in their lot right beside Route 16.

* * *

Forty minutes later, I sat on my own sofa with a pig underfoot and a lapful of corgi.

"Your instincts were right," I said to Melanie. "Racheal moved both vehicles around so people wouldn't notice one of them never left the garage. Neddel said the Denali was registered to Richard only. She can't sell it. But she could move the one registered in her name, and that's what she did. I'm sure she had a good reason. I also now know she has game cams, but not out front, so she knows I was in her backyard, but not her driveway."

"What is all this getting you?" Melanie asked.

"I'm positive that Ivan Henderson has another woman, maybe another wife, someplace else. I'm leaning towards his knowing this other woman before he married Edith Greene. Once he had his citizenship, he jumped into the wind. Finding him will be somebody else's job."

I laid out my notes, explaining to Melanie as I did so who I'd talked to and what I had found out.

"That ass," my daughter said. "That poor old lady will be heartbroken."

"Melanie, she's my age."

"Like I said, that poor old woman."

I threw a couch pillow and missed her by a foot.

"Did you bring in the groceries already?" Melanie asked.

Crap. I'd forgotten to stop in Tilton at BJ's.

Chapter Thirty-Six

I was back at my desk in the office the next morning when the landline rang. I didn't often receive calls at work and was a trifle surprised. Heidi came running in.

"It's Mrs. Henderson!" she gasped.

But I had already said hello.

"I don't want to interrupt your day, Doris," my on-leave boss said. "And I don't condone taking personal calls at work."

"I understand, Mrs. Henderson. What can I do for you?"

"It seems that I might have been less than forthcoming with Sheriff Neddel."

This was the first time I'd detected any hesitation from her.

"Okay." I waited for her to tell me where Mr. Henderson was buried.

"I have a bill of sale from when my father bought the freezer at Sears and Roebuck. It has a serial number on it. What would be the best way for me to get it to him quickly, as opposed to mailing it?"

Huge sigh of relief from me. No way I'd say he'd already seen it. I took the coward's walk.

"Two choices. You can walk into the police station and give it to him yourself. Or if you'd rather bypass the questioning by his subordinates before you get to him, you can ask him to come to your house." Anticipating her next question, I added, "I don't have any idea what to tell you to expect. And to be honest, it's not my business. But I can tell you, he may not be a local, but he's fair."

"Thank you."

She was gone. No goodbye. If I'd thought Neddel would let me get away with it, I'd have run up Main Street to his office so I could hear his side.

I had one client visit nearby. Then I could go back to making phone calls and getting people started on services I thought were appropriate.

When I returned from my client call and walked into the cubicle space I shared with Maryann and Hector, the first thing I saw was a note taped to my desktop monitor.

CALL ME–ASAP–HEIDI.

What now? I wondered.

Whatever it was, it must not have had anything to do with my fellow field agents. Neither had left a note or tried to warn me. I buzzed Heidi.

"Hold on, I'll be right there," she said.

"Hello? Heidi? Hello?"

The phone had gone dead in my hand. Faster than Houdini on roller skates, she was standing in front of me.

"S'up?" I asked.

"Remember a couple of weeks ago I told you that if you wanted to be considered for the vacant full-time position to get on it?" she asked.

"Yes, remember I told you I wasn't interested?" I rejoined.

"Okay. Well, news alert. Mr. Bennett sent a notice out to Concord on Monday. As a cost-saving measure, he is going to push to find a full-time employee and eliminate the part-time position."

"That doesn't sound like cost saving," I said.

"The full-time job is already incorporated into the budget. The job you're holding is not. If you want to keep working, you need to fill out an application."

She looked so hopeful. I didn't have the heart to tell her that I was already sorry I had taken this job.

"I can't, Heidi. First of all, I don't have enough hours in the week to go full-time. Second, it'll mess up the stipend I receive from Ian's social security." I reached over and grasped her clenched hands. "You know as well as I do, this job is needed. There are so many clients out there waiting. But if it goes away, there's nothing I can do about it. You'd be better off starting to look for the best possible candidate."

She looked miserable.

"How did you know Bennett sent that message out?" I asked, hoping to change the subject.

"I deal with his email sometimes. The man's an idiot. My name is on several of his group lists, and he doesn't even realize it. Every time he sends something out to the brass, I know."

"And you're not telling him? You bad girl." I smiled, and she relaxed.

"Yeah, it's my little piece of the pie."

She left. I made my calls. It ended up that I had to do an introductory visit in Tamworth Village around noon.

The house wasn't hard to find. Getting away from the elderly man and his daughter was more difficult. I was having a problem focusing on what they wanted me to do. Which by the way, was more than I could get accomplished without bringing in people from other services.

Then, too, it might have been because it seemed that every moment my brain was searching for some missing piece of data connected to Ivan Henderson and Richard Gerrish. With Neddel busy all day at work and then taking Duke to school in Twin Mountain three evenings a week, I didn't even have him around for a backboard I could bounce theories off of.

My way home brought me to a Double D, and I pulled in. My to-go thermos hadn't lasted long that morning. As usual, there was a line for the drive-thru. As my jeep inched around the corner to the ordering board, I could see the housing development behind it that Evie said Racheal had rented before buying the house in town. Nice neat rows of modular homes, mostly double-wides. Each street had a cutesy critter name. Rory Raccoon, Bungling Bear, Sly Fox. I wondered which one Racheal and Richard Gerrish had lived on.

RACHEAL!

My brain went from casual thought to, holy cow, look where I am. I held back for the next couple of inch-long progressions. As soon as there was room, I cranked the steering wheel to the right and pulled out of the queue. I headed straight toward the modular with the office sign out front.

"Hi." I smiled at the gentleman seated at the desk. "My name is Doris Flynn. Could you give me directions? I'm looking for the double-wide that Racheal Gerrish rents here. She told me I should do a drive-by, as I'm in the market." Bigger smile.

As soon as I indicated I was interested in a unit, the man's face took on a glow. Kind of golden, like pirates' booty.

"Well," he said. "I can certainly tell you where it is, but the Ms. Gerrish doesn't lease. She owns." Then he faltered. "I certainly hope she isn't looking to rent the unit. There are rules."

"No idea about that," I said. "So…?"

The guy penned a drive line on a photocopied map. When I left, I also had his business card, a brochure about the mobile home park, and two pamphlets for different companies that built units. My cheeks hurt from forcing a grin.

I had to admit, the mobile home park was nice. Most of the units were not the single twelve-by-sixty units I remembered from when I was younger, but double-wides that looked like ranch-style houses with small porches. Some even had attached garages.

The lots were moderately sized, with paved driveways and mowed lawns. My route took me all the way to the back of the park. I knew from what the manager had said that there were 170 homes. A tiny quick-stop grocery/ice cream bar/coffee shop somewhere would have made a killing.

The Gerrish unit was beautiful. I knew no one was living there, but it didn't look abandoned or neglected. They had to have a lawn person, because the grass and flowerbeds were professional quality and made mine look hokey.

I didn't see anybody peeking around their living room curtains to watch me, so I took the liberty of getting out and peeking in the windows. I also tried the doors, and all that. I mean, the guy knew I was down here. If a neighbor called to report me, I was covered.

I circled around the back. There was a deck with sliding glass doors. Unfortunately, the curtains were drawn. In addition to the two-car attached garage, there was a metal shed in the back.

Leave no stone unturned, right? The latch was set and twisted, but there was no padlock. I opened the door.

OMG! The stink. I saw a lawn mower and a few yard tools. And a haphazard stack of big plastic tubs, all just thrown in there. Instinctively, I backed away.

I had a four-inch mag flashlight attached to my purse. I got it from my car and went back. Using the light and my foot to move the buckets, I saw the streaky crud that let me know they'd been rinsed out, but not with care. That awful smell was familiar, but for a few moments I couldn't lay my finger on it. I shoved a tub outside for the natural light. When I moved it, I could see the back corner of the shed had been damaged, and the tin was peeled open.

Whatever had been inside the tub had been gone for a long while. I stuck my face down close and took a big whiff. My butt dragged the rest of me back in a rush. That stink was decomp. I couldn't get that bucket back inside the shed fast enough. I slammed the door shut and almost twisted the pivoting mechanism off the latch. I didn't want a neighborhood kid finding this.

I was back in my car, still trying to take a breath, when I thought about the damage on the back of the small metal building. That hadn't been done by a woodchuck. What if someone had crawled out of there? I had my hand on the key, my wrist trying to turn it, but I had to know. Common sense said it had not been an escapee, but who would break in the back if they could have just opened the front?

I looked around, and so no one in their yards, no peekers out from behind the shades.

I'll run really fast, I thought.

Neddel is going to kill you, Left Brain said.

When I got back out, most of my bravado was long gone. In the backyard, I circled around. The mowing stopped right where the back wall of the shed was, so now I stood in knee-deep weeds. I noticed a couple of trashed items there—a weedwhacker and a wheelbarrow missing one arm. When I got closer to the shed, I could see the big claw marks. The smell of the tubs had brought something brawny close. I inhaled, trying to separate one smell from another. There's a peculiar stench when bears are in the area, like spoiled garbage, or rotten meat. A crawly feeling went up my back.

I twisted to see into the sapling forest behind me. Fifty feet away was a piece of faded blue, not fabric, but something more solid. I made my way toward it.

This had to have been another tub, with pieces spread all over the grass where I stood. Most weren't larger than a bread plate. But a couple of them, especially the likely corners, were larger. I took photos with my phone, then went back to the shed and took more. I sent them to Melanie and told her when she got the message to download them before I accidentally erased them. It was time to call Neddel, but I hesitated. What if he didn't take the call, just forwarded it to voicemail? His office was on my way back to the agency. He was fifteen, twenty minutes away, tops.

In the manager's office, I asked, "Just wondering, do you have a problem with bears here?"

I sounded as if I were croaking.

"Well, this is New Hampshire. But we take each report seriously and respond immediately."

He still had his welcome to our neighborhood smile on, but something, maybe my cringing posture, alerted him that I was more than slightly curious.

"Why do you ask?" he said slowly.

"I saw some trash behi…I mean, on the side of the road that looked like it had been shredded by something bigger than a raccoon," I said.

The guy actually laughed at me. "Raccoons can do some pretty extensive damage."

"Oh, yeah, I guess that's true. Thanks."

As I backed out, I realized the guy had a file open in front of him when I went in. He looked tense, as though he'd just had a conversation that didn't work well for him. I remembered what he said about Racheal owning the unit. Just as the seatbelt snapped into place, all the parts of what I'd just seen did as well. The bear wasn't the issue; the fact that several tubs with the stink of decomp and a missing man were! I tried to shift into reverse before I switched on the ignition. An automatic reflex failed me because there were so many things whirling in my head. It seemed I bumbled out there for a long while, not just a few seconds. But I was there long enough for the rental agent to walk over to the window and part the blinds.

"Oh, for the love of Pete. He probably just called Racheal to burn her a new one about renting without permission."

Racheal, who knew where I lived, where Melanie was! I careened out of Wild's Community Mobile Home Park, cutting off a happy Double D customer. I had to get Neddel. I had to get home. Then, as quickly as I'd pulled out onto Route 16, I yanked over onto the side of the road. The person I'd cut off roared past me with a blast of the horn and an up-lifted finger salute.

Racheal was closer to Melanie than I was to Neddel. There wasn't time for me to drive to his office and go all Father Brown on him. I cussed myself out as I fished my cellphone off the floor where it had landed when I jerked the car over. My hands shook so badly, I had trouble pushing the buttons to make the call. I was almost sobbing by the time Dolores answered.

"Well, he's kind of busy right now," Dolores said when I asked for Neddel.

"Dead body, Dolores! Dead body! Now! I need to talk to him now!"

I think I might have been screaming. I was clammy with sweat.

When Neddel got on the phone, I told him about what I'd seen.

"I think Racheal dismembered Richard's body and put the pieces out in those tubs in the shed. She probably didn't realize what would happen to all that plastic when it got hot in there. That ungodly smell."

"Where are you?" Neddel demanded. "Get out of there! I'll have to get a warrant out of Ossipee. Get out of there NOW!"

My calm was tiptoeing back. "Listen, Neddel. You don't have time to sit there and wait around for a warrant. I had to ask the manager where the Gerrish mobile home was. He seemed to think I was checking it out to rent it."

"That doesn't matter. Get out of there!"

"Yeah, it does, because I went back to check on bears, and he looked like a bee had just stung him on the nose. If he called Racheal to tell her she can't just rent the unit out without permission, she knows somebody was there. All she has to do is get there first and get all that stuff out of the shed."

"Crap!"

"Exactly. If it were me, I'd be pushing the speed limit right now. Evie told me Racheal, not Richard, rented that mobile home. I don't even know if Richard ever lived there, for crying out loud."

The words were barely out of my mouth when Richard's big, black Denali raced by, doing well over the speed limit. And Racheal was driving. I watched in my rearview mirror as she hooked a left into Wilds' Community Mobile Home Park. No speed bump was going to slow her down.

I had no idea I started shrieking about it to Neddel. I barely heard him order me not to follow Racheal.

Chapter Thirty-Seven

I was safely backed in and camouflaged between other vehicles in the Dunkin' Donuts lot when the first state police vehicle did a nice low and fast approach into the mobile home park. No lights or sirens to alert the populace, or the criminal, just a quick ride to thwart her plans to remove evidence. I left my jeep and moved at a fast walk in the same direction, hoping Neddel was on his way with a warrant. When the second trooper whipped by, no siren, lots of flashing blue, I picked up the pace.

The troopers didn't stop at the manager's office. By the time Neddel's sheriff cruiser pulled in to the Gerrishes' and parked cockeyed on the lawn, I was safely ensconced on the front porch glider of a neighbor who was probably at work. As Neddel paused to visually sweep the area, I stayed low.

Neddel went around the house. I was two houses up, but I darted across the street, crossed the first backyard, bent over, and flat against the siding. The second one, right next to Racheal's, had a deck with lots of furniture. I belly-crawled on the planking until I could peek out from beneath a chaise.

Two officers stood in place, keeping Racheal away from the shed. She wore restraints but paced back and forth in the small area she had been allowed, like a border collie about to lose her sheep. I clearly heard her deny any wrongdoing, and her shoulders danced as she spoke.

Probably has an Italian or French grandparent and is having trouble talking without being able to use her hands, I thought.

Once again, she was decked out in one of those 1950s Betty Crocker dresses with all the crinolines. This one was a warm, buttery peach, probably made of satin, that threw off sparks of light with each move she made. The heels of her matching shoes were black with mud and slime. They weren't made for stamping around in the backyard.

The other two troopers and Neddel inspected the tubs they had pulled out into the sun, but they didn't go inside the shed. Right about then, the man I'd seen in the manager's office came jogging around the corner.

"Crap," I whispered, ducking down.

"What's going on here?" he demanded.

While all the players were occupied, I chanced an outgoing call. I hadn't seen a lot of residue in the tub I had taken out of the shed, but the bits of plastic back in the weeds were filthy.

"Dolores," I whispered. "Contact Neddel. Tell him there's another tub all ripped up about fifty yards behind the shed."

"Okay," she said. "Wait. Where are you? Why are you whispering?"

I cut the connection. Before she could call me back, I shut off the phone. The last thing I needed was for the ringer to alert all those law enforcement guys I was staking things out. As it was, one stood hands on his hips, surveying the neighborhood for witnesses. I put my head down and tried to press myself further into the deck.

The chaise was decorated with senior-citizen fringe. I could only hope it kept me hidden.

Neddel got a call. It must have been Dolores, because his attention was diverted from the tub at his feet to the sapling field beyond the shed. He and one of the troopers hurried off in that direction and were gone for several minutes.

When they came back, Neddel walked right past where I was hidden to his cruiser. I knew from experience that the black duffel he returned with had his crime scene equipment in it. This time, when he left the yard, he was gone for a long while, taking a second trooper with him.

They came back with two fifty-five-gallon trash bags of stuff. Neddel was also speaking on his phone again. He went up to the older trooper, probably the lead, since his insignia was different from the others. Neddel handed the phone over, and the man spent a good minute looking at the display before passing it back to the sheriff.

Cellphone in hand, Neddel walked up to Racheal and held it up so she could read the screen.

"Racheal Gerrish, this is the warrant to search and seize issued by Judge Albe. A hard copy for your records is en route from the Ossipee courthouse and should arrive momentarily. This gives us the right to search your domicile, property, and all outbuildings for any material or evidence that might relate to the disappearance of Richard Gerrish. Do you understand what I just said?"

It suddenly occurred to me that Neddel hadn't ignored my belief that Richard was missing. He just hadn't shared what he knew, or how the police investigation was working. They had a procedure; I just fumbled around.

"No!" Racheal, who had been allowed a seat on the deck, jumped to her feet, head shaking wildly. "No! Richard is not missing. Listen to me. He's just…gone. We argued. He left. Please listen to me."

Neddel was not swayed. "You are to remain here while the search is being conducted. It is your choice if you wish to allow us access. Otherwise, we will enter by the use of force."

Two troopers accompanied Racheal to her vehicle while they retrieved her purse. As if the yard weren't already full of cars, cops, and assorted crime crap, another cruiser pulled in. Behind it was the oversized New Hampshire green van used by the State of New Hampshire Bureau of Investigations, Crime Scene Unit.

I needed to get out of there. Discretion was quickly evaporating as an option. Crawling backwards got me a couple of splinters. And when I went to cross the road, I saw one of the troopers, standing beside Racheal as she unlocked the front door, look up. The handcuffs dangled from one wrist.

I headed between two houses, and from there took the shortest route possible back to my vehicle.

I thought I was safe until I got to the main entrance of the mobile home park. Two cruisers—one state, the other, sheriff's—blocked the way. They were meant to keep random people and the media, who were already arriving, out. But they also had me trapped inside.

As casually as I could manage, I walked south on Chirpy Chipmunk Lane until I reached the end. This put me on the far side of Dunkin', near The Tire Warehouse. That meant I could push my way through the scrub to where I'd left the jeep.

No one noticed me. All eyes were on the cruisers.

A mile down the road, I turned my phone back on. I'd missed half a dozen calls from my daughter demanding to know where I was because the sheriff's office was looking for me. There was also a message from Heidi.

"Doris, your daughter called. She seemed really upset. Call her or me, okay?"

I called the office.

"I got a flat tire in that dead zone over on Route 25," I said. "I'm on my way. Can you sign me out as of about eleven? I mean, the agency shouldn't pay for all the time it took me to change a tire, right?"

Heidi agreed, even laughing a little at the idea I could change my own tire, then hung up.

Melanie was more demanding. I told her I'd just watched the cops take down Racheal, and I'd tell all when I got there.

"What do you mean by took her down? Where are you? You'd better not be someplace where shots are going to be fired!" Melanie was getting wound up fast.

"I'm on my way. I'll tell you all about it when I get there, but I can't drive and talk about it at the same time." I pushed the end button before she asked me to pick up milk.

Next call. "Hi, Dolores. Yeah, sorry about that. I accidentally shut off the phone when I was flipping out. I went back to work, but I'm headed home now. Did Neddel find anything?"

"Right. Like I believe you. FYI, an arrest has been made. Neddel will call you directly." She sounded like my mother when I'd gotten into trouble and she'd warned me to be ready when my father got home.

I did exactly what I said I would. I went home, played with the pig, fixed suppers, fortified myself with a full pint of Cherry Garcia ice cream, and waited for Neddel. Melanie followed me from chore to chore, eating some of my ice cream and asking the same questions over and over. It's the kind of trap I used to use on her to find out what she was doing, really, like the truth, doing.

"I've told you everything I know," I said finally. "You're exhausting me."

"What about what Neddel was doing?" she asked. "What did he say?"

"I haven't talked to him since I called to tell him about the shed."

"But you saw him?"

"Yes."

"And he didn't step over and say a single word?" Her eyes were drilling into my head.

"He didn't actually see me," I said slowly.

She sat back. "You're kidding? How's that?"

"Ah, nope, not kidding. I might have been, you know, under a chaise lounge."

"Mom." Melanie shook her head. "When he gets here, he's going to kill you."

"He probably won't come by tonight," I told Melanie. "Duke has school."

"Yeah, right," she said sarcastically. "Did you eat that whole pint?"

* * *

It was close to nine when Neddel finally showed up. I was beginning to believe he actually wouldn't come by to see me. I gave him a hug, made him a big sandwich, then separated Duke, who hadn't made it to school, from the housedogs so he, too, could have some nourishment without other noses in his bowl.

"I truly didn't expect you to get over here tonight," I said.

"Yeah, I had to stop in and pick up Duke." He inhaled the first half of his sandwich, but I was already making him another. "Then I was so antsy, I figured we'd drive out."

"So, what happened?" I was going for nonchalant as I ripped open the chips bag.

"Well, you pretty much know the first of it," he said.

I cocked an eyebrow, wondering if he was going to tell me what had happened after my call.

He finished the last bite of the first sandwich before he spoke. "I was surprised when you disappeared off the next-door deck. It cost me five bucks to the lieutenant when you slipped out."

I blushed all the way to my toes. Melanie and Neddel both got a good laugh.

"Now that you've had your fun, do you want to tell me what happened?" I asked.

"We didn't find anything in the house, but there was gouge evidence on the concrete floor of the garage that several cuts had been made on something that had been lying directly on the cement. There was a circular saw on the workbench that had been rinsed and doused in Clorox. That'll never work again." He kind of tittered before he spoke again. "Testing in the area showed blood traces on just about everything up to chest height."

My butt sank into the kitchen chair. I'd seen the whole mess, yet I hadn't backtracked to figure out how it happened. This was late-night television stuff, not my idea of small-town New Hampshire.

"So, you've got enough evidence to arrest Racheal? Send her to prison?"

"Like forever?" Melanie asked.

"You'd think so, wouldn't you?" he said.

"What does that mean?" Melanie asked.

"It means that, according to Racheal, there are other factors in play." Neddel pushed his plate away. He wasn't interested in the strawberries I'd sliced for him, or the chips.

"Racheal's statement says she hasn't seen Richard since shortly after they moved here. He went south to handle some unfinished business. She didn't know where, and he never came back. According to her, she didn't notify the police because he wasn't in danger; he just wanted to leave."

Duke walked over and lay his head on Neddel's knee.

"She'd contacted the office they'd worked for under the guise of someone else and was told he hadn't been there. She further states she learned recently that a woman he'd had a child with had also relocated to this area. Racheal believed he had gone to be with her. According to Chris Gillespie at the bank, Racheal had come in to speak with a bank representative because she wanted to put the mobile home on the market. Even though she holds the mortgages on both houses, somehow, they're tied into the real estate agency, and Richard's name is on that. It's a catch-22 situation where she could lose out all around."

"Bit herself in the butt on that one, didn't she?" I remarked. "I mean, her big picture is all about the agency.

"Furthermore, because Richard hadn't gone back to Nashua, his girlfriend was up here, and the mobile was vacant, Racheal believed that was where he was living. There were a number of calls on the answering machine where she begs him to call her so they could try to work it out. I knew about the mobile home and have been out there twice. Neighbors said a car goes in and out of the garage, lights come on, and the lawn gets mowed. But no one actually saw Richard, and I didn't find him there. Our search today found evidence that the house has been occupied. The initial inspection indicated the occupant was a man."

I opened my mouth to ask how he assumed that, but he was still speaking.

"Guy's underwear in the laundry. Shaving gear on the bathroom counter," Neddel said. "During the interview with the manager, Les Harris, he said he'd seen Richard's Denali enter and leave several times. He could tell it was a man driving, but because of the tinted window, not *exactly* see the face."

I liked this story less and less.

"Excuse me," Melanie said. "But is Racheal saying somebody else could have killed Richard?"

"Basically, yes. However, we haven't established yet that the blood and, ah, remains we were able to collect in the garage were Richard's."

Duke came over. He wanted a treat. I took a soft peanut butter one out of Buttercup's container and split it between the three dogs.

"Did you ask her about the freezer that had been in her house in town?" I asked.

"She said it didn't work. It was locked, and she couldn't get into it, so she had it hauled away. At first, she said she couldn't remember who took it, but finally gave up her gardener." Neddel pulled a notebook out of his pocket.

"Man said he and his buddy hauled it to the dump. When they got there, they were informed the lid door had to come off. Using a cold chisel and a hammer, they shattered the lock. They got the guy from the dump to help them, which gave them an alibi."

"It gets a little interesting here because both men testified separately that when they finally got it open, there was an overwhelming rotten meat smell, even though the unit was empty. I called the people who had owned the house previously. They admitted the freezer was unreliable and refused to have it repaired. They had no idea why it stunk. End of that line of questioning."

"Wait, a minute!" I almost jumped out of my seat. "Was there a freezer in the trailer?" If there were a third freezer, this was going to be so confusing.

"Racheal said no, and the manager who sold her the unit furnished said no." He paused, seeming to consider. "Edith Henderson called me the night before last. I went over there, and we had a talk. She'd found a receipt for the freezer that she and Ivan had removed from her house. The serial number on the receipt matches the unit found on Chocorua Mountain Road."

Melanie gasped, fingers across the bottom of her face. "Oh, no."

"Neddel," I said. "We can prove Ivan Henderson was alive and is somewhere with a different woman. So, the body you found could be Richard's. You can prove Racheal's freezer actually went to the dump, but not Edith's."

"I know," he said.

"Where is Racheal now?" I asked.

"I had to release her. She called a lawyer," Neddel said. "It gets tricky because fingerprints taken out of the mobile home belong to Richard. He was there at some time. And we found damn few of Racheal's. Most of those were right around the front door. If she lived there, and he didn't, then he had that place scoured clean."

"Then what? Invited Richard to come in and touch stuff?" Melanie asked.

"That doesn't make sense," I said. "He posted that he had done all these repairs, of course, he'd be touching stuff. But if she was living there, so wouldn't she."

"But was she actually living there already?" Neddel asked.

"I don't know," I said.

Could she have bought it, let him move in while she was still in Nashua, I wondered. Then decided that a double-wide wasn't a good look for her new realtor persona? When she got ready for her big move, had she bought the blue house with the plan to sell the mobile Richard had gussied up?

"Right now, I don't have enough evidence to go with Racheal having committed a crime." He got up to go. "Will you be at the Humane Society tomorrow?"

"No. That ended last Friday. We're all done with the campers for this season. I thought I'd play catch-up here. That way, I'll have more time on the weekend if you want to do something."

"That's a nice idea." He had a happy smile. "But I'll have to wait and see. Hopefully, a smoking gun will show up."

Chapter Thirty-Eight

I went to bed believing I was exhausted. Then I slept for thirty or forty minutes, woke up, squirmed around, considered how Racheal had beaten us even if she didn't get to cash in on it. I worried about Evie for a little while, then dozed off again. My whole night went like that. Some of the naps were as short as twenty minutes. I felt hungover and sleep-deprived when I got up.

There was critter-inspired hurry-up with the breakfast noise all around me.

"I need coffee," I groaned.

No break in the whine-and-cat-chirp action.

"Coffee," I repeated.

Melanie wasn't an early riser, so she wasn't any help. When I finally got past the bare minimum of what I had to do inside, I shut Royally in the house and went out to tend Buttercup. It was absolutely pouring buckets.

"What the—?" I asked when I opened the kitchen door.

The yard was awash. The trees dripped a solid curtain of water. How had I not heard the thump-thump of heavy rain against the metal roof? Common sense told me to go back and get a slicker, but I had just gotten the door closed to the point where Royally couldn't follow. I forged ahead. It wasn't cold rain, but it sluiced over me.

"Maybe this'll wash the fog out of my brain," I muttered.

Buttercup didn't notice that I was soaked to the skin, only that I had brought food. When I stepped out, her nose was in the trough. I left the gate open as well as one side of the barn door. Even though it was raining hard, the air was hot and cloying. A bad combination.

Back in the house, I couldn't leave the windows open, so I opted for fans. Still uncomfortable. This type of weather was really hard on Melanie. Instead of signing on to work, she lay on the sofa with a wet washcloth covering her face. Lilo sat high on the back beside Pumpkin. They knew and were standing guard.

I left tea and half an English muffin with butter and jelly for her on the coffee table. The fan was set on low. The soft whir provided constant white noise.

I worked quietly. When Buttercup meandered through the rain and onto the deck, I let her inside, willing to clean up the mud if she wouldn't make a noisy fuss. I rubbed her down with a beach towel and made baby girl noises to her, which she loved, then paused to wonder how anybody couldn't see how loving she was. And smart! If she didn't understand something, she tried to figure it out. If I wanted Royally to fetch anything other than his dish, I had to throw it, but the pig could identify several items. Melanie would hide things and send Buttercup out to find them. The pig knew what a chicken was. If one didn't come in at night, she could find it. She was loyal. Recognized people, and had a nose any bloodhound would envy. And unlike a sighthound, she could follow a really cold trail.

When I stopped rubbing her, Buttercup assumed we were done. I hadn't replaced the dog gate, so she meandered down to the living room and got the English muffin off the low table. Then she found a space close to where Melanie slept and lay down.

"What a smart girl," I whispered. "You knew exactly where she was, and not to wake her up. And you cleaned up all the crumbs, so I won't have to vacuum later."

I was still sitting on my heels, using the dirty beach towel to clean up the floor, when I realized that, yes, Buttercup was smart, but like a child, she sometimes reacted to a remembered feeling rather than what had actually happened in the moment. Like associating Racheal with the pepper spray. Buttercup might not have remembered exactly what happened, but the next time she'd run into Racheal, the pig knew the woman was bad news.

I dialed the phone.

"Hi, you cute little son of a gun," I said in my big-smile voice.

"What do you want?" Neddel asked slowly.

"Nothing. I'm in a position where I could offer you a one-time deal on the answer to your biggest problem."

"You're scaring me," he said.

"If you wanted to ask Racheal Gerrish more questions, could you just bring her in? Or maybe have her go down to the state police barracks, like voluntarily?"

"If it were warranted," he answered.

"Okay. So, all that plastic and stuff you picked up from behind her shed? Where is that?"

"As I believe I told you, we sent a broad sampling out to be tested." Neddel didn't sound confused, but concerned I might do something foolish. "The rest of it is in Ossipee, being held under lock and key in the evidence lockup. And no, I don't have a key."

"But you know who does, right?"

Chapter Thirty-Nine

Four hours later, I pulled into the parking lot of the small antique shop next to the state police barracks in Tamworth. I angled for the best space that was also out of view, because I was hauling the trailer.

Before I dropped the tailgate, I stuffed the piece of garbage that I'd taken out of Melanie's car into the side of my shoe. It was a good thing she refused to accept responsibility for keeping the vehicle clean.

Then, with Buttercup harnessed and leashed beside me, I had to find a way across the barracks lot that did not offer a mud puddle on the way. We walked past four parked cruisers, plus Neddel's sheriff's vehicle. Among the cars in the visitor's area was Richard Gerrish's Denali. The one Racheal was driving because she'd sold her SUV.

"I don't know how you explained how you still had Richard's vehicle, Racheal," I said aloud. "But more power to ya."

Buttercup looked up to see if I was addressing her. When I didn't acknowledge her, she kept moving ahead. It was a good thing Neddel is such a good negotiator, because when we got to the door, Buttercup wanted to be inside out of the wet. I cracked open the door, and she forged ahead.

Instead of going in through the front, we entered through the annex for driver's license testing. Our arrival created a small commotion.

"What kind of license is she going for?" one guy asked, pointing to Buttercup.

"Motorcycle," I said.

At that point, we were ushered through the connecting door into the main structure. Buttercup got a pass into a public building because Neddel had vouched for her, and she was integral to our plan. There was a long, narrow conference room on the back side of the building. At the far end, away from the door, Neddel, the NH State Police Lieutenant, Racheal Gerrish, and a man whose presence screamed lawyer sat around the end of a table. Racheal was in the seat directly facing me as I walked in. Well, as *we* walked in.

When she saw Buttercup, Racheal literally squealed and jumped from her seat.

"Take it easy, Ms. Gerrish," Neddel said.

While she babbled about the pig being dangerous, the lawyer, identified to me as Max Shelbourne, demanded to know what was going on. Even the trooper, who was in on my and Neddel's plan, looked skeptical.

"This is Ms. Flynn," Neddel said. "Her companion is Buttercup, an award-winning competitor in search and, well, not so much rescue as find. Buttercup has proven in other cases that she can identify trace scents, even on a cold trail. What we are going to do here is offer her a chance to investigate some of the items we picked up. You know, to see if she can identify who they belong to, or who handled them."

"This is rubbish." Mr. Shelbourne was still trying to get Racheal back in her seat.

"It's your choice, sir," Lieutenant Trask said. "We can run this test here, or take it down to Judge Albee's chambers. He's standing by. He even said he wants to see the pig in action."

Shelbourne looked vexed, but nodded. "Go ahead. Racheal, sit down. It will be all right. You're safe from the pig. We're all right here."

A trooper wearing nitrile gloves brought in a sealed evidence tub. Behind him, Deputy Dolores and Stan, the hot dog man, entered. Without a word or a look at Buttercup, they went to stand against the wall across the room from Neddel.

The new trooper cut the seal on the evidence locker. I pulled out a Ziploc bag that contained a man's handkerchief. Without touching it, I let Buttercup get a good sniff. Then I let her hold it in her mouth.

"Take it home, Buttercup," I said.

This was a game Melanie played with Buttercup and the dogs.

A few moments passed while she worked out why we were playing this game. I was nervous. But finally, she dropped the handkerchief, lifted her snout, and sniffed. When she decided where Neddel was, she picked up the piece of cloth and took it to him. Then she waited.

"You have to acknowledge," I told Neddel. "Take it from her, but don't talk to her."

He accepted the handkerchief. She returned to me. I gave her a treat. When she was ready, I pulled a second Ziploc out. This one had a plastic candy bag inside.

Dolores loves peppermint candies. She's always eating them and shares with Mayfaire, her horse. She's also shared candy with Buttercup in the past. The pig sniffed.

"Take it home," I ordered.

Snout came up. Candy bag went right to Dolores, who almost broke the rules to pat Buttercup.

The pig returned to me. Another snack.

Third bag. This one held a used paper napkin smeared with mustard. I hoped Buttercup would get this right strictly by association.

When I opened the bag, I saw a little tremble along her spine. She absolutely knew. There wasn't much left of the paper napkin when she handed it to Stan, but he didn't mind. I think Buttercup might have been a little disappointed that she didn't get a Special, the mustard and ketchup hot dog bun he usually gives her, but settled for a treat.

Neddel said thank you to Dolores and Stan. They left the room, closing the door behind them.

"Do you have any questions about how this works, Mr. Shelbourne?" Neddel asked.

"I think this is an elaborate trick," Shelbourne said.

Racheal nodded as if she wanted to send her head flying.

Neddel slid a piece of paper over to the lawyer. "These are Buttercup's credentials. A list of the awards she's won for participating in this exercise at fairs, obedience trials, and with the Working Dog Unit."

"I don't believe any of this will be admissible in court," Shelbourne said.

"Nonetheless, we would like to proceed," Neddel replied.

The lawyer looked over the paper. "Go ahead."

Lieutenant Trask opened the door and spoke to the man waiting in the hall. The trooper who had originally brought in the evidence container removed it and placed a new one on the floor. Shelbourne was offered a chance to examine the seal before the trooper cut it. I moved Buttercup back when the lawyer approached. At his nod, the trooper cut the seal and left the room.

"This container holds items collected at the residence of Richard and Racheal Gerrish on Woodchuck Lane, The Wilds' Community Mobile Home Park, Route 16, Tamworth, New Hampshire," Lieutenant Trask explained. "Each evidence bag has remained sealed and marked since collection. No one has touched this evidence without wearing gloves. What we are asking Buttercup to do is to identify any residual scent left on the plastic scraps from earlier."

Shelbourne looked skeptical, but Racheal was having all she could do not to grin.

"Go ahead, Ms. Flynn," said Neddel.

I picked up one of the bags holding a larger tub corner piece. Restraining Buttercup while I opened the bag with gloves on was awkward and took me a bit. While I was doing that, I pulled the small scrap of gardening glove out of my shoe. I had picked it up weeks earlier in Racheal's yard. From where Racheal and Shelbourne sat, they couldn't see the piece on the floor, or my shoe, either. When I finally had the faded blue plastic scrap free, I placed it on the ground right next to the gardening glove.

"I don't know if she'll be able to pick this plastic up," I said, suddenly scared she'd pick up the glove.

"That's okay," Neddel said. "As long as she can indicate where it goes."

Now it was going to get tricky.

"Buttercup. Take it home."

To me, my command sounded shaky, but she understood. We had been playing a game. She knew I had another snack in my hand, ergo, we were still playing.

I had been right that she wouldn't pick up the blue piece. Instead, she took the section of fabric. I didn't have a chance to snatch it away from her. After sniffing the air, Buttercup made her way towards Racheal. I had been all ready to whisper, *Where's the bad dog?* or maybe give her a discreet knee shove, but she trotted off. I wanted a reaction from Racheal, but it wouldn't be good if Buttercup reacted as well. So, this time I went with her.

The closer Buttercup got to Racheal, the bigger the woman's eyes got. She had her fingernails dug into the lawyer's arm. He held up his hand to stop Buttercup's advance, but it was too late. Another two steps and Racheal and Buttercup were within hugging distance of each other.

Belatedly, I realized Buttercup would remember the pepper spray and recognize Racheal as having been involved. Just then, the pig gave a big, angry snort.

Racheal screamed loud enough to send Buttercup running. There wasn't room for the pig to maneuver, so she tried to go around the lawyer. Her bulk shoved his chair against the edge of the table. Not good. But no one heard him gasping for breath because Racheal jumped on the table. Luckily, she was wearing a vintage sailor outfit with pants instead of a dress, because she scrambled across the oak platform top on her hands and knees. Her toes of her red high heels squeaked on the polished wood surface.

What happened next was another bit of chaos that hadn't been in the original plan. Neddel, Trask, and Shelbourne all did the man thing that happens when a woman gets hysterical: First, they froze. Then they verbally attacked each other. In the middle of all the craziness, I scooped up the clue as I rounded the table.

Buttercup got to the door. She knew that was the exit.

"Everybody calm down!" Neddel roared.

I couldn't get the door open to get out. Buttercup was in the way.

Racheal slipped and almost fell off the table. She recovered, ran for the door, and realized that now she was rushing toward where the pig was stuck.

"Get away from me!" she screamed, and back-pedaled right into Shelbourne. It was a domino trail falling down.

I'd pulled a total faux pas. This had been my idea. My mistake. My brain clouded. I had a momentary mental image of Richard and Andy.

I said, "Relax, Richard, she's not going to hurt you."

"RICHARD! What do you know about Richard? That ass! He got exactly what he had coming to him. He was going to leave me for that slut! And on top of that, he wanted half of the money! I would have had to sell the agency."

Shocked, I practically sat on Buttercup.

"What?" I asked.

"It was an accident. We argued. It got nasty. I picked up the hammer from the workbench and... and he was dead. Just dead." Racheal was on the table again, curled into a messy ball. And sobbing.

Neddel's mouth was hanging open, as was Shelbourne's. Only Trask looked pleased.

This may have been what Neddel and I wanted, but it was way more than I'd expected. I felt my blood pressure spike. Buttercup butted me, hard. She wanted to leave right now, but then so didn't I. I put all the strength I had into shoving her aside far enough to get the door open. I don't know how she didn't take it off the hinges or break my arm.

It was raining again. Buttercup and I sat in the hay in the trailer. She wanted a cuddle. All the snacks were gone, and we still weren't going home. Eventually, Neddel and Trask showed up.

"That was awesome," Trask said.

Neddel's eyes belied that sentiment. "I absolutely can't believe Buttercup got anything off that plastic. It was mauled by a bear, left in the weather for weeks."

"A bear ate the remains?" Trask asked.

"No," said Neddel. "We only knew a bear had been involved because it ripped the shed wall open and left claw marks everywhere. But by the time the bear showed up, the remains were in the first freezer. I'm sure the brute was disappointed with all the empty plastic tubs."

"Can we go home now?"

I felt ashamed I had deceived him by not telling him I was bringing the glove, even though Racheal had confessed. I'd explain later when Trask wasn't standing right there. It wasn't evidence; I'd taken it out of her own yard, but I might have crossed some other legal line.

His look softened. "Oh, honey. Of course you can. I never thought to tell you it was okay. I'm sorry. But I can't thank you and Buttercup enough."

"That's okay. I would have had to wait for Buttercup to calm down, anyway. She's good now. But I left Melanie, and she's having a bad day. I'll see you Saturday, okay? I don't want Duke to miss any more school than he has already."

When I got home, Melanie was sitting in Ian's chair as Noah heated up chicken noodle soup for her.

"Who moved the chair?" I asked, surprised to see it in the other corner.

Ian's overstuffed chair, which had sat in front of the window for all the time we'd been together, had swapped places with the EZ Boy from across the room.

"I had Noah move it," Melanie said softly. "It's better over here. I can sit in it and work if I want to. And it doesn't fit Neddel as well as the EZ Boy does."

I knew there was more happening with Melanie than she said. In her own time, she'd

'fess up. It was only a piece of furniture and not worth a heavy conversation.

"Are you feeling better? Want me to tell you what happened at the state trooper's barracks?" I asked as Noah came in, carefully balancing a full bowl of chicken soup, what my mom always called farmer's penicillin.

Melanie nodded, accepted the soup, and then she and Noah sat on the sofa while I recounted the afternoon's events.

Outside, the rain continued to fall, though it had grown gentler. Buttercup, after all her exertions of the day, was fed and tucked in. I took a chance and cracked open a window on the porch for a bit of air, and caught the splash of water against the fender entering the drive.

I headed toward the kitchen door, unsure who I'd find there.

"I'm wet," Andy declared when the door opened. Without hesitation, he stepped inside. Or tried to. Royally had his nose right on Andy's belly, sniffing all the boy's good smells.

"I'm sorry. I should have called," Eve said, trying to stop her son's forward progress.

"No, no, of course not. Come right in. You didn't walk over, did you?" I asked.

Looking over Eve's shoulder, I could see her car in the drive.

"No. That nice young mechanic stopped by a few days ago. He found a car like mine that had been in a wreck and was able to salvage the parts I needed. Not only that, but I could actually afford it!"

She laughed, but I had the impression all the wet on her face was not from the rain.

"Well, you're right on time. Noah was just going out for pizza," I called into the living room.

"Dialing," Melanie called back.

"Leaving," said Noah, the pickup guy. As he passed me, he grabbed the pizza money envelope off the refrigerator.

"We can't stay, really," Eve said.

"Is it cheese pizza?" Andy asked. "I lub cheese."

"Cheese!" I called again.

"Got it."

"Yes, it's cheese," I told Andy. "Oops. How about we take those wet sneakers off right here, okay?"

The sneakers came off, but the socks were equally soaked. Little footprints ran down the hall toward where Lilo stood, nervously attentive.

"Hi, puppy!"

Lilo took off like a shot, Melanie-bound. If she needed protection, that was the place to go.

I cringed a little. Melanie's MS-spawned migraines could be crippling. Then I heard her laugh. A good sign.

With Noah gone to pick up the pizza and Andy busy telling Lilo about Prince while Royally tried to sit in his lap, Eve perched on the edge of the sofa. I poured hot tea, but she seemed tense. I waited. When she finally began to speak, very slowly, I heard the choke in her voice. I could see Eve's pain reflected in her eyes.

"I wanted to let you know that we—Andy and I—are leaving. Moving, actually. My family is just outside of Nashua, so that's where we'll go."

She took a couple of quick sips of tea.

I was taken aback. I guess I knew she had family somewhere, but she hadn't said anything about going to them before this.

"When will you leave?" I wondered if she knew about Racheal's confession this afternoon, or if she just couldn't take the strain of Richard being gone, and barely being able to support Andy any longer.

"Sometime tomorrow. My brother made arrangements for the furniture to be picked up then, that's how come we're going so fast. I spent most of today packing. All I have to do is put our personal stuff in the car in the morning."

Andy cut in. "My grandpa is going to let Prince come too, even though he's 'lergic."

"That's nice of your grandpa," Melanie said.

"Dick left Prince with us so he'd be safe. Racheal was mean to both dogs. She still has the other one, Baron."

That reminded me of the Jack Russell, probably shut up in Racheal's house. I hadn't heard anyone mention him. I needed to make a call. Before I could get up, Eve spoke again.

"I don't think I'll ever see Dick again. I just know in my heart something bad happened. But I came over here to say thank you for all your kindness." Her eyes filled again.

"Okay then, all that's done for right now. We're going to have pizza, and if Melanie has her way, root beer floats afterwards. I want you to sit back and relax. Enjoy the evening."

I was at a loss about what to say. The lab reports weren't back, according to Neddel. Somehow, this didn't feel like the right time for me to speak up. I could only hope that she would be with her family when she learned what had happened.

"That's right," Melanie said. "Tell us all about where you're going."

Eve told us the two Mr. Langs had offered to hire her back when she'd called, seeking a reference for her upcoming job hunt. The woman who'd taken her job wasn't cutting the mustard. So she had a job to go back to and a place to stay as long as she wanted or until she found the perfect spot.

I was sad to learn Evie and Andy would be leaving, but glad to hear she had family and friends willing to be there for her.

Noah returned with two pizzas and waffle fries. Also root beer floats, which Andy had never experienced. They got a thumbs-up all around. Even the dogs got a bite of cheese. When the rain stopped for a few minutes, Andy and I took a piece of pizza out to Buttercup. It was a rare treat for her.

"You did good today," I whispered before I followed the small boy back to the house.

After Eve and Andy left with the promise that they would keep in touch, and Neddel arrived, Melanie walked up and put her arms around him.

"I'm so glad you didn't show up ten minutes ago," she said.

After she'd gone back to her place on the sofa, where Noah brought her tea, Neddel said to me, "What just happened here? Why did she hug me?"

"You're an idiot," I said. Then I explained about Eve getting ready to leave the valley. "What happened after Buttercup and I left?"

"First of all, I don't know how you got Buttercup to go at Racheal like that…"

I started to speak, but Neddel held his hand up. "I don't want to know. Really. I. Do. Not. Want to know. But her lawyer couldn't shut her up. Once she got started, the dam burst."

We sat at the table, each with a cup of tea and a dog on our feet.

"It seems," Neddel said, "that Racheal knew about Eve, but not that she was living quite so close. I'm going to have to go over and have a talk with Evie, but I thought I'd stop in and see how you were doing first."

"You can leave Duke here while you go," I said.

Neddel was quiet for a bit, then he said. "Racheal and Richard were still living in Tamworth when she came home one day to find him loading his suitcases into his vehicle. When he told her that he'd had enough and was leaving, she reacted in anger and grabbed a hammer lying on the windowsill in the garage. That was one of the reasons she didn't want to sell the Denali. She wasn't sure if she'd gotten all the blood off it."

"I would have thought a couple of runs through the carwash and a good detailing would have solved that," I said.

Neddel shrugged.

"The tubs from moving were right there. She cut him up. I think Trask almost laughed when she said she got the idea from a killer on some TV show. Then, him out in the shed. She had the whole house cleaned. Twice. Total wipe down. I asked what she used as an excuse. She said she had told the cleaners she was allergic to a cat the previous owners had. Then she used Richard's hands to leave the prints."

I almost gagged up my pizza.

"When she bought the blue house and moved, he was still in the shed. She knew she'd have to deal with the tubs, but things came to a head when one of the neighbors called and told her about the stink and a bear that was seen prowling around. She went back. According to her, she had to get stoned to be able to clean up."

"I'm almost afraid to ask," I said.

"Racheal said she poured the remains into trash bags, loaded them into the Denali, and, because she couldn't deal with much more, took them back to the blue house and put them in the freezer. Later, she went back, rinsed the tubs, and threw them in the shed. It took days for the smell to dissipate."

"But it didn't," I said.

"I know. She still didn't know what to do with Richard's remains, but came home one day and found oil on the floor. The freezer had stopped working. That was when she took the trash bags up on Chocorua Mountain Road. Her plan was just to throw them in a ravine someplace, but she was gobsmacked to find another freezer dumped on the side of the road. Accepting it as a gift from God, she loaded Richard's remains inside and tried to use a screwdriver to turn the locking mechanism. We know how that worked out for her."

"Then she play-acted that Richard was still around?" I asked.

"Pretty much. She kept going back to the trailer to clean up. You know, stage the area so that when she filed for divorce, it would look like Richard had been living there the whole time. She was smart enough to wear gloves *every* time she was there, which shows premeditation, of a sort. And she knew she'd have to deal with the shed, but she said she just couldn't force herself to go inside."

I sat there gazing out the kitchen window to a place beyond the barn when Neddel reached over and took my hand.

"Hey, it's okay. You did a good thing."

"I wasn't thinking about Racheal," I said. "Or Eve, or Richard," I said. "I was wondering about Edith Henderson."

"It's a cinch that Ivan thought he'd save himself thirty dollars and not take the freezer to the dump," Neddel said.

"True, but not that." I told him about my visit to Concord and the pictures of Ivan and the smiling woman wearing a wedding band.

"Ouch," he said.

"Who was going to tell her what had happened to Ivan? She's going to be heartbroken," I said.

Neddel leaned forward, elbows on his knees.

"Are you okay?" I asked.

"Talking to Evie is going to be hard," he said. "But facing the dragon lady is going to be terrifying."

I laughed at him, but when he stood up, he pulled me up with him, arms coming around me, warm and strong.

"I have to see Evie tonight, now," he said. "I'll face Edith Henderson tomorrow, but maybe," he kissed me softly, "I'll stop back before I go home."

"I guess I'll just have to hold Duke hostage so that you do," I whispered.

Chapter Forty

Melanie and I were having lunch in the garden plot. The gate was closed, so all the critters, including the Blanche gang, were on the outside. They muttered and crowded the fence, but we didn't pay them any mind. Even though Baron, Racheal's Jack Russell, had come from a bad place, I'd heard he'd been rehomed with a guy in Bartlett who thought he was perfect. I had a new boarder myself, a Belgian Shepherd who looked dangerous, but so far had proven to be a softie. He was out on the run, daring a chicken to come within reach. Blanche knew better.

Neddel and I were back on an even keel. Supper about every night. An overnight here and there. Patty Monson knows he's on a diet and can't have more cookies. He told me that Duke was the smartest dog at school. We'd find out next week at graduation.

Eve and Andy were gone. Neddel said their conversation was rough. But the next morning, I took Buttercup down to say goodbye, and her family was there, solid around her. A new family with four kids had moved in. I waved every once in a while, but so far hadn't stopped by. The bulldozer and the sign down on the corner lot disappeared. Only the stumps from where the sign had been cut down with a chainsaw remained. There was a rumor going around about a wastewater plant. Who knew where that came from? I think Racheal's old secretary is spreading gossip.

Racheal was charged with Richard's death. She claimed it was a crime of passion. I didn't know how much water that would carry. And I didn't care, as long as I didn't have to be involved.

"Mom? Hello, can you hear me?" Melanie threw an ice cube into my lap.

"What?" I asked.

"How did your last day at work go?"

Oh, that was another thing. I'd gone in and given Mr. Bennett my two-week notice. Heidi had watched me with a sad look. But I didn't want to work there anymore. I didn't want to feel that someone was looking over my shoulder every minute. Or that my every move was wrong.

"Well, there was cake."

"Yeah, you already told me that part. And mentioned that it was pretty good." Melanie smiled.

"The best part was my final goodbye to the new agency director, Ms. Greene."

Edith had come back to the agency with her pride intact, her marriage annulled, and her hands firmly back on the controls. Heidi told me Mr. Bennett had been shipped to a satellite office near the Canadian border.

Outside the fence, Buttercup gave a soft see-me-mama woof.

Levering myself up from the lawn chair, I asked her, "Would you like to go down to the river and chase minnows?"

There were happy pig chortles and doggy woofs from Royally and Lilo. This was the best part of the summer.

Acknowledgments

There's a long list of people who help me, laugh with me, egg me on from one book to the other. In the long list of The Pig & I Series, it should be noted that Sarah J. Henry asked for a book that hadn't been written, but which I talked about all the time. Standing right beside me was Canadian Author, Gabrielle St. George, who announced to all and sundry that it was actually a three-book series. Now I was on the hot seat.

Verena Rose from Level Best Books picked up the series and, along with Shawn Reilly Simmons and Deb Well, keep me hard at it. Thank you all for making the book in my heart a reality.

Lisa Matthew, Kill Your Darlings Editing, who really, really tries to teach me.

The cover work, created by Shawn Simmons.

The giggles from people who read the first book and are waiting for the next.

My family, who wait for supper on the nights I'm really into it.

All these people! Hugs and Kisses to ya'all!

About the Author

DonnaRae Menard is a hybrid author with both self-published books and contracts with Level Best Books Publishing, as well as with Of Metal and Magic Publishing. She is the author of multiple series, including the An It's Never Too Late, circa 1970s series, The Pig & I series, and The Women Warriors. She writes in multiple genres from cozy/caper to traditional to horror, as well as historical fiction and thrillers. DonnaRae splits her time between Vermont and New Hampshire, has an affinity for odd jobs, rescued cats, and searching out new sites for her mysteries. Check out her website donnaraemenardbooks.com. Find and follow her on Facebook and Blue Sky.

AUTHOR WEBSITE:

donnaraemenardbooks.com

SOCIAL MEDIA HANDLES:

Facebook @ DonnaRae Menard Author

Blue sky @ donnaraemenardbooks.bsky.social

Also by DonnaRae Menard

Snuffling Up Bones

Murder in the Meadow

Murder on Eagle Drop Ridge

Murder in the Village Proper

Murder on the Small Farm

Murder on US Rte 160

The Affiliate

The Morality Issue

Beneath the Fountain

Dropped from the Sky

Patterns

Hunters

In the Shadow of Pharaoh

Strength of the Mayan Leopard

Wu-Lee

Willa the Wisp

It Takes Guts

Dreams of a Mad Woman

The Waif and the Warlord